CAST THE FIRST STONE

PETER FALCONE

This book is a work of fiction. Names, characters, places, and incidents are either a product of the author's imagination or are used fictitiously. Any resemblance to actual persons, living or dead, business establishments, events, or locales is entirely coincidence.

Copyright © 2014 Peter Falcone
All rights reserved.

ISBN: 1492107751
ISBN-13: 9781492107750

Library of Congress Control Number: 2013914925
CreateSpace Independent Publishing Platform
North Charleston, South Carolina

For Terri,
now and always.

PROLOGUE

On October 31, 1997, a large, aggressive-looking man entered the Cohen Brothers Jewelry Store in Schenectady, New York. He was nondescript, wearing jeans and a rumpled jacket. A Boston Red Sox ball cap and dark sunglasses rounded out the picture.

Mrs. Cohen was pleased to have a customer, as business had been slow since Labor Day. "What can I do for you, sir?"

"Get me the merchandise I ordered weeks ago," he replied gruffly. "My name's Petrofsky."

"My husband, Nelson, took your order, as I recall. I'll get him to come out to the counter and speak with you."

Nelson emerged from the back room and extended his hand to the customer. "Mr. Petrofsky, right? Look, I'm sorry it took so long to get your order, but there isn't much demand for charm bracelets and charms these days. My distributor didn't have the merchandise on hand and had to order direct from the manufacturer. The good news is that your order came in last Thursday. I tried to phone you, but you're not in the book."

"If you've got my order, bring it out. I'm busy."

"Coming right up, sir." Nelson scurried to the back room, emerging quickly with a small box. He placed it on the counter. "Please check the order, Mr. Petrofsky. There should be twelve fourteen-karat-gold charm bracelets and twelve extra crab charms. If you don't mind my asking, why one extra charm per bracelet? Are you handing these out as party favors, maybe for a celebration?"

"Yeah, a special celebration. What do I owe you?"

"The total is one thousand one hundred fifty-five dollars, including tax. Which credit card will you be using?"

"I'm paying cash. Make out the receipt." He took out a gold money clip from his rear pants pocket, held his thumb over the engraved initials—I.H.—and counted out the money.

Mrs. Cohen handed the customer his receipt and the box. Her husband said thank you, come in again. But the man was halfway out of the door, which he slammed behind him.

I.H. walked briskly six blocks down the street, hopped into a red Dodge pickup with a cap over the bed, and took off.

Inside the store, Shirley said, "I hope that guy never comes back. He's weird, angry at the whole world. He's got a really mad look on his face."

Nelson said, "As they say, If looks could kill, we'd be dead already."

In the truck, I.H. smiled, looked over at the merchandise, and whispered, "Showtime."

CHAPTER ONE

Stamford, Connecticut. Emergency Response Center. 8:40 a.m.

"You've reached 911 Emergency. If this is not an emergency, you will be given another number to call. Go ahead."

"There's a man in a field. I think he's dead. He's naked and bloody. It's horrible. Please—"

"I need your name and location. Where are you?"

"I'm Jane Hendricks. I'm on my way to work, and I spotted this guy in the field, naked and—"

"I need your exact location now. Where are you?"

"I'm on Long Ridge Road at the corner of Ambrose Street. There's a big field, and he's out in the middle of it. You need to send cops there now. Am I supposed to stay here? And what about—"

"Yes, stay there. And remain on the phone until the patrol car arrives. It was dispatched automatically along with EMS. I repeat: stay on the line. You're on a cell phone. Got a fresh battery?"

"Yes, I think it's OK. How do you know I'm on my cell?"

"Your number comes up automatically on the computer caller ID. How close are you to the victim? Did you move anything?"

"No. I'm not near the guy! He's in the field, as I told you, about thirty yards away."

"Oh. Are you sure he's dead? How do you know he's naked? Did you approach the body before calling? Hello? Hello, come back on the line."

"OK, I heard you. The police are here now, parked behind my car. I know this guy is naked, because someone placed him upright, tied to a cross. I saw the cross as I drove by. I wish I'd never come to work this way. It's horrible."

She hung up.

CHAPTER TWO

At 8:46 two patrol cars pulled up at virtually the same time, two uniformed officers in each car. A county sheriff's car arrived moments later, driven by a deputy, who had also tuned into the dispatcher's message.

Other than traffic accidents and drownings, none of these officers had ever encountered a corpse. They were certainly not prepared for the scene of this crime. First, a shaking middle-aged woman leaning weakly against the fender of a Chevy Cavalier. Then the unforgettable sight of a white man, naked, tied upside down to a wooden cross in the middle of the field.

After the initial shock started to wear off, the officers radioed in and learned that Assistant Medical Examiner Sheila Ryan and Homicide Detective Bob Farone were moments away. The officers began to seal off the area with yellow crime-scene tape, grateful that they had a routine task to perform before dealing with the crime.

Meanwhile, Deputy Sheriff Lyles was interviewing the woman, Jane Hendricks, who had called in the discovery of the body. Information about her was critical for the crime-scene report but also invaluable, the sheriff knew, in the unlikely event that she was connected with the dead man or the crime.

Her information was, in any event, straightforward and conventional. She was forty-one, employed as an assistant chef at the Merritt Farms Country Club in Darien. She had left her home in Stamford a little earlier than usual in order to pick up a present for her eldest child's birthday and had taken a route to work she rarely used. Much to her dismay. She told the sheriff that she had been shocked to see the body on a cross in the field and had guessed it was a fake, some dumb hoax dreamed up by drunken fraternity boys. But then she stopped, backed up, and surveyed the naked man. She realized he was really a dead or dying person when she saw blood seeping from his mouth, across his cheek and left eye, and into his hair.

There had been virtually no traffic on the road since an accident involving an overturned RV had blocked both lanes for over two hours. Unfortunately for Mrs. Hendricks, she had been the first to go through. Right now, though, traffic was flowing again—but slowly, because of rubbernecking and control by the cops. By 9:06, however, Assistant Medical Examiner Ryan and Detective Farone had arrived, separately but within minutes of each other. They made a minimal amount of small talk and greetings. They then surveyed the scene and interviewed the officers.

After speaking briefly with Mrs. Hendricks, Farone decided she was probably clear of any connection with the crime, but he told her they would be in touch later for a more detailed statement. She left immediately, went home, and called in sick. Real sick.

CHAPTER THREE

Farone and Ryan approached the victim carefully and alone. They didn't wish to compromise or obliterate any potential clues, and they wanted a very clear and uninterrupted first impression of the crime scene.

Dr. Ryan had decided to become a pathologist early on in medical school. She had an almost instinctive desire to solve mysteries, put together patterns of pathological evidence, and hypothesize on the causes, if not the nature, of death. She had another insight as to why she chose this field, insight she never shared with anyone: she feared that she was too "soft," as she put it, to spend a career breaking bad news to patients and their families. She just didn't have it in her to confront living patients. The dead, however, posed no problem. And the murdered or suicidal were best, since she was also surrounded by cops, state attorneys, and cynical defense lawyers in the courtroom—people with whom she could be very professional, as well as equally strong.

Detective Bob Farone, however, did not have to impress upon others that he was hard and tough. He was. At least in his professional life. The only son of a highly successful New York criminal defense lawyer, Farone grew up surrounded by stories of famous cases, many of them complex murders, with a host of fascinating people, ambiguous evidence, unclear motives, perjured testimony, and botched science.

His father, Gennaro Farone, aka Jerry, was angry and disappointed when Bob graduated from UConn and decided not to go on to law school. He entered the New Haven Police Academy instead, graduated with distinction, then served for three years as a uniformed officer. He studied hard for promotion to detective work and passed all his exams with flying colors. As a newly minted detective, he was assigned to vice. He then served for two years in robbery before getting the spot he really wanted: first-class detective in homicide, in his hometown of Stamford.

Single, hardworking, and motivated by doing an outstanding job, Farone combined his brains, his street experience, his heavy immersion in criminal law as a kid, and a strong drive to succeed. Which he did, with a greater ratio of solved crimes per year than the next two detectives combined.

...

The cross, such as it was, was stuck in the ground about twenty-five yards from the road. The victim was a middle-aged white male. The body had been lashed to the cross upside down. The feet were crossed at the ankles, bound together with quarter-inch, three-strand, white nylon rope. The rope was secured tightly over the horizontal crosspiece so the body would not slump downward.

Ryan was able to shake off the shock and revulsion first and approached the body. "Let me do a cursory check of the body first, Bob, before you bring in the forensics guys and the police photographer."

Farone was relieved that he didn't have to approach the body immediately and instead took charge of the two junior detectives, Sloan and Nugent, who had just arrived. "Scour the area for anything that could conceivably be evidence and clue in forensics and me. Ask the uniforms to canvass the neighborhood to check for possible witnesses, strange and unusual sights, sounds, or strangers this morning. You know the drill."

Bob couldn't help but remember his first impression of the young detectives: Sloan, a tall, dark-complected man who wore Ivy League clothes; and Nugent, a tall, cool blonde who dressed in loose sweaters, slacks, and thick-soled duty shoes so that she would not be taken for the gorgeous young woman she was. In a different setting, they would look like the two icons on top of a traditional wedding cake.

"Bob, come over here, OK? I'm ready to give you some initial impressions."

Farone joined Ryan by the body.

"First, look closely at the victim's face and neck."

"Good god, what a mess. What's the story with the blood that dripped out of his mouth?"

"Whoever did this cut his tongue out. I found it on the ground under his head."

"What killed him, Sheila? Did he bleed out?"

"Not a chance, Bob. His heart had stopped pumping before the tongue removal; that's why no blood other than that in his mouth was pumped out. Right now I'd say death resulted from strangulation. Look at the ligature marks around his neck. Very forceful—trachea's crushed, too. Someone with very large, strong hands did this. Most likely a man. The tongue removal was an added attraction, probably some form of revenge. Or maybe it has cult or ritual significance, leaving some crazy message. This guy's been dead for about two hours max, Bob. Tough case. I'm guessing you've got a nut on your hands."

Farone was momentarily distracted by Ryan's cool professionalism and her ability to communicate without lapsing into technobabble. "Yeah, Sheila, it's not a gimme. The guys haven't turned up anything at the scene, and the canvass probably won't yield much either. We've got to get an ID on the victim fast, in order to investigate friends, acquaintances, and, if we're lucky, known enemies."

The forensics team was called in to obtain fingerprints and to photograph the site. It was quickly observed that the cross was made of common pressure-treated four-by-four lumber, spiked together, and that the rope was the three-strand nylon type most commonly used in boating. It also became evident that the cross had been wiped clean of fingerprints. The dirt extracted from the hole was dried out, suggesting that the hole had been dug some time earlier in the week, in preparation for the killing.

Farone guessed—and the others agreed with him—that the killer or killers had committed the murder in another location, bound the body to the cross, driven to the site, and implanted the cross. The tongue was probably cut out at the scene. And if it was only one guy, Farone thought, he must be very strong. And very pissed off.

Farone's conjectures were interrupted by Detective Margaret Nugent, who had been checking the body for additional clues with her partner. "Excuse me, Detective Farone. We've found something. A bracelet on his left wrist."

The detectives and Medical Examiner Ryan pulled closer to examine the evidence, the first break they'd had all morning.

The bracelet was a gold chain with a small gold object attached. "Anybody know what this is?" Farone asked.

Ryan, embarrassed that she hadn't noticed the bracelet herself, came up with the answer. "It's a charm bracelet, Bob, with only one charm. A crab."

CHAPTER FOUR

Lt. Jonas James, head of homicide, called the meeting to order at exactly 10:00 a.m. on Tuesday, the day following the homicide. Bob Farone, along with Detectives Nugent and Sloan, was the first to arrive, having already briefed the chief in his office.

The meeting got started when Medical Examiner Sheila Ryan and Assistant State Attorney Catherine Weiss arrived moments later.

"Everybody here knows everybody else, so we can get started right now," James said brusquely. "We're all up to speed on the murder—at least the bare essentials—so let's go over what we've learned. Bob, you get us started. OK?"

The meeting room was bright, neat, and up-to-date with the latest computer and conferencing equipment. In fact, the entire homicide facility was the model of efficiency: rather severe—but not intimidating—interview rooms; secure, modern holding pens; and neatly aligned desks in the detectives' open space, each desk replete with multitask communications equipment and, of course, the ubiquitous computer monitor. The entire area was neat and modern by design, according to Lt. James, "to foster an impression of professionalism and to provide an efficient, nonintimidating, high-tech working atmosphere for our detectives and staff support."

Farone arose and began a detailed review of the case. He omitted a lengthy preamble and got right to the point. "Thanks, Jonas. You all were briefed yesterday with what little we knew of the crime. Today, thanks to forensics and basic detective work, we've developed significantly more information, but remember, we're still a long way from ID'ing or profiling a suspect. Let's get started with what we know. Sheila, dim the lights a little, please."

Farone's information was neatly summarized in one-line, numbered bursts, which he amplified with his whiteboard presentation.

"Number one, the victim's name is Robert DeJohn, pastor of a TV ministry called Servants of Job. He is white, fifty-one years old, married, no children. He lived just over the Connecticut border in Port Chester, New York.

"According to the Port Chester cops, Reverend DeJohn was the head of a very sick, screwball sect—about two hundred parishioners. It's their belief, according to the cops and the Reverend's own pamphlets, that God is still testing man's faith, the way he tested Job's. So these people congregate in this small building owned by the DeJohns about twice a week and take turns crying out what's supposedly tragic in their lives: being fleeced, lied to, cheated on, unjustly accused, that sort of stuff. At the end of the services, the good reverend comforts them—lots of tears and compassion. Everybody's crying and hugging. The stereo's cranking out Bach chorales for organ. And then the good reverend extracts cash donations—twenties and fifties—from each person or family, which he pockets. He also requires an annual membership of five percent, which he declares on his tax return, and gets extra fees for one-on-one counseling—presumably to listen to their complaints and offer hugs in return.

"So for openers, we have the possibility of a disgruntled member of the flock executing him. Could be a fruitful trail to follow, because of another interesting angle: the cops in Port Chester call this guy 'Ballin' Bill,' because they recently arrested him for at least fourteen sexual offenses against minors. Boys and girls. One of the kids told her parents—and they reported the assault to the authorities—explaining that the reverend said it was just another one of God's tests. The word spread, and the state attorney OK'd the collar. The pastor made bail two days ago. I've sent Markowitz and Foster down to Port Chester this morning to get statements from the parents of the kids and to dig up any other useful information to develop leads.

"Point number two: the forensics and medical examiner reports. Either of you guys jump in if you think I'm misinterpreting your findings.

"First, forensics. So far, no fingerprints anywhere. The killer probably wore gloves. The pressure-treated four-by-fours are common building materials, available in any lumberyard. Ditto the nylon rope. Mostly used on small boats for dock or mooring lines, sometimes for small anchor lines. Available at any ship's chandlery or the big Kmarts of the world. One interesting thing, though. The knots used to secure the victim are called sheepshank knots, named by sailors hundreds of years ago, and not commonly used today. It's a long shot, but we'll have some uniforms check out the local Greenwich, Stamford, and Norwalk boatyards.

"Kids play and hangout at the crime scene, so there are really too many footprints. However, we did find one, near the cross, and cast it for possible evidence. The reading on the print so far is that it was probably a boot, size thirteen. Not a kid's. Also, the depth of impression indicates that the boot was worn by a large person, no doubt a man, who weighs well over two hundred pounds."

"How about the neighborhood canvass? Anything on vehicles or strangers? Any odd noises?" asked Lt. James.

"So far nothing, sir. None of the homes have a direct view of the scene, so no reports on people or cars. Also, no one claims to have known the vic, which rules out a backyard-burial situation. But we'll continue the canvass."

Farone went back to his seat. "Sheila, you did the medical exam. Why don't you present the findings?"

Sheila rose and walked to the head of the table. *She looks more beautiful every day*, mused Farone. He had always found her attractive. Had flirted now and then. Against his better judgment about not getting romantically involved with people you work with, he had even asked her out. And to his surprise, she had agreed. It was an intense, passionate affair—the happiest days of his life, he often said—until the day she explained that she could not be seriously involved with someone in the same line of work. Farone had been left with a mixture of heartbreak and relief after she broke it off. He knew she was right and agreed with her reasoning. But he also knew she was the one woman he could love forever, and losing her was a crushing blow.

Ryan began her report directly. "You all know that the reverend was crucified upside down. The hole had apparently been dug days before, yet the concrete mix used to fill the hole around the base of the cross was still in the process of setting. Concrete takes twenty-four hours to dry and set, so it seems that the perp had first dug the hole and then strangled the reverend to death at another location days later. Then, about two to two and a half hours after the actual murder, he tied the vic to the cross, cut out his tongue, and cemented the cross to the ground, pouring the concrete mix, along with a container of water, into the hole. He might have only been on the scene for five to ten minutes, which would explain why no one noticed him."

"What's the story on the severed tongue, Dr. Ryan?" asked Assistant State Attorney Catherine Weiss.

"I'm sure the tongue was cut out at the scene. He was already dead, and that's why only local blood was dripping downward from his mouth. We are conducting a full autopsy now, but I suspect we won't learn anything particularly useful."

"Was there anything unusual about the tongue? Any chance that we're looking at a cult or revenge murder?" persisted Weiss.

"Yes, Ms. Weiss," Ryan replied quickly. "I was getting to that. The tongue bore traces of a white, filmy substance on it. Further investigation showed that the same substance was also in his mouth. Our first guess was that there had been an oral homosexual contact. But that notion was thrown out after further testing."

"Well then, what was it?" interjected Lt. James.

"Plain soap. Probably Ivory, judging by the so-called purity. Want my guess? Somebody washed out the reverend's mouth with soap. Just like they did in the old days with naughty children."

Farone cut in. "Dr. Ryan and I went over the soap scenario before this meeting. I agree with her that the mouth-washing act was symbolic. The guy was a preacher, supposed to spread the good news, help people. Instead the sleazy bastard abused kids. He didn't practice what he preached—that's the message. Someone wanted to rid the world of this guy and leave a not-too-subtle message to the rest of us."

"That certainly points a finger at the parents of the kids," Weiss said with some enthusiasm. "Who could have a better motive for revenge—child abuse and years of hypocrisy?"

"What about his wife as a suspect? Pissed off to discover what he'd been up to for years," asked Lt. James.

"Chief, the Port Chester cops who investigated him said his wife, Amy, is as corrupt as he was and knew all about the kids. Plus, she just returned this morning from a trip to Marblehead, Massachusetts, to visit family. Alibi checks out," Farone answered. "Detectives Nugent and Sloan interviewed her just before this meeting. Tell us what you learned"

Margaret Nugent, aka Peggy, was the more articulate of the two young detectives, so she responded. "Yes, we spoke to her for about one hour and had the feeling she held nothing back in the interview. As Bob said, her alibi is solid. She expressed zero remorse about her husband's death. Cool as ice. And while we were in her living room, her life insurance agent returned her call. Our impression was that she was as surprised by the murder as anyone else. The cops in Port Chester will continue to sniff around, but it looks like a cold lead."

Detective Brian Sloan's head popped up from the notes he was making as Lt. James directed a question at him. "Brian, as I remember it, you spent a year in the seminary, so that makes you our religion expert du jour. This Reverend DeJohn was crucified, right? And we can guess that it had something to do with his so-called profession, or it was an odd twist by the perp. I guess we'll figure out the connection sooner or later.

But what's the deal on the guy being hung upside down? What's this guy trying to tell us? Any ideas?"

Sloan actually had been giving the problem some thought but made sure his answer didn't sound too definitive or opinionated. "Well, I do have an idea of why the crucifixion was done as it was. I think you're right. The decision to crucify was a distorted reflection of the reverend's Christian beliefs. Why upside down? I'm guessing that the murderer knows something about early Christian history. When the Romans caught St. Peter and convicted him of heresy, he was sentenced to be crucified. As the story goes, his last request was to be crucified upside down, since the conventional way would be an insult to the memory of Christ. So they obliged him. I don't feel there's any connection past that."

Catherine Weiss shifted gears abruptly. "What about the charm bracelet you found on the body? I read about it in the report. Is it evidence in any way?"

Sloan replied, "Peggy and I called on four different jewelry stores in the Stamford area. Each one said the charm and bracelet were common. Nothing special. We showed the bracelet to Amy DeJohn anyway, to see if we could develop a lead. She told us that she had never seen the bracelet before, but it couldn't possibly be her husband's. Said the guy hated the idea of jewelry on men, made 'em look like fags. He never wore anything—no chains, tie clips, cufflinks, or even a wedding band. And the last thing he would wear would be a charm bracelet."

"So what, if anything, do you two make of the bracelet we found? Any ideas?" asked Farone.

Nugent replied. "No real ideas yet, Bob, but it seems to us that someone deliberately put the charm on DeJohn's wrist. We feel that if we can discover why—and what the significance of the charm is—we may have something to go on."

CHAPTER FIVE

Six days later. Hysterical cleaning lady in exclusive Round Hill area of Greenwich phones in apparent homicide. Her employer, a successful middle-aged corporate CEO, has been found dead in his own bathtub. He is naked. Hands and feet have been bound. His face and parts of his body have been disfigured.

The police report, provided by Detectives Sloan and Nugent, added the remaining gruesome details: According to the autopsy performed by Dr. Ryan, the victim had been placed, hands and feet bound, in the tub of water and left there for at least eight hours, probably overnight. Puckering of the skin consistent with this finding. He had been dead, however, for only about one hour, death caused by drowning. Tub filled with bizarre objects: several dead fish floating belly-up and a few malformed lobsters and shrimp. Also, discharge of urine and fecal matter. Of additional significance were large traces of hydrochloric acid in tub, which caused burns and disfigurement on the body. One other disturbing feature: bound hands were placed behind head, then secured with rope over the top rim of the tub, tied to faucets.

And on the victim's left wrist, free from acid attack, was a common gold charm bracelet with crab charm attached.

• • •

Bob Farone convened a late afternoon meeting in the conference room. He included Dr. Ryan and his two young detectives, Sloan and Nugent.

"Let's get started with what we know. And make it brief. The chief is getting hammered by the media over these two homicides, and he may need to call me out to assist or give him any further info he can reveal to the media without compromising the investigation. Sheila, we all read your initial coroner's report. I'd like your full impression of what happened."

"Well, Bob, the complete evidence is circumstantial, but I'm pretty sure this crime was committed by the same guy who killed the reverend. Can't believe it's a copycat, since you did a good job of omitting key details to the media yesterday.

"From a medical point of view, I believe the perp entered this guy's house around midnight, despite the fancy alarm system. What look to be bruises about the head and face indicate that the victim—Mr. Regis Pollard, as you found out—had been smacked around and subdued. He was ordered to strip, I've concluded, and, no, there was no evidence of sexual abuse. Tied up, then placed in bathtub, hands tied to faucets and tub filled with water. Incidentally, the sushi selection tossed into the tub had been dead for several days and probably stored on ice. As far as the defecation and urination go, you might say these were natural events, being that Pollard was left in the tub all night. My guess is he eliminated involuntarily, out of sheer terror, because the killer had tortured him by methodically pouring a high concentration of hydrochloric acid on different parts of his head and torso. He then pushed Pollard's head under to drown him—in his own filth—at about seven thirty this morning, just before the maid arrived. No way for me to tell if he came back to drown the guy or hung around all night."

"Thanks, Sheila. Yes, it's shaping up to be the same killer, but we have to keep an open mind to other possibilities, like gangs, cults, coincidence. Peggy, what did you and Brian come up with?"

"Nothing much yet, Bob," Nugent replied. "Brian's the religious expert, and he can't come up with any religious or satanic-type parallels between the two killings. No footprints, no fingerprints. The alarm system was never turned on. Guess he believed in the infallibility of being rich, smart, and tough."

Brian Sloan picked up the report. "On a positive note, Bob, the rope used to tie Pollard up was identical to the one at the reverend scene. The knots were different, but Officer Felice, who was at the scene, told us that they were classic, old-time sailors' knots. The cop hails from a Gloucester fishing family and knows a lot about this stuff.

"As far as the neighbors go, well, it's four-acre zoning out there, so no one recalls hearing or seeing anything unusual. He lived alone, as you know. Ex-wife in New York, three kids grown and gone. Girlfriend comes out on weekends to play house. We've called them all to break the bad news; no one had any ideas about any enemies Pollard may have had."

"Thanks. Keep banging away at this, the both of you. And let me know if and when we're going to need more detectives to help out," Bob added. "One obvious similarity to the DeJohn case is that both vics have been in the media spotlight recently. DeJohn for being exposed as a pervert, and Pollard for heading up a company that's been indicted for years of discharging industrial waste and carbolic acid into Long Island Sound. Great neighbors. Other than that, it's hard to see any tie-in between the vics, except being murdered. Which brings me to our most intriguing piece of evidence, the charm bracelet. It's been found to be identical in both cases, added by the perp as some sort of message or signature.

"The best I personally have to offer at this time is a hunch: some big, strong, smart, crazy guy is killing people in bizarre, grotesque ways. Motive presently unknown. Nylon line and ability with knots mark this guy as someone with a sailing or seafaring background. Add to this that his signature is a crab. I don't know what that tells us now, but I'm guessing that our best opportunity to develop leads lies in canvassing anything to do with boatyards, chandlers, bait-and-tackle shops, marina operators and yardmen, and so on. Ask about any man who's been acting weird or angry lately. You know the drill. Take as many uniformed officers as we can spare. We're back to basic detective work. Let's get something. Good luck."

CHAPTER SIX

Two months before.
 Dr. Ransom's office, FairfieldDermatologyCenter, southern Connecticut.
 "Thanks for coming in exactly when scheduled," Dr. Ransom began, somewhat nervously. "Wasn't surprised. Your primary-care doctor is a golf buddy of mine, and he said you were notoriously punctual."
 The man he addressed was a new patient, a tall, powerfully built white male, forty-eight years old. Conventional looks, brown hair with sprinkles of gray, blue eyes, even features. He was inconspicuously dressed in a navy-blue Lacoste shirt, standard tan chinos, and Sperry boat shoes. His face was unlined but quite tanned. He was composed but somewhat wary, Dr. Ransom noted. Pretty much as the internist who had referred him had described him.
 "Well, Mr. Hartman, as you know, the small mole we excised from your back and biopsied appears to be malignant melanoma, Clark's level three, with a point three millimeter Breslowe thickness. And last week you underwent a broader excision at the site, in which an additional seven point eight millimeters was removed from either side of the incision line—"

The patient interrupted, slightly sarcastically. "Upon completion of the excision, the specimen was sent to radiology for further review. They gave the results to you, and now you've called me in on short notice to 're-view'—as your phone message said—my case. So can we please get down to business and cut out the foreplay?"

Slightly annoyed that his attempt at professional diplomacy had been cut short, Dr. Ransom got right to the point. "Mr. Hartman, I'm sorry to report that the radiologist to whom we sent tissue samples has indeed confirmed that your malignancy is a serious form of skin cancer—melanoma—and unfortunately it seems to be progressing to other sites, notably the lymph glands and lungs. The spreading of cancer cells is called *metastasis*. It's very serious, so we need to discuss a course of treatment and begin it immediately."

The patient retained his composure fully, expressing only a questioning attitude with his eyes. "I get a complete physical exam every year in Connecticut. Why wasn't this problem picked up earlier?"

Dr. Ransom replied carefully, "Obviously we don't know the extent of the examination performed by your personal physician. Normally, however, the examining physician looks over your skin and asks you if you've noticed any new moles or skin irregularities. The doctor is looking primarily for any moles that are or have become irregular in shape, lumpy, encrusted, and so forth. That type of unusual skin lesion is what your doctor sent you to us for originally, requesting excision and biopsy. Then we made a deeper and broader excision for additional study and diagnosis."

"What if someone had noticed the growth earlier?"

"Well, Mr. Hartman, your initial difficulty would then, worst-case scenario, have been a class-two melanoma, which is also dangerous, but quite treatable through excision, since it's basically an epidermal condition and has not yet penetrated the system and advanced to classes three or four."

"I've spent most of my life out of doors in the sun, on the water. Is that why I'm sick, even though I use sunblock and wear a hat and do all that other crap you dermatologists harp on?"

"I don't like to guess at the cause of disease when there is no medical history of the patient. My guess, based on the medical data we have for all forms of skin cancer, is that your problem, as for so many others, was caused when you were very young. Playing in the sun too long, no sunscreen, no hat, all the other things you apparently disdain," the doctor replied, slightly annoyed at the patient's attitude. He was also aware that the allocated time for a consultation allowed by the insurance company was running out. "Does that answer your question, Mr. Hartman?"

"More than you'll ever know." Harman thought of his Father, a big-time blue-water sailor. When Hartman was a kid, his Father would take him out on the boat to teach him to sail. His mother hated boating; it made her seasick. She was happy to see them take off. She got to spend the whole day shopping and having lunch with socialite friends. What she didn't know was that his Father had a girlfriend, a lot younger than Hartman's mother, and that this girl, Rachel, would join the so-called training cruise. And after about one hour of sailing, the old man would enter Norwalk harbor, anchor, and go below with Rachel for a few hours of drinking and screwing in an air-conditioned stateroom. Hartman was left above decks, soaking up the sun.

Doctor Ransom fidgeted slightly in his chair and glanced sneakily at his watch. So many patients to see. "To be perfectly honest with you, Mr. Hartman, it's not too fruitful to try to identify the specific origins of your cancer. Probably the damage was done with repeated exposure to the sun, both on the boat and ashore. You probably had severe burns, possibly blistering, rashes, and perhaps feverous reactions."

"Well, now that we've dispensed with the past, Doctor, what do I do about this problem starting today?"

"Mr. Hartman," the doctor began carefully, "you're very sick. In my opinion, a drug called interferon, which may help slow down the growth rate of the cancer cells in your body, is called for. However, I'm going to refer you to an oncologist, whom you should consult immediately for your ongoing care. She may wish to start you on interferon or some other drug, such as interleukin-2. Radiology and surgery may also be prescribed. I'm certain that some of your lymph nodes will have to be removed to further reduce metastasis."

Hartman showed absolutely no reaction. "I sold my construction business last year for over two million dollars net. I also inherited a great deal of money after my father died four years ago. So I've got the time and resources to get any treatment, anywhere. If you were in my shoes, Doctor, what would you do?"

"Just what I told you," Ransom replied bluntly. "Your strategy is to retard the cancerous growth's expansion by utilizing some combination of chemotherapy, radiology, and surgery. The goal is to then enter a clinical trial, which may lead to a breakthrough in treatment. A variety of such trials are coming up, both here and in Europe. And it goes without saying that if you want a second opinion, your film can be sent to any other clinic you choose."

Hartman interrupted calmly and coldly. "So what you're telling me is that the so-called current treatment isn't good enough to cure my cancer but will instead guarantee that I lose my hair, suffer constant nausea and vomiting, and live without a lymphatic system. And all to hang in there until I sign up as a guinea pig for a trial, most of which result in failure."

Dr. Ransom rose to his feet and closed the chart on Hartman. "Mr. Hartman, please take the steps I've planned for you. I can understand that you're frightened, anxious, and confused, and we can prescribe tried-and-true medications to help deal with your feelings. But please don't lapse into denial. Every minute counts in your treatment. Do you understand?"

"I'm neither frightened nor confused," Hartman answered coldly as he stood up. "If I can't buy my way back to good health, I'm not going to poison myself with palliatives and pray for some trial to come along. Tell me directly: if I do nothing, how long have I got to live?"

"Hard to say. At least eighteen to twenty-four months. But don't dwell on that. Take a day or two and think about what I told you. Don't make a rash decision just because you're angry."

"Thanks for leveling with me, Dr. Ransom," Hartman replied as he extended his hand. "I've felt for years that some form of big-time calamity such as this would hit me. I'm more emotionally prepared than you'll ever know. You can seal my chart. I intend to live out my days feeling well, strong, and productive. As they say, I've got places to go and people to see."

Dr. Ransom and the patient left the examination room together. Ransom once again urged Hartman to reconsider, said good-bye, put Hartman out of his mind, and checked with his assistant to learn whom his next appointment was with. His last thought about Hartman was that the man had reacted oddly—differently from any other patient he had ever had to be blunt with. Cold, yet obviously enraged. Shrewd and decisive but, curiously, almost as if he was expecting terrible news.

Hartman headed for the parking lot, a picture of health bathed in late-spring sunshine. His truck, a customized Dodge Ramcharger crew cab, also served as a traveling office, a carryover from his contracting days, although the truck had originally belonged to his father and had become part of the estate when his father died. It was equipped with cell phone, fax, GPS, weather radio, and ordinary items, such as paper, pens, architect's ruler, measuring tape, tool kit, and mariner's rigging knife with marlin spike. The bed of the truck was fitted out with a large, lockable tool and equipment container and also contained several neatly coiled lengths of rope, a folded tarp, and assorted long-handled tools, shovels, and the like. None used much recently, since he'd sold his house.

Hartman sat in his truck for ten minutes, enjoying a cigarette—*Not good for your health*, he noted ironically—and ruminating. Most people who learned a little about Hartman's life would be impressed, even envious. He was a seemingly pampered only child, born to a wealthy family in South Carolina. Behind the scenes, however, was the daily pressure of living in a very dysfunctional family. Mr. Hartman Sr. worked only a few hours a week running his commercial construction company. He delegated authority freely to several respected, highly paid managers who, in turn, ran his company with great precision, providing increased revenues and profits each year, leaving him even wealthier and allowing him full time for his greatest pleasures: blue-water sailing, alcohol, and wild, young girls. He considered his son to be, at best, a potential boat hand, maybe a crew member. But the kid was so skinny, he wondered if he would ever be able to handle the lines, the halyards, and the sheets. He paid absolutely no attention to his wife, writing her off as a giddy socialite, wasting her life on clothes, charity work, and bridge parties. He found out later in their marriage that she had made time for additional activities: sleeping with a variety of pool boys, tennis pros, and men she met traveling to bridge tournaments.

Divorce pleased both Hartmans. Plenty of money to share and complete freedom to live without hypocrisy. The only glitch was their son. Neither really wanted him. Joint custody was arranged by the court. The result was two satisfied grownups, and one unhappy, skinny, and lonely little boy—Ivan Hartman.

School was a disaster for Ivan. As he was growing up, in conservative Beaufort, the other kids reflected to Ivan's face their parents' views of the Hartmans: the father a drunken playboy, the mother a tramp in fine clothes. When Ivan lost his temper, the resulting playground fight was a wipeout for him. Too slow, too small. The ultimate childhood insult was making fun of his odd name. He was routinely referred to as Ivan the Terrible. When his father impetuously moved to Lyme, Connecticut, Ivan went with him. He did not miss his mother. The feeling was mutual.

Much to his father's surprise, Ivan suddenly started growing bigger, probably owing to some inherited gene from his mother's family. He shot up to six foot three inches, still skinny but heavily boned.

Big as he was getting, Ivan had no interest in team sports. Nor did he care about his studies. He had no close friends, except the girls in his high-school class did become increasingly friendly as they noted how goodlooking he was becoming. The obvious advantages of wealth—nice clothes, plenty of money, credit cards, and a new Corvette Stingray convertible—enhanced his popularity but not his self-esteem.

In addition to a growing interest in girls, young Ivan had two other serious interests: his new nineteen-foot Ensign sailboat, which he raced every weekend, and daily trips to the gym, where he spent hours at a time lifting weights and taking martial arts courses. Ivan had many secrets. He had kept a notebook from fourthgrade onward, detailing each outrage he felt he had experienced at the hands of his parents, schoolmates, and strangers. And for each offense he had assigned one of six different "torture and death protocols" to enact upon the offender. In ninth grade, he burned the notebook and turned to less serious—but more practical—revenge. His mother's "lost" car keys. Gull shit strewn on his father's forty-four-foot Morgan sloop. Knocked-over mailboxes, tires slit on schoolyard bikes, unsigned hate mail sent to classmates.

After graduating from high school in the lower third of his class, Ivan was counseled to enroll in a trade school or enlist in the military. He was considered to be a "waste" in the school system, because—although he had a high IQ, was wellread on his own and, though quiet, could argue forcefully and articulately when pushed to in class—he was always bored, rarely studied, and had little interest in his classes.

With his father's contacts, he got a job on a construction crew building tract homes in Danbury. He rose quickly through the ranks, from rough carpenter to finish carpenter to foreman. By the time he turned twenty-seven, he was ready to start his own contracting business, building high-end residences in affluent Fairfield County. Other than sailing, Ivan had never had any particular relationship with his father. But now he could turn to him for business advice and start-up capital.

Looking back, Hartman realized that his early twenties had been the best part of a shitty life. He lit another cigarette and fast forwarded to what the next twenty years of his life had meant: nothing, nothing at all. A successful business, certainly, but one made increasingly difficult by architects, who designed houses with little regard for difficulties in construction, and impatient homeowners, who wanted everything done immediately and then asked for changes on a whim. Building materials increasingly shoddy, demands for benefits increasing, building and environmental codes more and more complex and restrictive. Glad to sell out.

Lousy personal life. Two wives, both whiners and both unfaithful. One child, dead from leukemia. Friends only interested in his money. Father, on his deathbed, refused to see him. So what's left? Money, which he wouldn't live long enough to spend. Powerful body, now rotting away. Maybe it was a blessing in disguise, a comment on a society that was rotting away, too. Corruption, immorality, hypocrisy, theft, lying—the media reported it every day. And yet these scum were still in business? The ultimate "Why me?" joke.

And suddenly it hit him. The plan for his remaining days. Hartman flipped the cigarette butt out the window and began to enjoy the same feeling of power he had with his secret vengeful acts as a kid. He would scour the media and rid society of the corrupt and the vicious, as many as possible in the time he had left. His final mission. Useful, responsible. The cure for cancer.

CHAPTER SEVEN

Exactly six days after the death of the polluter, Regis Pollard, was discovered, another body turned up, in the parking lot of Stamford Hospital. Naked, middle-aged white male stretched out on his back, feet tied together with nylon rope. His hands were free. His right hand lay across his chest, clutching what looked like a large, bloody kidney bean. A large pool of blood had spread around the body. No evidence was found at the scene.

The autopsy report concluded that the victim had died of massive blood loss. The cause was odd by any medical standards—his right kidney had been crudely removed, placed in his hand, and propped onto his chest. Bruises on his stomach indicated that he had been held down while bleeding and that it had taken approximately nine minutes for him to bleed out.

Several hospital employees, canvassed by Detectives Nugent and Sloan, quickly identified the body as a doctor named Elliot Rabin, a staff surgeon at the hospital.

The media clustered like flies. They had covered the long malpractice trial of Dr. Rabin, who, it had been proved, had removed the wrong kidney from his patient, a young boy who later developed an infection and died.

One reporter in particular was very persistent in asking the detectives if any items had been found on or near the body. Both Sloan and Nugent had been well trained in the art of appearing courteous and open with the media while not giving them any serious information that could spoil potential leads and jeopardize the investigation. Which is why Margaret Nugent did not even consider mentioning the gold crab charm bracelet, covered with dried blood, that she had slipped into an evidence bag and then into her purse .

CHAPTER EIGHT

The homicide review meeting conducted by Chief James was somber, to say the least. Bob Farone was grateful that Jonas had refrained from hectoring his team for coming up with so little on the murders—few clues or leads—particularly since the lieutenant had been so heavily pressed by the chief of police and two county commissioners. Of course the pols had endured their own questioning, with intimations of ineptitude, by the media. *Flows downhill,* thought Farone, *and Jonas is showing a lot of class in not taking it out on us.*

Before Farone could begin his review of the homicides, Jonas James told the group that he had an announcement to make. "In light of the fact that each victim was apparently forcibly picked up and later removed to the crime scene, we've got to look at these crimes as abduction and kidnapping, as well as murder. To me that means asking the FBI to step in as our partners in this investigation. And since it's fairly obvious that we're dealing with a psychopath—a serial killer—their experience in both profiling and sophisticated detective work will help us break this case that much faster. Three agents from the Hartford office are outside and will be joining this meeting momentarily.

"Their head agent is Raymond Snyder. He will act as Detective Farone's partner, so to speak. The other two agents will report directly to Snyder. All of you, including Sheila and her pathology staff, will remain on the team. And, of course, Catherine Weiss, from the state attorney's office, will be involved. In fact, she's coming over here at the end of this meeting to get up to speed on the case.

"As you may imagine, the judicial group is increasingly concerned about the finger-pointing that may be started by the media, so keep her clued in. Remember to be cooperative with the media, but don't give them anything that might screw up our case.

"One last thing. Before I ask Agent Snyder and his team to join us, I must urge you to cooperate fully with them and not to regard their addition to our team as a rebuke to you or in any way as taking over the case. In short: no turf wars. After they join us, and we get acquainted, I'd like you to begin the briefing, Bob. Thanks."

Farone maintained his composure, but his stomach was churning. Jonas obviously had no choice regarding the addition of the FBI, but it still rankled. Farone felt that his team had done a very thorough, very professional job so far, even though no solid leads had been developed. A break would soon be forthcoming, he felt, just as they usually did. His father, who had made a great deal of money defending all sorts of clients, had once told Bob, "The reason I'm always busy isn't that I'm so smart. It's the basic fact that even the most clever criminal screws up."

Farone swallowed his disappointment and greeted the federal agents gracefully. The two junior agents were dressed alike in Joseph Bank-type Ivy League clothes. They were cool yet pleasant. Eager to begin.

Head agent Raymond Snyder was a different type altogether. When introduced as "Ray," he explained that he wished to be called Raymond. He wore a pinstripe Brioni suit, a custom-made Austin Chang shirt, and an Armani necktie. A silk pocket square, Gucci shoes, and an Ebel wristwatch completed the picture. Margaret Nugent, who followed fashion closely, concluded that Snyder was either living over his head on an agent's salary, or he had family money behind him. The latter turned out to be true.

Detective Sloan began the meeting with a brief review of the various crime scenes, using blow-up copies of street maps, forensic photos, and lists of evidence and demographic information on the victims. Everyone agreed that there was no particular consistency with respect to the locations of the bodies other than the obvious fact that an attempt had been made to make a symbolic statement using the scene of the crime as a "setting"—for example, the hospital parking lot for the doctor.

Farone next asked Detective Nugent to outline the basic information they sought but hadn't yet found. As Nugent got to her feet and began her presentation with acetate overhead slides, Farone noticed that Snyder looked approvingly—even lustfully—at the young, attractive detective. *At least our Mr. Raymond is straight*, he thought.

Nugent quickly and efficiently ticked off the information they either had in hand or lacked. First, they had turned up no witnesses. There was no evidence of robbery or sexual molestation of the victims. One footprint had been found, possibly indicating that the killer was a large male. There was no history of any familial, social, or professional connection between the victims. In fact, the only similarity between the victims was that they had received adverse media publicity recently, for crimes, or alleged crimes, that could raise a cry for revenge.

The pattern of the crime scenes that Sloan had shown on his maps was also inconclusive at best. No weapons had been found anywhere, nor were there any full or partial hand or fingerprints or any potential samples of DNA.

Farone took on the challenge of reviewing the only real pieces of evidence from the crime scene, the nylon rope and the charm bracelets.

"As far as the nylon rope goes," Farone began, "it's the most common type of line used in this area, three-strand nylon. It's used for general applications but is found commonly on boats and docks. Used primarily for dock lines, mooring lines, anchor lines, et cetera. Since it's nylon, it resists breaking down by the sun and salt air. It's also somewhat elastic, so it gives a little—actually stretches and rebounds like a rubber band—which makes it ideal for boating applications that face severe winds and other stressors.

"The unusual knots used to bind the victims also point to a boating orientation. Margaret, be good enough to pop up the slide showing the various knots this guy used."

The slide showed six different knots, as photographed at each scene by the CSI team. A second slide showed the knots as drawn in a sailing manual.

"The knots you're looking at are used in boating, primarily on sailboats. They've been identified by our coast guard contacts in New London as the clove hitch, the sheepshank, the bowline, the sheet bend, the anchor knot, and the halyard bend. So there is some indication that our killer is or was a sailor—skipper or hand. And this indication is possibly supported by the crab charm on each charm bracelet. Is there a link to the sea, the name of a boat, professional shell fishing? We've had six uniformed officers visiting the various places and people connected with local boatyards. So far, nothing that appears useful. We've also checked local jewelers. The charm and bracelet are not at all uncommon. Right now it appears that we've got to pursue the boating connection, review every scrap of information we've acquired, and, frankly, hope for a break."

"Well, I hope we're not tying our success to Lady Luck, Detective," interjected Agent Snyder. "Our profiling people in Washington are ready to develop a description of the killer, but 'large male with possible sailing background' isn't exactly a running start.

"On a different tack, if you'll pardon the pun, what else do we know or surmise about the bracelets?" Snyder continued. "For example, perhaps there is an actual link between the victims. They were each found with the same bracelet. Why conclude prematurely that the bracelets were placed on the victims by the killer? Maybe these men were part of a cult or secret club. They wear these bracelets the way fraternity boys wear badges."

"Don't believe that's the case, Ray," rebutted Detective Sloan. "We talked to each of the victims' families, and they confirmed not only that these guys didn't know each other but that none of them wore much jewelry, if any, and they didn't own these bracelets."

"I believe that further professional investigation will resolve that particular question, Sloan," Snyder said with an icy smile. "I think we may have a potential clue in the time lag that occurred between killings. A topic I haven't heard broached yet, Detective Farone."

Farone asked calmly, not betraying any hostility, "What exactly did you have in mind, Raymond?"

Snyder dropped the tone of his voice in order to better convey the import of his thought. "The second murder occurred exactly six days after the first. And the third murder took place six days after the second. If there's a fourth murder, I'll bet it will take place six days after the third crime—three days from today. The intervals will provide three sixes—a pattern fundamentalist Christian sects fear as the sign of Satan. If I'm right, the man we seek will be identified as a satanist, probably the member of a screwball cult. We will then have a specific trail to follow."

Snyder looked down the table at Peggy Nugent, expecting to see a look of respect, a sign that she was duly impressed with his insights. Her only reaction was to turn on her cell phone and prepare to leave the meeting.

The next murder took place exactly seventeen days later.

CHAPTER NINE

Lester Wulkan strode aggressively from his office, through the exit door, and across the parking lot to his Toyota. He was impatient to get home to his apartment, shower, and get dressed in his Scout leader's uniform. The weekly Boy Scout troop meeting was the highlight of his otherwise boring life, an escape from his dull job, and an antidote to living alone. And in the closet.

Wulkan was hardly aware of footsteps that approached quickly from behind, until a sharp object was pressed against the small of his back and a large hand was placed across his mouth. He was ordered to remain silent and to walk slowly to a red Dodge Ram pickup truck parked nearby, away from the overhead lights of the parking lot. Upon reaching the tailgate of the truck, the object was quickly withdrawn from his back, and two hard whacks of a fishing bat across the back of his head knocked him cold.

He regained a small amount of consciousness as the truck headed down the highway at a moderate speed, with him in the bed. Wulkan's ankles were securely lashed together and tied to the interior tailgate latch with a clove hitch. His hands were bound behind his back, he was gagged, and he was covered with what appeared to be a large, heavy piece of canvas. He was terrified. In a panic, he writhed around and pulled at his restraints, to no avail. He tried to scream but failed.

The truck pulled into a remote campsite, used by Scout troops and other organizations to pitch tents and camp out overnight or for a weekend. An army-surplus pup tent with ground cover had been set up and staked down. A small Coleman lantern was glowing inside the tent.

Feeling euphoric, Hartman killed the engine, hopped out of the truck, and pulled down the tailgate. Wulkan was momentarily relieved as his kidnapper cut away the ropes securing him to the truck bed and then removed his gag. His relief was quickly cut short as Hartman dragged him from the truck bed, struck him several more times with his aluminum fish bat, and tossed him onto the ground in front of the tent.

"Mr. Wulkan, it's a real pleasure to meet you, despite the circumstances," Hartman said. "You've had a lot of coverage lately in the Danbury media for allegedly sexually molesting young scouts in your troop. Probably a pack of lies, right? Or maybe not. I was a young Boy Scout years ago. Really admired our troop's scoutmaster, too. Seemed to be a much nicer man than my own father. Until he asked me to come into his tent one night at the jamboree camp-out and raped me. I didn't know it at the time, but I wasn't the only kid he attacked. Must have been only thirteen or fourteen, but it seems like yesterday. It had a beneficial effect, though. Got me into body building and martial arts. I vowed that I would never be touched again, and I wasn't.

"But you know, big and strong and tough as I got, the shame and rage never left. Right now, for example, I'm seething. And we're alone, Mr. Wulkan. See this knife? Don't worry, I'm not going to cut you. But I am going to cut away your clothes. No rape, though. I'm obviously crazy in my own way, but I'm no gay predator. Like you. Let's get started."

Hartman, wearing double layers of latex gloves, cut away the clothing and, along with all the victim's other effects, stuffed them into a garbage bag for later tossing out. He then removed the gag, allowing Wulkan to protest his innocence and beg for his life. He lied, whined, and finally pleaded that the boys "wanted" it.

Hartman listened, his loathing and contempt masked under an icy calm. He calmly interjected, "You know, I don't believe anything you've said. You are an evil man, one who no longer belongs on the planet."

Wulkan began sobbing desperately as Hartman continued with a smile on his face. "Don't feel so bad, I apparently don't belong on the planet either. Everything that I ever valued in life went sour, Mr. Wulkan. Rotten parents, bullying in school, whores for two wives, child dead, and now the final joke—I'm a walking dead man. Like you. But there's a difference between us. You're checking out as the perverted scum that you are. But when I die, my legacy—and believe me, every act is recorded in my diary—will show that I took as many rotten human beings to the grave with me as time and opportunity allowed.

"Now hold very still. I'm going to free your hands and give you an opportunity to repeat the Boy Scout oath."

With his hands free, Wulkan tried to resist, but with ankles tied and a large smiling man striking him in the face with painful slaps, he soon gave up struggling. That is, until Hartman began cutting off his right thumb. Wulkan writhed and screamed in agony, his voice lost in the night air. Then Hartman cut off the little finger on the same hand.

"Three middle fingers left, Scoutmaster, just right for presenting the Boy Scout salute. Hold still for chrissake. I'm going to place your hand on your forehead so you can make a proper salute. C'mon, cooperate. Take the Scout oath and stop your goddamned screaming," Hartman urged with a smile.

He then castrated Wulkan with one swift knife stroke and shoved the bleeding penis into his mouth, ending the screams of terror and pain forever. Moving efficiently now, Hartman knotted an old Scout neckerchief—his own saved from years ago—around the victim's neck. Two flashes of his knife made diagonally across Wulkan's wrists assured a more rapid bleed-out. And before dragging the writhing body into the tent, Hartman affixed a small gold bracelet around his bloody left wrist.

CHAPTER TEN

The twelve-hour days, almost completely fruitless, were beginning to wear everyone down. Tempers flared, civility waned. Farone knew it was time to take an emotional break, so he called the primary team together for a "working lunch" at the Merritt Farms Country Club in Darien.

"How does a guy on a cop's salary afford a fancy club like this?" Snyder asked bluntly as they were seated. "Rich wife?"

"No wife," Farone answered calmly. "Rich father, junior membership."

Detectives Sloan and Nugent smiled nervously, sensing obvious friction between the two senior men.

Farone decided to set the tone of "time-out" by asking if anyone would join him in a Bloody Mary, a glass of wine, or a beer. Sloan and Nugent opted for white wine. Snyder proclaimed a Bloody Mary to be a waste of good tomato juice, pointed out that FBI investigators never drank on duty, and ordered a Perrier.

Social preliminaries were quickly dispensed with. Brian Sloan announced that he had become engaged, no set date for the wedding. Congratulations followed. Snyder then artlessly segued into asking Peggy Nugent if she were "involved" with anyone. "Married to the job, probably like you are, Raymond," she replied, pleased to dismiss him with a cliché and not-too-subtle shift of the conversation back to the investigation.

Snyder took the hint, flashed annoyance, and turned to Farone. "This small posse of extra detectives and officers assigned to the case by your boss—any results, or are you still treading water? Families of the vics are screaming to the pols and the media for results, and it's obvious we have nothing concrete to give them. Where are we right now, Farone?"

"Sounds like you used the 'we' word, Agent Snyder. 'We' means the FBI, too. So why don't you report what, if anything, your people have discovered? And remember, we are scheduled to make a complete report to Lieutenant James, eight o'clock tomorrow morning."

Snyder picked up the challenge. "The FBI has a lot to report. First, our profiling people have rounded out their picture of the killer. As discussed, a big guy, very strong, learned a lot from watching TV and movie detective shows. Crazy, homicidal psychotic, but in full control. A planner, cold and efficient. Most likely a loner. Boating background, probably sailing, judging from the knots he used. Probably a local, since he's very familiar with the Fairfield area."

"That's an excellent summary of what we've already been through," Nugent said innocently. "Anything new?"

Snyder was annoyed but eager to meet the challenge. "As a matter of fact we have. Our people easily identified the local wholesale distributor of the bracelets by going directly to the manufacturer in Wisconsin. Apparently they're the only people left producing these types of charms. The wholesaler gave us names and locations of three jewelry stores, one in upstate New York, the other two in northern New Jersey, who had ordered bracelets and charms within the last three months. One of the jewelers in Jersey was a dead end. She hadn't sold any of the bracelets. The other Jersey dealer, as well as the guy in Schenectady, both sold out their entire inventory of the bracelets and charms in the same week. Nine items from one store, four from another. Paid for with cash. Each bracelet came with twelve charms, the signs of the zodiac. Probably marketed to astrology screwballs."

The detectives were impressed. "Any description of the buyer or buyers, Raymond?" Farone asked.

Snyder expanded on his briefing with a flourish of command. "As you might guess, Farone," he answered patronizingly, "a small purchase made months ago would not ordinarily provide easy recall of the buyer. But the purchase of the entire inventory of charms in each store was unusual enough for the store owners to remember the transaction. As we've learned, these items move slowly, one at a time, mostly at Christmas and June graduations. Birthdays are also hot. Both stores have reordered new merchandise, but there have been no sales. We have, of course, descriptions of the buyers, and it looks to be the same guy. Tall, sandy hair thinning on top, ruddy tan complexion, really big. Over six foot three, about two hundred forty or fifty pounds. A bit flabby, but heavily muscled. Ordinary WASP-like features. Khaki or some form of tan pants in each case. One jeweler, the guy in Schenectady, couldn't remember anything else, except that the customer was wearing a blue Lacoste-type shirt with a logo or design on it. He remembers the logo because it looked something like Miami Club or Yacht Club, so he asked the guy if it had anything to do with the local sailing club, some small-time summer club on the Mohawk river. The guy just laughed."

"What did you learn from the other jeweler, the one in New Jersey?" Sloan asked respectfully.

"He gave us the start of a concrete lead," Snyder replied. "Seems the customer was eager to leave quickly for some reason and left his change—a few dollars—on the counter. The store clerk hollered at him to give him his change, but the guy was already exiting the parking lot. He was driving a full-size red pickup truck, shiny and in good shape. Probably a late model. The clerk guessed it was either a Dodge or a Ford. No make on the tag number, except he did note that the plates were not from Jersey."

"We've got a good portraitist in New Haven, Raymond. I'll ask him to start work on a composite rendering immediately," Farone volunteered.

Snyder laughed openly. "This isn't a small-time crime, Farone. We've had our own gal on the job for two days. We'll have a complete portrait, along with one thousand copies, available for our meeting tomorrow. Are there any questions? And, if I may be so bold to ask, do you people have anything new to report? Leads, clues, hearsay? Anything?"

"I'll defer to you, Peggy," Farone said grimly.

"We've dropped the concept about tying the crimes or the perp to the fishing industry, or to crab harvest, or to boats with crab or other shellfish transom names. Too general, too amorphous. And nothing coming up anyway," she stated succinctly.

"It's a long shot, but we've stumbled onto the obvious: the crab is a zodiac symbol called cancer," Sloan interjected. "We're taking a stab at linking the vics to the disease, some form of cancer. Maybe instead of, or in addition to, being some form of avenging angel, the perp, in his crazy way, thinks he's ridding the area of cancer, or punishing these people for being sick."

"Stay on that track, Brian," Farone suggested. "It's hard to believe these three brutal murders were motivated by anger directed at cancer patients, but with crazy people you never know. I suppose you've already requested to see the medical records of the vics?"

Sloan answered yes and promised results by morning.

Everyone had ordered some form of presumably healthy salad except Snyder, who requested an egg-white omelet with dry whole-wheat toast and a side order of cut fruit. He was the only one who ate with any relish. "Since you people are rolling into high gear on the investigation," he said sarcastically between bites, "maybe you're ready to give this guy a name, something to call him until we find and arrest the actual person. Any ideas?"

His question was met with a frosty silence.

"Given his call sign, and the fact that he's a bona fide mental case who is prone to violence and driven by anger, I suggest we name him Crabby." He laughed at his own joke.

No one else smiled or said a word.

CHAPTER ELEVEN

Two days later, the police got a reprieve of sorts from the media. Instead of a continual rehash of the recent spate of homicides, with speculations about the serial killer or killers and increasingly pointed criticism of law enforcement, the news now focused on a particularly vicious crime. A young black male, Ronnie Harper, was accused of the abuse and torture of animals, particularly dogs. A Rastafarian, Harper was considered by police to be a cult person with some twisted interpretation of a ritual which included the sacrifice of animals. They also concluded that he was nuts.

Harper had been released on $10,000 bail, the bond posted by a group called CPC—Coalition of People of Color. The group was headed by the Reverend Hal Leathers, who, in his press conference on the steps of the Stamford Courthouse, declared the arrest and arraignment of Harper to be racially motivated and an insult to all African Americans. The apparent dog bites on Harper's left forearm were caused, Leathers went on, by typical police brutality.

Harper lived in a squalid room behind the "Temple"—a dilapidated and abandoned old stucco building that the cult used for meetings. The building had been condemned for six years, but city budgets never seemed to allow for its razing. Neighbors had reported hearing the anguished barking of dogs at the temple on at least five occasions. The police had finally responded and had discovered the decomposing bodies—some quite recent—of nine animals, mostly dogs. The animals had been brutally tortured with, it was conjectured, cattle prods and possibly a blowtorch. The blood had been carefully drained after their throats were slit and apparently reserved for some later ritual. In any event, Harper refused to say anything, mumbling in a foreign tongue and alternately laughing and crying.

The police referred to the scene as the "Temple of Doom" and openly wondered whether Crabby would get angry enough to avenge the deaths of the animals. Was animal mutilation enough to set him off?

Seven days after his release on bail, Ronnie Harper again became featured in the morning news. His brutally mutilated body was discovered by the owner of a local junkyard. The corpse was well inside the high chain-link fence that surrounded the property.

A crab charm bracelet had been found on Harper's wrist. Possibly the work of a copycat, but the police consensus was that the murder and abduction had, in fact, been done by Crabby himself. It had taken a man of considerable strength to hoist and toss the live body of Harper over the fence. And the wrists had been bound behind Harper's back in the same way as the other crimes, with meticulously tied nautical knots. The legs had not been secured, police noted, so that the victim could walk or run inside the yard. The victim was fully clothed, at first an inconsistency in the pattern of slayings. But detailed investigation of the body by Sheila Ryan and her assistant showed that raw hamburger had been stuffed into virtually every space between Harper's body and his clothes. A generous serving of raw meat had been massaged into his dreadlocks and on what was left of his face.

Ryan's autopsy report would later show that Harper had been set up as bait, then tossed into the yard, which was patrolled by three large so-called "junkyard" dogs. A long trail of his blood indicated that he had run and stumbled forward for about twenty yards before collapsing to the ground. A further examination of the stool samples of the two lanky pit bulls and one German shepherd confirmed that the victim had been run down, bitten repeatedly, and partially consumed by the dogs. Sympathy for the victim among the general public, at least as measured by comments on talk shows and random media street interviews, was virtually nonexistent. Reverend Leathers wrote the murder off as another example of racial intolerance. He did not receive much support for his views. The judge refused to order the destruction of the dogs, as the prosecutor had halfheartedly requested.

Two days later, the media rehashed the four killings and demanded that law enforcement come up with some results. "The people demand answers," the media proclaimed, looking eagerly for increased broadcast ratings, newspaper subscriptions, and newsstand sales.

CHAPTER TWELVE

The express commuter train takes about fifty-five minutes to complete the journey from Stamford to Grand Central Station. As he boarded the train, Farone looked forward to some uninterrupted time reviewing the details of the case over lunch with a man who was knowledgeable about homicides, openminded, a creative thinker, and the best legal mind he knew: his father.

The men met for lunch in Grand Central Station to save time but also to enjoy the traditional, delicious foods served in the Oyster Bar. A bottle of well-chilled Pinot Grigio was a luxury for Farone—who rarely drank wine at lunch—and, according to his father, a "tribute to civilized man." A refined man with old-world appetites, he enjoyed a few glasses of wine at both lunch and dinner.

Both Farones knew that lunch would be the setting for at least two discussions: Bob's murder case and his personal life—or lack of one. Bob hoped the latter conversation would not take place but realized that his father would be hounded by Bob's mother for the latest report of her son's progress in "starting to lead a normal life," as she put it.

Fortunately, it was business first. Bob reviewed the latest homicide in detail and then quickly rehashed the earlier murders. His father knew all the details anyway, since they had discussed the case via phone and e-mail repeatedly. Nonetheless, Bob's father listened very attentively to the review. Thirty-one years of successfully practicing criminal law had taught him a number of lessons, one of which was to always listen carefully to reports of events and people, even if you had heard the information several times. The insights for examining the motives and details of a crime came, as often as not, from inconsistencies in the reports.

Another lesson was that almost all investigators—even the most objective and experienced ones, like his son—consciously or subconsciously formed an opinion of the case early in its development and, without realizing it, began to fit the clues and evidence into a pattern that proved their hypothesis. Sometimes it worked, if the investigator was particularly intuitive, or just plain lucky. But more often, the elder Farone had learned, an objective view of a case, with no preconceived notions, led to the development of a variety of possibilities and, subsequently, solving the crime.

At the conclusion of his informal but careful presentation, Farone asked, "That's about it, Dad. Any questions?"

"Yes, Bob. Three. Why are you letting your oyster stew get cold? Why are you nursing your wine? And when do I learn about your personal life?"

Bob responded with slight amusement, "If you can do some of the talking—after all, you're a lawyer—I'll concentrate on the nice lunch. As for my personal life, you'll hear one hundred percent about it when you take five minutes to walk me to the train track. C'mon, Pop, help me out."

"Let's go over the potential evidence one piece at a time, Bob," the lawyer answered, his demeanor increasingly professional. "I believe you've concluded, rightly so, that the crab charm is not directly related to the shellfish or the fishing industry. The sailors' knots do obviously support some form of nautical tie-in, but I think the connection is accidental. As I recall, a different interpretation of the crab was developed by your friends at the FBI. Something about the fact that the crab, as a zodiac sign, is known as cancer. Did anything develop from this approach?"

Bob answered with a smile, "Thanks for the shot about the FBI guys being my so-called friends. You know better. To be fair, all of their people have been helpful, professional, useful, et cetera, except their asshole leader, a guy named Snyder. I don't really care that he's patronizing us local cops. I kind of expected that. But he's arrogant and opinionated, and he is into serious one-upmanship. Wants to be a star. He's a team player, as long as he's the leader of the team. He's also annoying some of us by crudely hitting on young detective Nugent—a female, by the way—and she has to waste time politely rejecting him.

"Anyway. The FBI people did a good job in tracking down the names of the jewelry retailers who most likely sold the bracelets to the killer. Got a partial ID on the guy's vehicle, a truck, as well as a composite rendering of the guy. Looks like a million other big, middle-aged white guys. The jeweler from Schenectady recalled that a logo on the guy's shirt said something like Miami Y.C. Detective Sloan guessed that the shirt said Mianus, so we checked the Mianus Yacht Club in Greenwich, and they don't have any boats registered to their members with names in any way connected to crabs or the like.

"We also showed the artist's composite to some staff and members of the club but didn't get any useful reaction or ID. The club's general manager said that while they sold logo shirts and other merchandise with the club's name and burgee on them, members often bought the items as presents for nonclub members, so it's possible that if the shirt our guy was wearing actually came from the club, he might have gotten it from someone else.

"Snyder did come up with the zodiac angle, that maybe the killer's calling card, as it were, was connected to the disease. We checked the medical records of all five known victims, and unbelievably the first two were, in fact, cancer patients. But not the other three men. We don't think there's any connection to the victims' medical condition. Snyder also proposed that we check to see if the zodiac sign, which covers all people born between June 21 and July 20, applied to the vics or the crime. No dice on the crime, since the homicides have spilled over into three months. Also, none of the vics was a cancer, so there doesn't appear to be any tie-in there either. What do you make of it, Dad?"

"Just as in all crimes, the key questions are obvious: who did it and why? Sometimes it's easier to determine who if you can figure out the motive first.

"In this case, since the signature bracelet is your best clue, I would seek motive by trying to figure out what he's trying to tell us with the charm. I think he's leaving a message, trying to explain why he's killing these people, and probably seeking credit, as it were. To us, that's crazy. But to him, it's perfectly reasonable. In my opinion, the crab's designation as 'cancer' was never intended to represent anything to do with the victims. The only connection between those murdered, as I see it, is that they were all apparently pariahs, men who had egregiously violated the mores and laws of society. And someone had to punish them. That's how the killer saw it, I think. So is he some form of avenging angel? That's the direction you're headed in, I feel.

"Not me, though, son. I think there's more to it than that. This guy's really angry. Psychotically angry. Angry enough to kill. Has a sense of bitter irony, since his punishments fit the crime. He has, in his own way, a strong moral code, since he only vents his anger on people he views as deserving of death, as opposed to random strangers. In his own mind, he's ridding society of real scum and wants to get credit for it; hence the charm he leaves. He could be more overt, of course, which suggests to me that he feels he has more work to do while he still has time.

"Why the crab charm? In net, Bob, my wild guess is that this guy himself may be the victim of cancer. If so, he only has so long to live, and it's made him crazy and violent. Who knows? In his tortured mind, he's decided to do something for the good of society. To get rid of as many rotten human beings as he can, to make their deaths a warning to others, and, on a much deeper and more personal level, to take as many people down with him as possible."

Farone felt that his father's guess was way off the mark, but he remained silent while his father continued.

"If you feel my views have any merit, Bob, I would recommend that your people interview health professionals in FairfieldCounty, particularly doctors, and primarily oncologists. You've got related materials to work with—the truck info, the sketch, the sailing background. You need to develop a list of those men fitting your preliminary profile who have been diagnosed with some form of deadly cancer in the last six months and correlate it with your other evidence. I'm fairly optimistic that despite all the hard work my suggestion will create, you will wind up with a few substantial leads. Move fast, though. This guy is smart, resourceful, and by no means through with what he thinks is his last chance for revenge."

CHAPTER THIRTEEN

The train trip back to Stamford provided the junior Farone with another uninterrupted opportunity to mull over the case. But recollections of his discussion with his father about his personal life—or lack of it—got in the way.

He had been divorced for a little over two years; fortunately, no kids. But the marriage had lasted seven years, and it was difficult for him to adjust to being alone. In fact, he dreaded it. And for the first time he'd admitted to his father this difficulty—what he called his "weakness." Bob Farone was a man who, though not really cynical, considered most personal advice to be bullshit. But owing to his immense respect for his father, he considered what the elder Farone had advised. First, to do the obvious: keep your job as a cop in perspective. It's an important job—sometimes a mission—but it's still only a part of your life. Take time off. Think about other things outside the job. Renew acquaintances and resume lifelong hobbies. All clichés, to be sure, but hard to argue with.

The second part of Jerry Farone's advice was more original. "Bob, when you go back to your apartment after work, disabuse yourself of the idea that you are alone or lonely. Your companion is you. Cherish the company. Your evening is a series of pleasant activities, something to look forward to, not dread. Have a drink, fix something simple to cook, and limit pizza deliveries and Chinese takeout food. Forget about work. Read something fictional. Watch a TV movie or a ballgame. Make sure you have at least one thing to look forward to with real people each weekend, be it a round of golf, fishing for striped bass, or having dinner with a nice girl. With something to look forward to, the quiet nights you spend at home will become just another part of a balanced, interesting week. I know that corny saying 'Be your own best friend' has whiskers, but there's a reason that it's still around. It makes sense, and it works!"

Bob tried to analyze his father's advice, first by trying to strip away the forceful and convincing presentation the old man had made—after all, he was a famed trial lawyer—and concentrate on the substance.

Conclusion? Easier said than done, but sound advice, and the only strategy he had for getting his life back. Nothing exactly tricky to do or to overcome. His only barrier: inertia. He made a vow to befriend himself and start to get on with his life.

What Farone had consciously omitted to tell his father was that there was a woman in his dreams. A wonderful woman. Unfortunately, she was no longer a part of his personal life.

He had been wildly attracted to Dr. Sheila Ryan, then the assistant medical examiner, right after his divorce was granted. And she had been equally interested in him. Several months after his divorce, he was working a case involving the murder of a housewife, with yet-unproven suspicions that the victim's husband had committed the crime. Ryan's painstaking investigation had turned up significant scientific evidence from the corpse. Although State Attorney Weiss would not approve an immediate arrest, Farone had enough information to pick up and interview the suspect. He got an almost immediate confession from the man. Farone's professional respect for Dr. Ryan matched his fairly obvious interest in her as a woman.

Sheila Ryan was not a beauty in any traditional sense. Basic brown hair, cut short and professional looking, along with hazel eyes and chiseled features. She would probably be described as "handsome" when she reached middle age. But for now she was twenty-nine, barely out of med school and residency. Tall, broad shouldered, and very curvaceous, she gave the dual impression of being athletic and sexy at the same time.

Ryan and Farone had spent little time socializing, with the general exception of drinking with other cops after work. The first major point of contact between them was a meeting that Farone not only could not erase from his mind but which he recalled often with a mixture of pleasure and regret.

One night at about nine, Ryan had finished presenting her findings from an autopsy to her boss, Farone, and three other detectives. Ryan's boss, the head of pathology, congratulated her on doing a good job, pointed out that it had been a long day for everyone, and added that he would buy a round of drinks for all who wanted to meet him at his favorite bar, on Bedford Street. Everyone joined him, with the exception of an older detective who had to get home to "the old ball and chain."

One drink turned into four or five, and the conversation had finally drifted away from police work into what the cops did in their civilian lives. Farone learned that Ryan lived in a small house in Old Greenwich, which she rented. It didn't seem as though she had any specific man in her life, although you never knew. The evening out began to come to a close at about eleven. Ryan's boss, who had driven her to work because her car was in the shop, announced he would drive her home. She protested, which made sense, since his home was in Darien, the opposite direction from Riverside. Farone interrupted smoothly and offered Ryan a ride home, which made sense since he lived in an apartment in downtown Stamford. She agreed and, after saying goodnight to her boss, who left, she and Farone remained for a nightcap, which she insisted on paying for. The drink lasted for forty-five minutes.

Farone inferred from Ryan's remarks that she not only lived alone but had no man in her life, at least right now. She was from Seattle but preferred the East Coast, primarily because of the greater diversity of the people. *Wait till she's lived here long enough*, Farone thought.

Farone revealed that he was recently divorced, a local boy. He had completed one year of law school before becoming a cop, and he occasionally considered going back to school and getting admitted to the bar. He wasn't sure if his motive to become a lawyer stemmed from an emotional and almost puritanical drive to seek justice, in which case he would become a prosecutor. Or perhaps he would work the other side of the courtroom, as a criminal defense attorney, and join his father's firm. He had admitted, though, that he would rather be a detective than a lawyer—or anything else, for that matter.

The drive to Ryan's house was filled with banal conversation, quite strained, which was evident to each of them. Farone pulled into her driveway and noted approvingly that she had left some lights on in her house, probably on a random-set timer. They said goodnight, he made a foolish attempt at humor, she laughed nervously, and then he held her close and kissed her with evident passion. He was more surprised than delighted when she returned the same intense passion he had smoldering in his heart. What followed was a brief session of kissing and fondling—*Making out like teenagers*, Farone thought to himself. He wondered if she would invite him in to make love, which he was wild to do.

But she had pushed him away, gently. "Did you ever read the *Kama Sutra*?" she asked. "One of the passages says that passion drives out reason. That's what's happening now to us, Bob. And I know it's not just the alcohol and the late hours. There's chemistry between us, and we both know that."

Farone responded as gamely as possible, "Somehow I get the feeling I'm being rejected. Tell me I'm wrong, Sheila. You can guess how I feel about you."

"I'm not interested in casual affairs, Bob. I'm looking for a life, not a lifestyle. We work together, and you know as well as I do that that would create a problem."

"Sheila, please. Sure, we'd have to be discreet, cool, and professional. The whole nine yards. But other people working together have been involved, with no real problems. Besides, we're both single. And everyone we work with knows the long and crazy hours we put in. Where is there time and energy left to meet new people?"

"Bob, please. Don't practice your lawyer skills on me." She smiled and held his hand in both of hers. "There's one other reason that makes me feel we shouldn't be seeing each other. You've still got that lost look in your eyes. You're still emotionally unsettled. I'm not sure you can resolve your pain, your loneliness, and your need to love someone in so short a time. I honestly don't want to be the woman who helps lead you back to the real world, and then you realize it's some other kind of woman you really want.

"Do not take this as rejection, Bob. You're smart and objective. Think about us from my point of view. And please always remember the attraction and chemistry we felt tonight was mutual. I've been thinking about you for months. But this is not our time."

She quickly kissed him on the cheek, put a finger over his lips to keep him silent, and slipped out of the car, heading to her front door without looking back. He never saw her tears.

The following week Bob had experienced a flash of what the French call "backstairs wit." The notion is that when someone hits you with an original insight, or worse, a nasty insult, you are stunned and can't come up with an immediate retort. When you are alone, "on the backstairs and leaving," that's when you come up with the perfect retort.

The most painful part of Ryan's explanation—rejection—was the famous *Kama Sutra* line about "passion driving out reason." Bob had no rejoinder for that, ironically noting that his favorite author, Tom Clancy, probably offered no one-liners to help him out. But tenacity, a valuable trait in a detective, led Farone to check out and read the *Kama Sutra* himself, at the local library. And in it he found a counterbalancing insight about love: "Reason drives out passion."

Several weeks later, he invited Ryan to lunch at a local restaurant with outdoor seating. Very low key. Iced tea and salads, sober and sunny. Farone had made a warm yet reasonable argument for "getting back together," as he called it, leading off with his newly acquired one-liner from Indian philosophy, the irony not lost on Ryan, who did not try to repress a smile. Farone also had had the good sense to acknowledge all of Ryan's antiaffair arguments without being overtly contradictory.

Meanwhile, Ryan was thinking that this guy was smoother than she would have guessed, and very persuasive. It rattled her decision to keep him at arm's length.

Ryan accepted his invitation to go boating on the following Saturday morning, a leisurely cruise across Long Island Sound, anchoring in the harbor at Northport, Long Island, and stopping for lunch at one of the local dockside restaurants. A promise to be back in Connecticut by four thirty, with no interlude for fishing, had sealed the deal.

Luck counts, thought Farone, as they cruised home from Northport. Perfect weather, smooth water, starboard engine not acting up for a change. Easy, warm conversation as if they had been together for years. And a punctual arrival back at the slip in Stamford, just as promised.

Good behavior is its own reward, but sometimes you get a bonus, thought Farone, while walking Ryan back to their respective cars. Just after he finished tying up his boat, she had impulsively grabbed his arm, spun him around, and kissed him passionately. She had then directed him to follow her home. "This date's not over until I say so, Bob!" she said with theatrical menace in her voice. Farone was continuing to learn that Ryan, like most women, really called the shots in the world of romance. Yes or no. Start and stop.

They had remained in Ryan's bed for most of the weekend, arising finally on Monday morning to get ready for work.

For the next four months, Farone felt happier than he had in years. But once again, the curse of the "passion drives out reason" idea arose. Ryan gently explained that there was no clear plan for them to build a life together; she wasn't really interested in pursuing a desultory love affair. And the fact that they worked together was an added strain. She also pointed out that neither of them was totally happy with their chosen profession, or even the decision to build a life in Fairfield. In fact, she confessed to lingering thoughts of returning to Seattle.

So they had agreed to take a breather—go back to being friends and colleagues, and maybe leave the door open for a real romance some time in the future.

Of course, Farone had no choice in the matter. He reasoned that time might be on his side, and if he was positive and optimistic, the tide would turn. Her decision to break off the affair was really for the better.

But in the harsh light of reality, Farone acknowledged that he honestly didn't believe in his "self-help" or "things happen for a reason" rationalizations. Total bullshit. He was in pain. Better to accept that sometimes reason drives out happiness.

The train pulled in. Bob briskly walked to his car, eager to get back to work and forget his personal problems for a while. But he did make a pact with himself: to seek pleasure in being alone and not to describe his existence as lonely. He also promised to call a few old friends—not cops—whom he had been neglecting, and make plans to go fishing over the weekend. Bluefish were running out by Lloyd's Neck, according to the paper. And he couldn't help but wish that if and when he got his life in order, there might be a chance to try to win Sheila Ryan again. If she was still available, he warned himself.

CHAPTER FOURTEEN

The Planned Parenthood meeting held at Dr. Childs's Clinic ended a little early, just after dusk. The head of the group, Marjorie Failsome, said good-bye to her friends and colleagues and thanked several newcomers for joining the group. She then locked up the office and headed diagonally across Atlantic Street to purchase some items at the pharmacy. A divorced woman with two teenagers, she had little in the way of a romantic life, with the exception of brief flings while on vacation.

On the other hand, her social calendar was quite full. The presidency of Planned Parenthood was only one of her many activities, which included membership in Greenpeace, PETA, and the Clean Up Long Island Sound committee. But having a man in her life would be much more satisfying emotionally, she thought, than all of her well-intentioned group activities put together. Which is one reason why she paid special attention at the meeting to an attentive, attractive middle-aged man who had attended the meeting alone. He seemed to be a rather serious man, quiet, unsmiling, and apparently completely absorbed in the material she and Dr. Childs presented. The man, however, did not pause to say good-bye at the end of the meeting, which disappointed her, as she had intended to learn his name and perhaps engage him in light conversation— "the interview process," as she ironically would describe it to her still-married friends.

As she returned from the drugstore, her sense of awareness heightened automatically, as it always did when she walked across an empty parking lot or in an underground garage. She relaxed a little when she realized that no one was lurking about the lot, and the only other vehicle was a red pickup truck, parked a few spaces past her Lexus, with no one inside.

As she reached into her purse for her keys, a large man approached silently and noiselessly behind her. She turned around slowly, sensing his presence, and was both surprised and relieved to discover that the man was the attractive fellow she had noticed at the meeting.

He broke the ice with a disarming smile. "Sorry if I startled you, Mrs. Failsome. I wanted to speak with you after your meeting, but you seemed to be busy with the others, and I didn't want to intrude. Hope I didn't frighten you."

"Please call me Marjorie," she answered. "And, if I may ask, what is your name?"

"Call me Joshua."

"That's an unusual name; nice name, though," she replied, slightly uneasy that he had not given a last name.

"Yes, it is unusual. Means 'savior' in Hebrew. I've sort of adopted it recently for my personal use."

"What brought you to our meeting tonight?"

"Curiosity mostly. I drive by here now and then and notice these women, mostly young girls, filing into the clinic to have their unborn children murdered. I suppose they've been brainwashed by your group, kind of like a recruiting organization for the abortionists."

"We're not that at all," she rebutted, trying to be calm, her voice steady, a pleasant smile on her face. "Anything but. Our job is to help make sure that all babies born today are welcomed and cherished and loved and properly taken care of. That's our only mission. I'm sorry that our philosophy didn't communicate that well at tonight's meeting."

As she spoke, Marjorie edged closer to her car, keys in hand. There was no immediate reply from the man. He merely stared at her retreat with slightly veiled amusement. Then he brought forth a short length of three-strand nylon rope.

The man who called himself Joshua began to walk slowly toward the now unsmiling woman. Her eyes were focused on the rope, her memory locking in on media reports of the details of a series of recent, bizarre murders.

"My real goal tonight was to have a short chat with your hired killer, Dr. Childs. But he left too early. No problem. I'll get around to him sooner or later. Finding you as a substitute is truly serendipitous, sweet angel of death. Maybe better, since all those useless protesters who picket the clinic and threaten doctors will now learn who the real enemies of innocent babies are.

"You're about to join an exclusive society, one with real growth prospects. I call it the SCOTE Club. Stands for Scum of the Earth. The initiation ceremony is a bit painful, though I'll try to make it unique. Also, just like joining a fraternity or sorority, where you get a little gold pin to wear, I've got a lovely gold bracelet in my pocket, just for you, to commemorate this little ceremony."

Just as Joshua made an abrupt lunge for the woman, she stepped nimbly aside and pressed the small panic button on the Lexus black plastic door-opener key. The infinitely reliable car responded instantly. The flasher lights began to blink rapidly on and off, and the horn started to honk over and over. The car's sound and light show momentarily distracted the man, giving the potential victim a chance to scurry around to the other side of her car, keeping the noisy, blinking vehicle between her and her tormenter. He tried in vain to apprehend her, but she was quick, very coordinated, her eyes locked on his. For every move he made around the car, she moved also, keeping the same difference between them. She also began to scream for help, over and over. And only moments later, of all things, an auto wrecker heading home from work saw her car in apparent distress, and hoping for a final tow job for the evening, swung into the parking lot to hook up her car.

Joshua the savior now had to act fast to save himself. He jumped into his truck and tore out of the lot, cursing the change in his luck.

The tow-truck driver hopped out to find a shaking woman, still able to talk, and with enough presence of mind to kill her car's panic button. She described what had happened and asked the truck operator to call the police.

The 911 response was almost instantaneous, with three patrol cars, a total of six officers, showing up within minutes, their Xmas lights flashing, sirens wailing. When they obtained her statement about the potential attack, they immediately ordered the dispatcher to issue an all-points bulletin to pull over any red pickup truck in the immediate Stamford vicinity operated by a large, middle-aged white male wearing a dark-blue shirt and chinos.

Mrs. Failsome and the tow-truck driver were asked to follow the police back to the local precinct to be interviewed by detectives, write out and sign a formal statement, and, perhaps, look at mug shots.

The tow-truck operator had little to offer the detectives, since his arrival at the scene had provoked the assailant to drive off. He did at least provide a better description of Joshua's vehicle—a red, late-model Dodge Ram cab crew pickup with a built-in tool box in the bed. Looked like custom oversize tires, but he was unable to note the brand. Neither witness offered any help on the tag number, but both agreed that it looked like Connecticut plates.

The information supplied by Mrs. Failsome was obviously more detailed and helpful. When she got to the part about the rope and the charm—along with her fear of the serial killer mentioned repeatedly in the press—the detectives realized the actual nature of the case. They broke off the interview temporarily and called Detective Brian Sloan on the phone. Fortunately, Sloan was home, watching the Mets game on TV. He thanked his colleagues for the heads-up, promised to round up his partner, Margaret Nugent, and head down to the station.

Nugent, as it happened, was out on a rare date. But she had sensibly mentioned where she might be—Pelicci's Restaurant—and took her cell phone with her. At some point between the vitello tonetto appetizer and the pasta special, linguini cestaro, Sloan got Nugent on the phone and quickly filled her in on the big break they had gotten on the case. Nugent apologized halfheartedly to her date—a smart, shy computer whiz at a local think tank—and asked the captain to call her a cab. The computer whiz was stuck with two meals, his request to go with her having been summarily denied. He was also stuck with the bill, which surprised him, since most women he knew insisted on paying their share. Which he liked. If he had gotten the chance to know Peggy Nugent better, he would have discovered that she was a social throwback, particularly when it came to dealing with men. Their invitation, their treat. And don't forget the flowers, good manners, and respect. "Works for me," she told her friends. *Works because she's beautiful*, they thought, but let the subject drop.

By the time Sloan and Nugent arrived at the interview room, the tow-truck operator, having completed his statement, had been excused. He was asked to leave his phone number in case there might be further questions. Meanwhile, Marjorie Failsome had been provided with the FBI profiler's composite rendering of the unnamed suspect, which she was now studying closely.

The detectives, after expressing genuine sympathy for what the intended victim had endured, went over every comment in her written statement, making supplemental notes as needed. As a formality, they asked her to sign a complaint and assured her that the entire episode would be reviewed with their superiors in the department, as well as senior people in the state attorney's office. What they didn't add was that a few details of the case would be leaked to the media by police brass in order to get them off the department's back. As Lieutenant James had earlier remarked, "Toss 'em a piece of hamburger now and then, and you can buy a little time before you become lunch. It's like feeding the alligators. Keeps the bastards in the water."

"Now that we've got the name Joshua to work with, I hope the uniforms will stop referring to this guy as 'Crabby,'" Sloan said. He began to go over the composite with the woman and his partner.

Mrs. Failsome evaluated the composite as "fair, not great" and agreed to come in the next day to work with the police artist to improve it. She felt that the man should be shown as a little heavier, but not fat. And his mouth should be neutral, not mean looking, as in the present rendering. But the most important aspect of the portrait was the eyes, she insisted. They should be a little larger, and neutral and blank. Devoid of any expression, just like a shark's. Her general description of Joshua's appearance also included his clothes—the boat shoes, lack of any jewelry. Nothing to help the investigation except to corroborate the other descriptions they had elicited. Unfortunately his blue shirt was plain, longsleeved, not short, and bore no insignia, yacht club or otherwise.

Detective Nugent asked the woman, without much enthusiasm, if she had—or had recovered from—cancer. A solid, "No, thank God!" put another nail in the coffin of the already discredited "victims have cancer" theory.

A brief discussion followed, in which several of the detectives who had originally investigated the complaint participated. One of them asked if the name Joshua would be officially used in the next steps of the investigation. And would anybody be checking out the bit about the savior?

Peggy Nugent ducked the question by stating that the decision to use the name—at least as a working name—would have to be made by Sergeant Farone the following day. Her partner, Brian Sloan, surprised her and the others by saying, in a self-effacing manner, that he was the precinct's leading religious authority and was best prepared to present the matter to Farone. Sensing a put-on, the other detectives started to smile, with the exception of Nugent, who pointed out that her partner had spent time in the seminary and was very well versed in scripture. She pressed Sloan for an explanation of the name.

"As this guy told Mrs. Failsome, Joshua is the Hebrew name for savior. What he didn't say was that in the splintering of Judaism into Christianity, the name Joshua was translated to Jesus—the Savior. So if you believe, as many did, that Jesus accepted the sacrifice of his own crucifixion in order to atone for the sins of mankind, you can make a stretch and conclude that our guy also sees himself as doomed in some way, and he is driven to leave his mark upon the world. It's our little problem, though, that our Josh makes a rather perverted interpretation of the scriptures. Instead of atoning for all sinners, he wants to make some of them pay for their sins. Probably as an example to others. Instead of sacrifice and sympathy, he's driven by anger and no small dose of vindictive, puritanical rage. Something or someone has probably made this guy snap. He's fearful of something important, like losing his mind, or his life. And he wants to take as many bastards with him—present company excepted, Mrs. Failsome—as possible. That's what I intend to tell Farone tomorrow morning."

The meeting broke up at 11:22 p.m. Mrs. Failsome received a police escort to her home, along with a promise to keep an eye on her premises. She was encouraged to phone in with any further information that came to mind, as well as to report any changes in her daily routines.

CHAPTER FIFTEEN

Brian Sloan was the first detective on the scene. A busy intersection normally, but not too heavy with traffic now, at shortly after midnight. The neighborhood was quiet. Mostly small businesses, a grammar school, a Lutheran church, and a handful of small single-family homes, all dark. *Not a promising spot for a canvass of witnesses,* Sloan thought, as he approached the two police patrol cars and their shift sergeant, who had called him.

"What's the story?" Sloan asked, as he registered the scene: a middle-aged white male lying battered and obviously dead in a fetal pose in the middle of the street. The scene was sealed off and an assistant medical examiner and forensic photographer had been called in, as well as an ambulance, now just arriving. The ambulance would have no lifesaving miracles to perform, as the victim's head was crushed and flattened.

The sergeant on duty, an old-timer, replied in a flat, professional tone of voice, "A motorist called in about twenty-five minutes ago on his cell phone. He was driving down Hyde Street when he observed the deceased lying in the street. He was a little hysterical, since he realized the guy was dead. He didn't have any other information to give us, so we took his statement and instructed him to phone in if he recalled any other pertinent information. Which is highly unlikely. Our first impression of the scene, Detective, was a hit-and-run felony, so we immediately began to canvass for potential witnesses. But there were no pedestrians about; most of the surrounding buildings were dark, closed. And no one in the few houses had seen anything, although we're still in the process of waking people up to question them. Two more patrol cars are on their way to provide extra manpower."

"When you called me," Sloan said, "you said there was a special reason to ask for me by name."

"It was either you or Detective Nugent," the sergeant replied bluntly. "We're all aware of the investigation of the 'Crabby' serial killer case. C'mere and take a close look at the victim's left wrist. Looks like a bracelet on the side we can see. We haven't touched the body or moved the arm, waiting for you to arrive."

"We need to get crime-scene pictures before we do anything else, but I'm going to bend the rules a little," replied Sloan as he pulled on a pair of latex gloves.

The torso of the crumpled body lay on its left side, obscuring most of the left arm. But the man's shirt, an expensive long-sleeved dress shirt with French cuffs and engraved gold cuff links, had ridden up slightly to reveal a gold Patek Philippe wristwatch and a gold bracelet. Sloan rotated the man's limp wrist and found what the sergeant had obviously guessed at—a gold crab charm.

"Good guess, Sergeant Morelli. Thanks for the heads-up on the case. I see Sheila Ryan ambling over. What favor did you do for her?" Sloan asked with a smile, as he rose to his feet.

"No favors yet," Morelli shot back. "But if I ever get to know her better, I will strongly advise her to get out of this line of work and help out the living. And I would also point out to her that with her looks and smile, she could get tons of guys asking her out at normal hours; guys who don't carry guns and handcuffs. Guys who still believe in the worth of life—whatever that is—and make big bucks. Like my son, the stockbroker," Morelli concluded with a smile.

Sloan knew that the old cop was just breaking his balls, but he had to admit it, the guy wasn't all wrong.

Right on cue, Dr. Ryan walked up to her colleagues, beautiful as billed but with no trace of a smile. "With you here, Brian," she remarked as she quickly examined the overall scene. "This hit and run must be something special. What's going on?"

"Look at the left wrist, Sheila. I moved it slightly to get a better look. It's the crab. Looks like we've got another tough one on our hands. The vic's still dressed in his power suit, though, and his hands and feet weren't tied. Also, why a hit and run? Lots of easier ways to kill people."

"I've got a few questions, but first let Larry finish with the photos. Then we can fish out his wallet and ID him. Sergeant, did any officer or civilian clean up blood evidence here tonight?"

"Of course not," Morelli answered, slightly offended. "There isn't any typical pool of blood seeping from the body, just that small amount drying about his mouth and nose. Or what's left of them. Nobody's touched or moved a thing. Larry's done with the pictures, and the crime-scene guys are here now. I'm going to ask them to secure the guy's wallet and start an ID. Let's talk later."

"Sheila, what's your take on the lack of blood? I agree, it seems weird," Sloan said.

"First guess would be that he was literally bled out and was dumped here. Who knows why? The autopsy will either confirm or reject my theory, so we'll know for certain tomorrow morning, about ten. If this man had been killed on the spot, there would be a pool of blood, as his heart would finish its pumping cycle. This fellow was brought here already dead, and dumped. The fact that you've already found a bracelet on his wrist may suggest a copycat, but I'm betting that our friend Joshua has left us and the media another message. The body's seriously crushed, particularly the head. Let's check with the crime-scene guys to see if they have any initial impressions."

Two middle-aged crime-scene investigators had already interviewed the police and had read the passerby's statement. Nothing. The perimeter around the body also revealed nothing unusual. The pattern of tire tracks across the victim's body, however, was of great interest.

There were three tracks. One had passed over the victim's legs, breaking both in the middle of the femur. The middle track traversed his chest. His lungs were crushed, as were his major organs, the autopsy report would later reveal, causing his death. The third track had crushed his head—a gesture of anger on the killer's part, Sloan presumed. Also, minute nylon fibers had been found imbedded in the victim's wrists, which also bore the indentation of having been tightly bound. There was no evidence of robbery or sexual molestation. Oddly, small amounts of gravel were imbedded in the back of the victim's suit jacket, as well as the back of his trousers. The CSI lab would report two days later that the gravel, while common, was the same as that used to pave the parking lot at the public marina on the Mianus River.

As the ambulance pulled away, the body bound for autopsy and morgue assignment, Sloan and Ryan stowed their notebooks and surveyed the closing down of the crime scene for the night: the media vans pulling out, awaiting their next opportunity to record someone's misery; the patrol cars heading out to finish their shifts. The crime scene was secured with a second perimeter of tape in order to preserve any evidence that might be more visible when the CSI guys arrived back at seven to recheck their work in the light of morning.

"Sheila, I'm sorry, but I'm going to have to take a rain check on that drink you offered to buy. I've got to call Bob and give him a detailed report, especially before the media deluge tomorrow morning," Sloan said, deadpan, as he walked Ryan to her car.

"Thanks, but I'd rather wait till your fiancée can join us anyway."

As he pulled away, Sloan considered the fairly obvious insight that if his boss had made a subtle pass at Ryan, kidding or not, she would have said yes in a nanosecond. The affair, now cold, between Ryan and Farone was not known to everyone in the department, just most people—typical of "secret" office affairs in any business, and even more obvious in law enforcement, where everyone was trained to be observant and nosy.

Sloan walked over to his car, the only one left on the street, and called Farone on his cell phone. Farone was not at all amused at being awakened at 2:40 in the morning, but he quickly became both alert and professional when he heard the nature of the phone call.

Brian Sloan was not only aware of the fact that he was making an official report, albeit via phone, but that he was also addressing the man who would be responsible for preparing the next personnel evaluation on his performance. So he planned his remarks to be laid out to Farone in the best possible manner—brief, factual, and with a minimum of conjecture but displaying some insight and a clear annunciation of the next steps to be taken.

After quickly skimming over the amenities, Sloan began his report. He announced the discovery shortly after midnight by a passing motorist of the body of a fully clad white male lying crumpled against the curb near the intersection of Hyde and Washington Avenues. The motorist had no further information to offer, and police officers had not gleaned anything from the neighborhood, which was quiet and basically empty at that hour. The first appearance of the scene was that the man was a victim of a hit and run. But the CSI people, as well as the ME, held the view that the man had been picked up, hands bound, and run over several times at a remote location. Farone interrupted to ask for more specific evidence, which pleased Sloan, since he was well prepared and had anticipated each question.

He related Dr. Ryan's observations about the lack of blood at the scene and reviewed the forensic findings with respect to the binding of the victim's hands and the tire tracks across the body. He noted the traces of gravel pressed into the victim's clothes and concluded that the preliminary impression of the crime was that the man had been picked up, tied up, taken to a remote location, tossed on the ground, and run over at least two, maybe three times. The body was then driven to the scene and dumped. Because of the trauma, the ME was convinced that the vehicle used to murder the man was either a very heavy car or, more likely, a truck. Forensics was attempting to get a tire track off the man's suit, but success did not seem likely. Another avenue to check was the gravel on the guy's suit, also a long shot.

Farone had already determined in his own mind what the nature of the murder was, but he waited patiently for the rest of Sloan's report before making up his own mind. And the balance of the report, both conjecture and evidence, guaranteed that Farone would not get much more sleep.

First, and certainly foremost, was the discovery of the crab charm bracelet on the man's wrist. Next, the fine wristwatch, solid-gold cufflinks, and a wallet with over three hundred dollars in cash and three credit cards showed that hate, not robbery, was the killer's motive. From the wallet an ID had been made and verified. The victim was a Mr. August Bronfstein, an affluent bar and club owner in WestchesterCounty. Further sniffing disclosed that Mr. Bronfstein had been charged with DUI vehicular homicide three weeks earlier, released on $100,000 bail. The hit-and-run victim had been a twelve-year-old boy from Stamford.

Bronfstein's body had been dumped exactly where he had hit the boy.

CHAPTER SIXTEEN

Bob Farone prided himself on his ability to leave law enforcement problems in the office—at least on Sundays, his only real day off.

His morning ritual on Sunday was pretty ordinary, which pleased him in some curious way. The day started early, with a short drive down to Tod's Point in Old Greenwich, a beautiful beach and park on the Sound just recently opened to nonresidents after a bitter court battle. Farone warmed up his legs, retied his Reebok running shoes, and began a leisurely six-mile run around the point and back.

The only normal distractions were the wheeling gulls, a few other runners, joggers, and walkers, and the occasional boat heading out to Eaton's Neck to troll for bluefish. But this Sunday was not that typical. Farone's mind was busy scrolling through all the recently acquired information, theories, and evidence swirling around the "crab" or "Joshua" killer. Farone also recalled the last piece of advice his father had given him recently via phone: "Sometimes when a problem, or in your case an investigation, seems so complex, with so many uneven pieces of information floating around, it's often best to make some hypotheses that are almost ridiculously simple, even obvious. These ideas will, at minimum, push the ongoing investigation into a few new directions. And even if nothing pans out, you may at least have eliminated some phases of the case and hopefully have created several new paths to follow. In this case, Bob, you have a killer, a maniac, who is trying to tell you something. Keep it simple. What is his message? Who is his audience? What motivates his hatred?"

The run completed, Farone stood sweating and lost in thought out in the parking lot beside his car. He knew his boring and beloved Sunday ritual was spoiled: the Bloody Mary with bacon and eggs, the Sunday edition of the *New York Times*, the frustration of working the crossword puzzle in the back of the magazine section, and the choice of heading out fishing on the sound or wasting the afternoon in what he called his "Barcalounger stupor," watching whatever sports were being broadcast on TV.

Instead he opted for a quick shower and shave, an energy bar, and coffee. He phoned Dr. Sheila Ryan, halfhoping she would not be in, so that he could hide behind the remoteness of a recorded message. But she was in and happy to hear from him.

After an acceptable exchange of small talk, Farone abruptly shifted gears in a tone of voice that Ryan knew signaled the "let's get down to business" phase of the conversation. It was a trait she liked and admired in Farone, his ability and determination to plow into the heart of a topic with little preamble or verbal foreplay. *This guy is definitely better suited to be a cop*, she thought playfully, *than a pinstriped career diplomat*.

"Sheila, I'm trying to come up with some new angles to the crab case, and I need your help in thinking them through."

Slightly disappointed that Farone's motive for calling was not of a more personal nature, Ryan was nonetheless flattered to be chosen as a colleague in arms, rather than a coldly scientific pathologist. Yet she replied rather disingenuously, "I'm only a plain-vanilla ME, Bob. Why don't you work out your theories with a real detective, someone like Snyder, the hard-hitting G-man?"

Farone didn't strike at the bait. "Doctor, my preference is to speak with you on this case today. I've learned that in matters requiring great mental acuity, creative if not inspired thinking, and remorseless objectivity, you are head and shoulders above any cop I've ever worked with. And that goes double for Raymond Snyder, a jerk whose best ideas are yet to see the light of day. And there's one other thing, Doctor: I prefer to see you because you are the embodiment of feminine appeal—gorgeous face, perfectly formed body, and especially—"

Ryan cut him off, suppressing a laugh. "OK, Bob. That's enough. Save your material for *Saturday Night Live*. Why don't you drive over here? Bring along the case file and a six-pack of beer for yourself. About one hour, OK?"

"Thanks, Sheila, about an hour is fine. Look forward to our meeting. See you later."

Farone had made a conscious effort to end the conversation in an impersonal, businesslike manner, especially because he was surprised—but pleased—to be invited to Ryan's apartment, where he had not been a guest since their breakup over seven months ago. He had planned on a neutral place to meet, probably his club or a local restaurant. He never would have suggested his own place or imagined he would be visiting hers. Too much history, too much disappointment. He laughed at himself for feeling like a schoolboy.

Ryan lived in Riverside, in a new condo near the tiny downtown area, which she liked, since she could easily walk to do most of her shopping. A great advantage over the mindless pleasant suburbs, where a car was one's second home and traffic jams a given, and where the strip malls had taken over the landscape. Her condo was comfortable and filled with very nice Colonial antiques, a few replicas, and seasonal flowers.

After Farone parked his car in her parking lot, he reminded himself that the decision not to bring flowers was a good one. So he ambled up the steps, attaché case in one hand and a brown paper sack in the other, bearing a six-pack of Bud Lite and an apple "for teacher," as he nervously put it.

After engaging in conventional pleasantries, short but warm and sincere, Ryan suggested that they begin working at the table in her small dining room. Farone broke out the case material, as well as two legal pads and two Uniball pens. Ryan had made herself a cup of green tea and had insisted on pouring Farone's beer into a proper lager glass, rather than having him down it straight out of the bottle. As a doctor, she couldn't help but agree that forgoing a glass, as most beer drinkers chose to do in today's world, was more hygienic in public places. Yet her sense of good manners overruled germ warfare, and she insisted her companions use a glass. Ryan also got a kick out of Farone's appearance—generic Fairfield County. Worn but pressed chinos, no socks, brown Timberland boat shoes, and a goofy nylon belt with anchors as a motif. His shirt, a pima cotton, Oxford-blue button-down was what he typically wore to work on the days when no court appearances or personal interviews required a suit and tie. Thus, she rightly concluded that he was negligent in doing his laundry, a thought she found curiously endearing.

As for her own appearance, Ryan had chosen a white cotton Donna Karan shirt, well-fitted Calvin Klein blue jeans, modest jewelry, and just a touch of perfume. It worked. Farone had momentarily lost his poise when she greeted him at the door.

The case itself was a strictly impersonal source of contact, particularly since each of them had been involved in it since the first day, when Reverend DeJohn had been found crucified upside down.

"Sheila, let's get started by reviewing what we have to work with right now. Then I'd like to try an approach my old man suggested a few days ago. Here's a list of the current information we have in hand. Please go over it and ask me anything you need to better understand some of this stuff. Better beware, though. I've been over this stuff so many times, my head is spinning."

Ryan finished her tea and picked up the list. It was short and blended fact with conjecture, which, she knew from experience, was the information blend in most investigations. It was ultimately the state attorney's call to assess the quality of the case the police provided—that is, whether there was sufficient evidence to make an arrest and obtain a conviction.

The list was titled "Facts and Suppositions Currently on Hand With Respect to the Serial Killer Investigation Known as Crab."

What do we know about victims?

1. They were all prominent in the media recently, for proven or alleged felonies.

2. All had potential enemies because of their behavior and crimes; however, investigation points to one man as abductor/killer, because of evidence gathered to date.

3. Though they were abducted, there was no evidence of sexual assault or robbery.

4. The victims had no ties or links to one another. There were no demographic commonalities either, such as race, religion, occupation, social class, age, and sex. (Most were male, but there was one female, who escaped.)

5. All victims were executed in a preplanned, cold-blooded fashion. All executions were unique; however, each bore a crude but clear reference to the felony the victim had been accused or found guilty of. A "let the punishment fit the crime" theme.

6. Each victim was left with bracelet with one crab charm on it.

What evidence and/or clues do we have to work with at the present time with respect to the perpetrator?

1. Vehicle is red Dodge crew-cab pickup truck. Connecticut tags, looks fairly new. Partial tire print.

2. Nylon three-strand rope used in killings. Primarily used by boaters. Complex knots suggest sailing background.

3. Charm bracelets bought in quantity for cash by one man. Only charm attached is the crab, zodiac sign called cancer, designates people born between June 21 and July 20.

4. Good artist's sketch of killer due to firsthand appearance before Ms. Failsome and three jewelers. Garments generic/casual.

What do we know about the killer?
1. He is big, strong. A middle-aged white male. Average looks.
2. Name may be Joshua.
3. Crazy, but intelligent and careful. Executions well planned.

4. Shirt logo suggested Mianus Yacht Club. FBI investigated, found no recognition of killer via artist's sketch. No tie to any sailboat. (Nugent/Sloan to try YC again.)

What motivates killer, triggers murders?
1. Seems to select vics from media. Quite probable he doesn't know them personally. Because of vics' notoriety, killer may fit avenging-angel profile.
2. Zodiac theory #1: Crab means June 21 to July 20. First two vics killed in that period. Therefore, expect next vics (killed in next zodiac periods) to wear charms for their killing period—e.g., Leo the lion, July 21 to August 21. But all wear crab. Conclusion: clue not related to month of death.
3. Zodiac theory #2: Period is cancer. Taken literally, victims suffer from cancer and are put out of their misery; killer somehow knows they're ill. Maybe he's a doctor, angry at the disease, takes it out on victims. Looks promising, first two vics being treated for cancer. But not the rest. This theory abandoned.
4. Zodiac theory #3: Forget zodiac. Crab literally means crab. A signature of some kind for killer. Typical of this breed, they want "credit" and recognition for their work. All boatyards, seafood dealers, and fish markets checked out with no success. No boat registered with name of *Crab* or any related type name. Cops to again recanvass using new sketch.

Ryan read the summary with some interest, recalling that crimes that lacked clear and apparent motives were generally difficult to solve. Bob had also reviewed the insights his father had offered, and Ryan, who knew and respected Mr. Farone Sr., made a short note paraphrasing what Bob had told her his dad had suggested: What is the killer's message, his audience? Why is he full of hate?

Farone, finishing his second (and last, he vowed) beer, confessed, "I'm fresh out of ideas, Sheila. I know we need more basic cop work, but there's only so many officers, and we don't really have any new directions to follow. Neither do the FBI partners we've acquired, although to hear Snyder tell it, they've almost broken the case. Any bright ideas? Or any ordinary ideas? We're kind of stymied."

"Bob, I don't know if I have any bright or even ordinary ideas, but I do have a fairly obvious one. And your dad did advise looking for a simple answer. Here's what I think. The notion that you came up with, the one that says there is no zodiac implication of the charm, well intuitively that may be the right conclusion. Plus, your investigation along those lines has drawn a blank. Lets say the crab means the crab: well, I would recommend you keep following that idea, even though the information is thin, and you've picked over the boating and seafood industry. This guy is signing his work with a crab, and that may be to tell us something about him.""Do you think this is one of those cases where the killer is trying to get caught?" Bob asked.

"My guess is no. He's either feeding his ego with the crab signature and telling us that he's taking credit for the killings, or there's another message in his madness, and I have a good hunch as to what that might be."

Farone, interest piqued, pressed her to go on, hunch or not.

"Well, it not only answers your father's three questions but mirrors Jerry's first impression of the crimes. And although you weren't interested in Jerry's theory, it's relatively easy to run down. Want to hear more?"

Farone nodded. His penance was to pour Sheila a glass of Pinot Grigio before she would speak up. He poured himself one, too, from an already open bottle in the refrigerator.

"This is real simple, Bob. Think about what your father told you. This guy signs his work with a crab. The crab means cancer, OK? So let's say that he's a victim of cancer. Maybe terminal. And that's how he defines himself, in his crazy way. I agree with your father; I think our killer is really angry that he's dying, and in some insane way wants all of us to know that he's performing good acts for society by murdering those people the media have made monsters out of, especially making them die of their own sins, metaphorically speaking. His motive is simple: If I, a good man, must be condemned to die of cancer, then my last good act on Earth will be to take as many loathsome people with me as possible. And leave a not-very-subtle message while doing it, both to get credit and make a point to the general public."

Ryan sipped her wine and tried to observe Farone's reaction to her concept. But her impatience for an answer got the best of her, so she asked, with an attempt at being playful, "C'mon, Bob, what's up with the pensive mood? Trying to think of a tactful way to shoot down my idea? Remember, your dad's smarter than both of us, and that's where he came out on this originally."

Farone continued to stare into space, then finally put his thoughts together. "This guy is dying of cancer and is really pissed off, and his notions of morality get scrambled. So he decides to take a few people across the River Styx with him. He selects his victims from the media 'bad guy du jour' coverage and takes them out. I think this is a good slant on the case, Sheila, and long shot or not, one we're going to pursue. But expand on one point: why does he go to all the trouble and risk of setting up these little death scenes if all he wants is a few scalps to take to that great marina in the sky?"

"I think it goes back to what your father guessed regarding motive, Bob. His killings go well past anger and revenge. In their odd way, and in his cold, crazy mind, the killings are tales of morality. Let the punishment fit the crime, an eye for an eye, that type of thing. He's hell-bent on warning other pedophiles, polluters, sadists, et cetera, that they can expect to pay horribly for their crimes. Over-the-top vindication. In his twisted mind, he thinks of himself as sort of a moral garbage man, taking out the trash and making sure everyone gets his message."

"We should consider one other idea. What if the killer is a cancer, actually born during that time period and who feels cancers like himself have some special mission in life? Tying the guy to his birth date would be a real boondoggle of the needle-in-a-haystack variety, but it should be followed up. Perhaps we could ask Snyder and his people to follow it up. The FBI is quite good at that kind of factfinding."

"Where would they start, Bob?"

"Well, the four people who've had a good look at this guy all make him out to be somewhere in his early forties. So the first place to check would be the county clerk's office to get a run of all white males born in Fairfield between 1960 and 1965. They can eliminate the dead ones, but after that it's a real project to cull the list. Right up Snyder's alley."

"Well, I guess for starters they could compare the list with DMV boat registrations to find any quick correlations," Ryan added quickly. "You can't fool me that easily, Robert. You're not really crazy about this idea, are you? That's why you plan to dump it on Snyder."

"It's a shot worth taking. Maybe we'll come up lucky. But we'll be looking at an enormous list of names, and even with available software it'll be very tough to shorten the list without making a career out of it. And we've got that big problem of not really knowing where this guy was born. There's a reasonable chance he's not originally from here. Just as well. Your hunch is much better than my idea."

Farone smiled warmly, finished his wine, and remarked that in the next life he should be the pathologist and she should be the detective.

"I've got a better idea, Bob," she responded, trying, not too successfully, to keep a light tone in her voice. "We become agronomists, dedicated to developing perfect organic produce. We live on a farm in Virginia, have two perfect kids, a few dogs and cats, and absolutely no connection to crime and punishment."

"You better be kidding, or else I'll do everything that I can to make your fantasy a reality."

"Why would you do that?" Ryan asked seriously. "Are you losing your interest in detective work?"

"No. I still love it. But maybe I love you more. And I'm not kidding."

A few tears appeared in Ryan's eyes, but she maintained her composure. "Please, Bob, let's leave some kind of fantasy life off limits. We've been over this before, and now we've got to get on with our separate lives, OK?"

"You're right as usual, Doc. Sorry I got serious. Hard habit to break with you alone with me. Time to change the subject, isn't it? Got to use the facilities, be right back."

He rose stiffly, weary from the run and the stress of the week, and headed down the hallway to the bathroom. As he passed her bedroom he couldn't resist a look inside. His glance went straight to one of the nightstands next to the bed. He remembered the best afternoons and nights of his life, lying in bed with her. And it wasn't just the sex—he had never felt closer to a person than when he just held her in his arms and dreamed of a life together.

He paused for a second, seeing the large dark-blue candle on the nightstand. During their affair she had ritualistically lit the candle every time they made love. Jealousy and fear gripped him momentarily as he checked the room quickly for a new candle, one that had been used. There was nothing there. He felt ashamed that he had snooped. After all, her life and her decisions about men were none of his business. But he was honestly relieved to see that his candle had not been used. *Nice material for a shrink*, he thought.

Leaving Ryan's apartment was awkward for Farone, as well as for Ryan. He asked her to meet with him the following morning in the conference room and to try to bring with her a list of all the cancer treatment clinics in both Fairfield and Westchester counties. He also requested a copy of the *Physicians' Desk Reference*. She agreed, relieved that their meeting was ending on a professional note.

But she was wrong. Farone suddenly put his arms around her, kissed her with great passion, then released her slightly to look into her eyes. He then kissed her gently and left without a word.

CHAPTER SEVENTEEN

At 11:00 a.m. sharp, Farone kicked off a meeting in the conference room at homicide headquarters. Dr. Ryan, as promised, showed up. So did Catherine Weiss, although she warned Farone that she had a date in court at 11:45.

Detectives Nugent and Sloan also appeared, having sensed from the urgency in Farone's voice that perhaps a break in the case was forthcoming, or at least there might be a new tack to take.

Ryan was slightly embarrassed as Farone got into the agenda, since he began by praising her for coming up with some new thoughts about the case. *Thank God*, she thought, *he didn't lay it on too thick.*

"This notion that the crab simply means that the killer is a cancer—born between June 21 and July 20—is of some interest," Farone began. "It may be his way of leaving his imprint on each homicide. I briefed Senior Agent Snyder and his people about an hour ago and they agreed to try to develop a list of white males in our county who were born between 1960 and 1965—that's the age range we got from witnesses—and who are cancers, so to speak."

Sloan interrupted, trying not to sound skeptical. "How will they go about it, Bob? And won't they get a ton of names? Who's got the manpower to eliminate the thousands of unlikely suspects?"

"That's the part of the job we've reserved for you and Peggy, Brian."

"Is it too late for me to go to medical school?" Nugent quipped.

"OK, guys, let's get back to an adult level here," Farone said, picking up the thread of the meeting. "My plan is that Snyder and his people will pull all the county birth records for those years and perhaps correlate them to names on boat registrations provided by the DMV. I'm also guessing that they've got some special software in DC, maybe tied to social security records, that will help in developing a list of likely names. Catherine, why are you waving your hand at me? Is my fly unzipped?"

"I'm trying to remind you, Sherlock, that I've got to be in court soon. Judge Parker gets really nasty toward people who show up late or unprepared. And the state has a shitty enough case already without me having to aggravate His Honor. So if there is anything in this briefing that is going to involve me, please get on with it."

Once again, with another acknowledgement of Dr. Ryan, Farone offered up the theory that the crab charm had no other meaning than the killer actually was suffering from cancer. "Which means," he went on to explain, "that our job is to obtain a listing of all local white males, aged early forties, who have been diagnosed and may be being treated for cancer."

The concept of a deranged cancer victim killing bad guys as reported in the media seemed a little farfetched to the two young detectives, but they managed to keep their mouths shut. Weiss, a pragmatist and considerably more brash, asked, "I still don't see where this is going with respect to accumulating sufficient and specific evidence that I can use to justify a warrant. What is it you want of the state, Bob?"

"Catherine, I'd like you and your staff to be prepared to issue subpoenas to various medical facilities—cancer clinics, private MDs, anyone in the health network. We're going to be asking these folks for the records of any male diagnosed with cancer, whether he is undergoing treatment at present or not. Since I believe some or all of these clinics will try to block our efforts on the basis of privacy rules, we'll need you to get them to comply legally. I know you have to run, so I will ask Peggy to give you a list of the clinics we plan to be interviewing later this afternoon. Also, Sheila has been kind enough to provide us with a list all of the docs practicing here and in Westchester. Of course we're particularly interested in cancer practices, radiologists, oncologists—you know what I mean. I hope we can have this list ready by noon tomorrow. The plan is to get about six detectives, under the temporary supervision of Sloan and Nugent, to join them in phoning every doctor and clinic on the list, to persuade them to turn over the medical records that fit our profile. So that's where you will no doubt have to fit in. Thanks in advance, Counselor, and good luck with today's case."

The meeting was interrupted by the appearance of Lt. Jonas James. "Bob, I hope you're ready to break up and get your people started on this new theory of yours. We're slated for a press conference on the case in about ten minutes, and I'll need you there. Believe me, this conference was not my doing. The higher-ups need to fend off the press and TV people until we get some concrete leads. So to get them off my back for a few days, I leaked the information that you gave me earlier this morning—that is, there are two new aspects to the investigation that look promising. But don't worry, I didn't give them any details. So let's go out there and stick to generalities, but act real confident with our new approach and the great boost we're getting from the FBI."

Part of the job, Farone thought, *The lousy part*. But he wisely kept his mouth shut.

Lt. James headed for the door, then turned to his favorite, Detective Nugent, and asked, "Tell me honestly, Detective, how do you feel about looking for some nut case who happens to have cancer?"

"We're all very enthusiastic about it, sir."

Jonas James knew when he was being put on and had an exit line ready. "Enthusiasm's great, Detective, but it never beat the Yankees. Better get busy."

CHAPTER EIGHTEEN

While Special Agent in Charge Raymond Snyder and his team waded through reams of data to try to isolate the perpetrator on the basis of his zodiac sign and age, Sergeant Bob Farone and his squad of local Stamford detectives manned the phones to attempt to obtain lists of white male cancer victims from local MDs and clinics. It was a difficult assignment for both teams.

Snyder and his people had little difficulty in amassing thousands of names. To narrow the list down, the FBI team began a time-consuming match of birth records with boat registrations. Their cohorts in Washington sympathized with the problem but could not come up with a "black box" solution to assist them in their investigation. After sixteen days, with no time off, eighty-seven men who fit the age, zodiac, and race profile were isolated on the basis that they owned and operated boats in the greater Fairfield area. Snyder knew that the challenge of running down each name would be exhausting and timeconsuming, but he had no choice, since he had no new ideas for investigation. Worse, he knew that the search he was in charge of might be an expensive witchhunt, because there was always the possibility that the perp was born somewhere else, thus well off the Stamford-area radar screen.

Farone's team fared better but still had a lot of work to do. It had been slow going at first, because most MDs and clinic heads refused to turn over their records. However, the threat of a subpoena from the office of Catherine Weiss brought most of them in line quickly. The clinics especially didn't want to incur the cost in terms of time and money to wage a constitutional-rights war with the local government. And for the few holdouts, the actual serving of a subpoena quickly convinced them to give up any rights protecting personal privacy. It had become quite clear that the government was increasingly defining and limiting those rights of citizens supposedly guaranteed by the Constitution of the United States.

The first cast of the net turned up well over two hundred names of men diagnosed and/or being treated for any form of cancer. The number of those declared to be end stage, or terminal, proved to be much lower, only twenty-four. Five of these men were immediately eliminated because they were not Caucasians. The investigators then eliminated seven men who were shorter than five feet ten and weighed less than 150 pounds, and eight who were physically handicapped or over sixty-five years old.

Farone and his team pored over the remaining four names on the cancer list. As leads, this raw list of names was pretty anemic, Sloan pointed out, with a slightly discouraged look on his face.

"Anemic or not, they're the only leads we have to follow," Farone answered with a little more anger and frustration in his voice than he would normally betray. "Let's go over the list one more time, and then we'll break it down among us by assignment. Cathy Weiss suggested turning it over to Agent Snyder and his people to get correlation of names, particularly those who've registered boats locally. But I intend to hold off on that, because I would bet my last dollar that once the FBI got their hands on our list, we'd get knocked aside. I don't mean to be too parochial, but I think because we're locals, we've got a better shot at turning up a solid lead than anyone else. So let's go over Sloan's so-called anemic list."

Detective Nugent dimmed the conference room lights and flipped on the overhead projector. The first transparency listed the names and brief description of the first two patients:

Richard Battaglia lived in Darien. Married with three children. His wife was listed as next of kin. His business phone number had been disconnected, but his home phone and cell phone numbers were available. He was fifty-two years old, six feet even, and weighed 210 pounds. His last treatment date had been six weeks ago, and he had declined further radiation and chemotherapy treatments at that time. He was dying slowly of prostate cancer. It had been diagnosed too late and had metastasized to his liver and lungs. It was estimated that he had about twelve to sixteen months left to live. There were no other maladies. The only remaining medications were painkillers, which dulled rather than "killed" pain, and Ativan, a medication designed to combat anxiety, an affliction that consumed him. Detective Nugent did not bother to relate the information to which the clinic had given greatest priority, notably his insurance and social security number (the new, de facto national ID).

Next on the list was Bart Daly, dying of liver cancer. Age forty-two. Mr. Daly was divorced, lived in downtown Stamford, and was being treated as aggressively as possible at his request, although his doctor and oncologist privately thought that he had only about nine more months to live. He was also suffering from a mild case of congestive heart failure. Daly was a large man, six feet four inches tall, and weighed over 230 pounds. He was subjected to radiation treatments every ten days, which, when combined with a typically reduced appetite, was resulting in a gradual loss in weight. Both daytime and home phone numbers were available.

Ivan Hartman was next on the list. He was listed as divorced, no next of kin, residing in Greenwich, age forty-eight. His record indicated past treatment for bipolar disorder, treatment having been provided in expensive private hospitals. His melanoma was labeled malignant and had begun to metastasize, but he had declined any treatment, specifically to remove six of his lymph glands. He was big and robust, six feet two and 240 pounds. His case was odd because, although his treating physician, Dr. Ransom, had not indicated that Hartman was terminal, the patient himself had declared that he was dying and refused to accept further treatment, or even to appear for an exam. The clinic was also frustrated because their radiology department had recently been staffed with a new chief radiologist in charge, and she questioned the accuracy of four recent diagnoses, one of which was Hartman's. His film consequently had been sent to MemorialSloan-KetteringHospital in Manhattan for a second opinion. The patient had been phoned several times to be brought abreast of the new development, but he had not picked up. Dr. Ransom therefore decided to wait for the final report from Sloan-Kettering and then phone Hartman again. He also planned to send the report with a cover letter via registered mail to Hartman's home, as much to inform the patient as to protect the clinic.

A married man named Nestor Johnson was last on the list. Johnson lived in Darien with his wife and three children. To his doctor's chagrin, Johnson persisted in his habit of smoking two packs of cigarettes per day, despite his incurable lung cancer and a terminal prognosis. His other maladies were unrelated, a torn rotator cuff in his left shoulder and recurring episodes of diverticulosis. He stood six feet one and weighed 195 pounds. His medical treatment was palliative in nature; however, a nebulizer and possibly a lung machine would be required within three months.

Sloan turned on the room lights, and Nugent gathered up her materials. "Thanks for the basic briefing, Peggy," Farone said matter-of-factly. "It's time to hand out the assignments. I want Peggy and Brian to pursue the first two leads, Battaglia and Daly. I've decided to tackle the next two myself. I've gone over all of this with the boss. He's opened every door we'll need—top priority—so let's get started. Call me anywhere if you hit snags or find major evidence. And forget about time off."

CHAPTER NINETEEN

"What lousy timing," remarked Farone in a short morning meeting with Chief James. "Just as we're making a dent in nailing Crabby, that missing-person case in Greenwich has been closed out and moved to homicide. They found the vic, about four days dead, bound to a headstone in the Kings Road cemetery in Greenwich."

"What was the cause of death, Bob?"

"Nothing obvious. No sign of a struggle. The medical examiners are working on it and should have an opinion by tomorrow morning."

"As I recall, the vic was a big-time criminal lawyer from New York City," James commented. "What information do you have on why he was in FairfieldCounty? And what are the details on the scene?"

"Here's the rundown, Chief," Farone answered laconically. "The victim, Leon Kroll, was a so-called celebrity lawyer. Defended only the rich and sought high-profile cases, especially ones in which he could manipulate the media. Represented everyone from wise guys to big-league jocks to society people. Fought dirty in court but usually got an acquittal or a hung jury. Hated, feared, respected, and rich; you know the type.

"Anyway, he kept a weekend house in Greenwich—four acres, six bedrooms, pool, tennis court—on North Street. Top shelf all the way. When his housekeeper reported him missing last Thursday, the investigation of his property showed nothing stolen, no evidence of a break-in or foul play. Cars in garage, neighbors too far away to spot anything strange. So the case was opened as a missing person, but the local cops were skeptical. His three cars were still on the premises, that area is too far to walk anywhere to shop, for example, and he was a paunchy guy who took no exercise. Looks like he was picked up by someone—friend or foe, who knows—and subsequently done in."

"How did the homicide lead develop, Bob?" Chief James asked, a growing look of apprehension on his face.

"Very straightforward, Chief," Farone answered. "One of the cemetery workers was picking up dead flower arrangements in the area and noticed the naked body of a man tied to a new headstone. The poor guy fainted with fright. I mean, the discovery was bad enough, but to find a corpse above the ground in a graveyard was too much. But he pulled himself together, drove back to the office, and told his boss about the discovery. The worker apparently has a serious booze jones, so the superintendent decided to check out the body himself. That's when he called it in to the Greenwich police. The police report will be available in about two hours, and one of our uniforms is standing by in Greenwich to pick up our copy. I'll summarize it for you then.

"I know you're going to ask me the sixty-four-dollar question, and I've already checked. There was no crab bracelet on the man's wrists. The idea that the graveyard superintendent or his worker might have removed it is highly improbable, since Kroll was still wearing a Rolex President watch and a fancy gold medical ID bracelet—for diabetes mellitus—when found. Plus, the cemetery guys told the detectives at the scene that they had not gone anywhere near the gravesite. The super said he learned that from watching *FBI* shows on TV."

Chief James removed his glasses and rubbed his eyes slowly. "Well, I guess network TV is good for something, Bob. Yeah, give me a complete briefing as soon as you get the report. I hope to Christ that Crabby isn't a part of this. Maybe he is, though, and ran out of charms, or forgot to sign his latest work of art."

• • •

At three o'clock, after giving Jonas James a complete briefing on the graveyard slaying, Farone called his squad into the meeting room, got them to clear away the debris of pizza boxes, paper cups, napkins, and crumbs, and then proceeded to review what was known of the Kroll case, which the New York tabloids had already dubbed the "Man With the Golden Tongue."

"Is there anyone here who doesn't know about this dead lawyer, Kroll?" Farone asked as he opened the meeting.

"Just what we read in the New York papers and get through the media, Bob," answered Peggy Nugent.

"Speak for yourself, darling," interrupted Jim Sisk, one of Raymond Snyder's agents, who was representing the FBI at the briefing. "We don't get to watch that much TV."

"Except on Saturday mornings," Nugent quipped.

Brian Sloan knew it was time to interrupt and get the meeting back on track. "If you don't mind, Bob, I'll give a rundown on this Kroll guy to get everyone up to speed. I'm knowledgeable because I am a media junkie, but also because my girlfriend is a trial lawyer and fascinated by Kroll and some of the cases he's won. His tactics are—or were, I guess—very similar to the ones used by Johnny Cochran, Bruce Cutler, Scheck, Shapiro, and the rest of these high-profile criminal attorneys, which means he basically attacked virtually every witness the prosecutor brought forward, particularly witnesses from law enforcement and forensics. Kroll was especially resourceful at finding his own so-called expert witnesses—articulate people who were highly qualified in their field and handled questions well, and who had a limited—or better, zero—track record of ever before having appeared in a trial. Kroll would get them to create the possibility of error or sloppiness in the findings of the prosecutor's primary witnesses. Kroll's personal examination of the people's witnesses was great theater, everything from sucking them in to making grudging acceptances of his expert's testimony by expressing empathy with how hard it must be for them to do their job, to serious world-class badgering and intimidation. Particularly on testimony involving physical or circumstantial evidence. He tried the same tactics on cops on the witness stand, with less success, although the word got around that a lot of these guys were really pissed off and wouldn't mind seeing Kroll dead. And he could jump from his adversarial argumentum ad hominem role to a friendly, velvet-soft presentation to the jury without shifting gears."

"Would you mind leaving out the parts in Greek? The ad homo stuff. I don't think many of us speak it," interrupted Sisk sarcastically.

"It's not Greek to me, Agent Sisk," Nugent interrupted. "Actually, the phrase is Latin, and it generally means attacking someone on a personal basis rather than making any factual rebuttal of what they presented or what they may have advanced as an opinion. Do you follow me, sweetie?"

A few muffled laughs, none from Farone, followed.

Sloan decided to relate the specifics of Kroll's most recent case. "I'm sure the name Lawrence Gunn is familiar to you. He's the client whom Kroll got acquitted recently from a murder charge. The state attorney had arraigned Gunn and charged him with the murder of his girlfriend, Nancy Coble. Gunn is rich, a Greenwich socialite, and unhappily married. Coble was a good-looking young travel agent who worked in Stamford. I don't remember how they met, but she was his mistress for about fourteen months. I mean mistress—not girlfriend. He kept her in a fancy apartment, bought her a nice car, the whole works. She had everything going for her—except for her drug habit. Injectable heroin. And the habit was moving out of the recreational stage to a real screaming jones at about the time she was killed. Cleaning lady found her body, naked and starting to bloat, on her weekly visit. Death was overdose by injection, but the Greenwich ME and detectives suspected foul play.

"The syringe, for example, was found in her right hand, yet she was left-handed; the most recent puncture mark was in her right arm. Also, there was some recent bruising on the face, primarily. It looked like she had been slapped around pretty hard. Didn't take long for the connection to Gunn to be made. And worse, for him at least, were some drunken remarks he had made to two friends in the bar of the Stanhope Country Club, to the effect that he had investigated his girlfriend's whereabouts and confirmed the fact that she was cheating on him. Said in so many words that he knew how to put a stop to it. And on top of all that, there were some other conversations and related physical evidence that led Gunn to be charged. Turns out one of his weekend golfing buddies was Leon Kroll, who took on the case and made mincemeat out of the prosecution's case, which wasn't that strong to begin with. So the girl is dead, Kroll adds to his golden-tongue reputation, Gunn is headed for divorce court, and the media has had a field day."

Nugent said, "Oh sure, it was certainly a fascinating case and trial, Brian, but Kroll could have been killed for any number of reasons by any number of people. Does anyone here feel that this was a revenge murder? Specifically for getting Coble's killer off? I remember she was from Texas or Oklahoma, didn't have any family up here. And if I recall correctly, the trial brought out the fact that she did not have a boyfriend other than Gunn. Her cheating was confined to occasionally sleeping around, so there wouldn't seem to be any immediate candidate to step up and murder Kroll out of revenge."

"That's good thinking, Peggy, and thanks, Brian, for the review. Let me take over and give you all the latest findings," Farone said gravely. "Kroll, as you know, was found by the cemetery custodians naked, dead, and tied to a headstone in the Greenwich cemetery. Local cops sealed off the scene immediately and, amazingly enough, there have been no leaks on the case to the press. This will answer some of your questions, Peggy. After the body was removed to the morgue, the headstone was shrouded by the detectives. The reason was that it was the gravesite of Nancy Coble, the murdered girl. Gunn had paid for the plot and the services after it came out that she had been involved with him. He had nothing more to lose by the gesture and maybe something to gain, to show he grieved for her and had nothing to do with her murder.

"Forensics easily concluded from the condition of his body that Kroll had died somewhere else and was taken to the gravesite. It took the MEs in Greenwich a long time to decide upon the pathology, but their conclusions are now on file. Apparently, Kroll had been attacked initially in his yard or somewhere nearby. A thirty-thousand-volt Taser gun had disabled him. He was then put in a vehicle and taken to a remote location, most probably. He was stripped then slapped around somewhat. The Taser was probably used several different times, since its effect generally lasts only twenty to thirty minutes. Turns out he was a serious diabetic, needed three to four injections daily. These were obviously withheld, because of his captivity, and the best guess is that he slipped into a diabetic coma within twenty-four hours. However, he actually went on to die of renal failure—kidneys quit. The examiners learned that he had had only one functioning kidney anyway; the other was long gone, a result of his condition.

"He had numerous injection marks on his thighs, the result of several daily treatments of insulin. However, one mark was found on his forearm, and it looked fairly recent. Autopsy then confirmed that he had been injected while in a coma, and the shot was what finally knocked out his remaining organ. The substance was ethyl glycol, the active ingredient, so to speak, in auto antifreeze."

"Looks like the asshole won't be overheating anymore," remarked Sisk with a low laugh.

"Bob, we know from cop scuttlebutt that Kroll did not have a signature crab bracelet, so are we at least concluding for now that Crabby is not implicated here?" asked Sloan.

"Unfortunately, quite the opposite, Brian," Farone answered slowly. "The killing fits his MO. Vengeance is a likely motive, directed at the rogue lawyer, not Gunn. Sophisticated knots like the clove hitch were used to bind the body to the grave, and just to wrap things up neat and tidy, and push us a little harder, the ME found a gold bracelet, complete with gold crab, tightly cinched around Kroll's tongue."

A brief pause ensued. Notes were made. Finally Sisk said, "You'd have to call it a real mouthpiece."

"Or a comment on his nickname," Nugent added.

CHAPTER TWENTY

Ivan Hartman pulled slowly into the Mianus Yacht Club parking lot in his 1989 vintage Jaguar XJS roadster. *One of the best-looking cars ever built,* he thought. *Too bad it's such a dog.* Twelve cylinders seemed like a lot, but the car was heavy, and pickup was unimpressive. But so what, he often thought. Between New York to New Haven the traffic on both I-95 and the older roads was so heavy that performance goals were strictly theoretical. Not like sailing, where wind, current, boat, and crew still mattered.

In addition to being sluggish, the Jaguar was also notoriously unreliable. Overheating, particularly the engine and exhaust system, were the main problems, due largely to the US-mandated catalytic converter, which was completely inefficient when married to the obsolete large engine. The electrical system, which had a mind of its own, could never be depended on to function as designed. And worse, for some reason no one could permanently repair it. The system had been designed by the Lucas Electrical Company in England. Among mechanics and auto buffs, Lucas was called the Prince of Darkness. Hartman had been dwelling recently on the Jaguar's many deficiencies, since to him, at least, the car was an obvious metaphor for his own condition.

Hartman's father's Dodge Ram pickup truck was locked away in his garage, now too risky to either use or get rid of. *Too bad*, he thought. The truck had been an important part of his crusade for justice. He had become furious with himself over the failure to capture and punish Mrs. Failsome, the abortionist. Had gotten cocky because his first victories in the crusade had gone so smoothly.

He got out, put on a Greek captain's cap, which he had always loathed, and wraparound Serengeti sunglasses with polarized lenses. He was about ten minutes early for a meeting with Tod Morgan, current vice commodore of the club, a meeting that Morgan had asked for, a clear hint of coolness in his voice.

Hartman strolled past the small, well-maintained clubhouse down to the dock and seawall at the river's edge, not far from the open water of Long Island Sound. The few powerboats in the club were tied to cleats on the fingers of the dock. The majority of the fleet were sailboats, for the most part swinging on moorings out on the river. A small launch at dockside was used to ferry members back and forth from their boats. Not a great day for sailing, Hartman observed. Almost a dead calm, with high humidity.

"Sure glad we're not racing today. Lousy conditions," Tod Morgan announced as he strode toward Hartman and offered his hand. Morgan was sixtyish, silver haired, tanned, and fit; very impressive looking. He took his job at the club quite seriously and was good at it. He also took himself seriously, and, though friendly, even occasionally charming, he gave off an aura of faintly suppressed condescension.

The two men walked back up to the clubhouse, making small talk about sailing, and seated themselves outside in the shade. Morgan made no move to invite Hartman to have a drink and generally gave the impression that their meeting would be short and cold.

"Ivan, there's something I need to ask you with respect to your involvement, or lack of involvement, with this club," Morgan began abruptly. "Your father was a member here for over thirty years. A fine man, an exceptional sailor, and a close friend of mine, as you know. We all miss him. You, as a legacy, have a right to join this club, but I've been informed by the membership committee that you have ignored several inquiries to join. Yet your father's boat remains here. May I ask exactly what your intentions are?"

"I haven't meant to ignore your solicitations," Hartman replied in a level voice. "I've been very busy lately with some personal chores, which look like they're coming to a close. But to answer your question, Morgan, I have no intention of joining this club, legacy or not. And, I might add, the boat is now mine. May I ask why you asked me down here and didn't handle this matter with a short phone call?"

"It's not just a simple matter of membership, Hartman. In all candor, I'm personally pleased that you won't be joining this club. You're an excellent sailor, but you fall short of the type of socially responsive, enthusiastic, and pleasant person we enjoy associating with. Frankly, in all the times you've been here over the years, I cannot recall one instance in which you made any effort to greet your father's friends, socialized in any way, or even smile, for God's sake. Your father always made excuses for you, and I am truly sorry about your many psychological and social difficulties over the years, but one would have thought that you would respond to treatment, mature, grow as a person. You were a great disappointment to your father."

Hartman exhibited no emotion or any reaction to Morgan's remarks. "I'm not interested in your personal opinions about me or my family. I've got bigger issues on my mind. Oddly enough, you'd be surprised if you knew how my father really was as a person, but that doesn't matter anymore. Once again, why did you drag me out here?"

"Last week I was visited by an FBI agent," Morgan said. "The first time in the club's history we've had any member of law enforcement knock on our door, so to speak. They would not reveal what they were after, but merely wanted answers to several specific questions about someone who was seen wearing one of our shirts. I pointed out that our items of apparel are not only worn by members and employees but are also given as gifts to nonmembers. And who knows what becomes of these articles of clothing when they are finally given away?

"Their next question came from left field. They wanted to know if we had a boat at the club with a name on the transom such as *Zodiac*, *Crab*,

Claw, or, God forbid, *Cancer*. I pointed out that Zodiac was a manufacturer's name for high-quality, inflatable small craft, but that we had no boats here with even a modest fit to what they sought."

"What does any of this crap have to do with me, Morgan?" Hartman asked quietly, looking at his watch with calculated impatience.

"Hopefully, nothing. But they also inquired about a red Dodge Ram crew-cab truck with Connecticut plates and a silver toolbox in the bed. And they showed me one of those police composite drawings and asked if I recognized the man in it, and, if so, was he a member here? Frankly, the picture looked somewhat like you. Not fully, but somewhat. They also described the man as tall and heavily built, also like you. And many others, too. Their description of the truck, however, clearly suggested to me that there was a possible link to you, because the vehicle they described is almost an exact fit to the truck your father used in business. Incidentally, you didn't drive that truck here today, did you?" he asked apprehensively.

"No way," Hartman responded smoothly. "That truck is long gone, part of the old man's estate sale."

Morgan seemed to be a little relieved to hear Hartman's lie. "Well, in any event, I want you to know that I did not offer any specific answers to their questions, particularly since they seem to be wasting taxpayers' money, as usual, with this foolish search for a boat. However, I want you to understand this very clearly, Hartman. If these men return, I will cooperate. I was perfunctory in my response to the agents for two reasons, and two only: protection of our club's excellent reputation and my loyalty to your father's memory. One of the agents gave me his business card and requested that I phone him if I recall any information they seek, or if anything new develops here vis-à-vis their case.

"If there is any problem with the IRS or drugs or whatever that leads to you, I don't want to hear about it. I assumed that you would have no interest in joining this club, so I instructed the harbormaster to reserve the travel lift for you so that you can launch *Coy Mistress* and vacate our premises. Two men and the lift will be available this coming Thursday at three thirty, which gives you three days to find a new berth for her. You should also clean out your father's locker, if you haven't already done so. Are these arrangements understood, Hartman?"

Morgan's question was met with an odd, cold smile. "You're a lucky man, Vice Commodore Morgan. You're a pain in the ass, but not an affront to society."

Morgan turned away and headed for the club bar. "Just make sure that you're here Thursday afternoon," he snapped. Under his breath he muttered, "Crazy bastard. His father should have tossed him overboard."

Hartman had little trouble in making new arrangements for the boat. After several calls to commercial marinas, he made arrangements to lease a slip at Harbor Marine in South Norwalk, up the coast about ten miles from Greenwich. Confirmed he would arrive about six o'clock on Thursday.

Meanwhile, he had a little preparation to do at the nearest ships' chandlery. He bought sixty feet of half-inch chain anchor rode, plus two fifty-pound plow anchors, and loaded them effortlessly into the trunk of the Jaguar. The clerk in the store had made some dumb remark about the last time they had sold anchor gear that heavy it was for the *Queen Elizabeth*.

On Thursday afternoon Bill Russo, MYC harbormaster, and his assistant, Kenny Fusco, prepared to launch the *Coy Mistress* and hoped that Ivan Hartman would be on time to sail her away. It was busy on the sound. Fridays off—*At least for big shots*, thought Bill—meant that a lot of members would show up after work on Thursday and make demands on both the facilities and his time. He also hoped that this big, unpleasant owner would be as generous as his father had been. Although tipping was not allowed, members like the senior Hartman slipped an occasional ten or twenty to the workers to ensure a little priority for their personal boating needs.

Hartman pulled into the club parking lot exactly on time and headed directly for the *Coy Mistress*, which loomed largely overhead, resting in a heavy wooden cradle. *Funny how big they always look in dry dock*, mused Hartman, *and how small at sea, particularly in a gale*. He waved to Russo and his assistant and said, "Let's go."

Two heavy canvas slings were guided around the boat's hull, one in front of the large keel, the other behind it. When the boat was fully cinched, Kenny Fusco expertly lifted it up from his position at the controls of the travel lift. The boat was then moved to the launching dock and lowered gently into the water. Dock lines were secured by Hartman and Russo, and the heavy cinches were unfastened and lifted out of the way. Hartman told the men he would launch immediately, under power, but would need some help with the ground tackle in his car. The chain and anchors were brought to the boat in a dock cart and stowed carefully in the cockpit. Russo thought the gear was foolishly excessive for the Morgan, especially since she already had fifty feet of quarter-inch chain, backed with three hundred feet of anchor line, all attached to a twenty-pound Danforth anchor. "Well, they always said that the Hartman apple dropped far from the tree," Russo muttered to Kenny. "A real nut case."

Hartman surprised both men with a smile, a thank you, and twenty dollars apiece as they helped him cast off. But he had avoided their questions about where he was headed. And he left word with the office that he would pick up his car later that night.

The Yanmar diesel engine started on the third try. Hartman noted that the tank was over three-quarters full of diesel fuel, more than enough for his needs. He put the engine in gear and swung out into the MianusRiver. The water was slightly turbulent, and the moored boats were rocking up and down. Not a reflection on the water conditions, which were excellent, but a sorry comment on the two idiots ahead of Hartman who were running their power boats at well in excess of the posted 5 MPH No Wake Zone signs posted every one hundred yards down to the mouth of the river. Swift Clorox bottles, Hartman, a boating purist, called them.

As he cleared the MianusRiver and entered GreenwichHarbor, Hartman steered to port to head east around Tod's Point. He decided to motor up to Norwalk and keep the sails furled. Winds were too light, and time was getting short. Though not a very nostalgic man, he took what he knew to be a last glance at Captain's Island with its treacherous rock-strewn bottom and over to the port side at the beautifully wooded Tod's Point picnic area, the jewel of tiny Old Greenwich.

The cruise east to Norwalk took about one hour. The only other boaters were primarily guys out fishing, trolling for abundant bluefish with wire lines and umbrella rigs. As he entered the harbor, he left the helm briefly to secure the bow, aft, and spring lines to the starboard cleats. He finished his docking preparations by hanging two large fenders over the starboard side. He raised the harbormaster on his VHF radio and requested a dock hand to be at his new slip to help tie up the boat. All went smoothly, and thirty minutes later Hartman had paid for two months' slip rental and ordered a cab to take him back to the MYC, where he would pick up the Jag and head home.

Mulling over his plans to flee, Hartman bitterly observed that *Coy Mistress*, scene of many afternoon delights for his father—and misery for him—would shortly go from being a guest boat to a ghost boat.

CHAPTER TWENTY-ONE

In the two-day interval between his unpleasant interview with the stuffy, condescending vice commodore and moving the boat to Rex Marine, Hartman had been busy. Not, however with administering justice and issuing a warning to malefactors—this work would have to wait—but rather with finishing up his personal affairs.

He paid a visit to his broker, Ryan McGovern, a man who had served the Hartman family well throughout the years. McGovern greeted Ivan warmly, although he secretly despised him, and explained that he had done as asked with the Hartman estate, although he was still mystified at the liquidation.

"Ivan, if I may repeat what I told you over the phone last month, there really is no practical reason to liquidate your father's—excuse me, I mean your—estate. It's been growing reasonably well in the last few years, despite a choppy market, and I believe that our investment strategy for you has paid off. Now, if you're planning to take your business to another brokerage, that's fine, but as a courtesy I would like to know to whom and why. Also, as I told you, there was absolutely no need for us to liquidate the entire account and convert it to bearer bonds. A simple transfer could have been arranged with the new firm, and then they could pursue whatever new strategy you agree to. It's extremely odd and very dangerous for you to walk out of here with over one million dollars in bearer bonds. Any thief could sign and cash them.

"Nevertheless, we have complied with your instructions to the letter. Account closed, bonds in this attaché case, and all of our fees deducted, including the cost of the fancy Halliburton alloy case you requested. If you have any questions, please call my assistant, JoAnn Baxter. We hope to serve you again, should you decide to make another change, and we wish you well.

"Ivan, would you please do me a favor and explain your plans? I owe it to your father's memory, if not to you, to offer any financial advice possible—it's free—before you walk out of here with such a large sum of money."

"There's no great mystery," Hartman replied coldly. "My father earned it, I spend it. As I overheard you tell him years ago, 'That kid of yours is a sulky, lazy, oversized punk. Make sure he goes off on his own or he'll squander every dime you've got and screw up your business in the bargain.'

"No, no don't deny it." Hartman waved at the other man, just as McGovern was about to defend himself. "I was pissed off at the time but objective enough to admit that you were probably right. And you're not the only friend of my father's to run me down, although most of them at least ascribed my deficiencies to being crazy. What a shock when I made it in business all by myself. Since you brokerage assholes size up people in terms of net worth, you might be surprised to learn that I have earned more money, and invested it for greater return, than my father ever did; in fact, I sold my business for mucho millions that are safely invested, fortunately not with you." He picked up the briefcase. "And I've been a hell of a lot more frugal, too. Don't worry about losing face with your partners over the Hartman account being moved to another brokerage, McGovern. I'm actively involved in a new enterprise with definite growth prospects. Have a nice day."

Ryan McGovern, ever the gentleman, began to rise in order to escort his guest to the elevator, just as he always did. But this time he sat back down as Hartman strode out and had the comforting thought that the fucking nut would blow all his money and wind up broke. Good riddance.

Hartman had long ago sold his own condo in Greenwich along with his father's house and furnishings. He now lived in a very attractive old stucco house on Sweetbriar Road in North Stamford. He was the only single person living in the neighborhood—a fluke, since the rental was offered by a couple who had been transferred by IBM for two years to France. They planned on returning to their beloved home and therefore wanted a renter that wouldn't leave a mark. Hartman was perfect—single, no pets, and, best of all, he paid in advance.

His father had died four years ago, and for two years prior Ivan was so depressed that he vowed to kill himself. But the ethical notion that suicide was the ultimate form of selfishness had been implanted in him somewhere, and he could not face up to OD'ing with the many bottles of prescription drugs he had squirreled away. He thought increasingly about the meaning of suicide and decided that it was primarily a means of escape. From physical pain, mental anguish, failing of the spirit, whatever.

And that's when it hit him: escape. No need to die, just vanish. Take off. If anyone really cared about you, you wouldn't be in this shape today.

Hartman had gone about creating a new identity with remarkable energy. His plan was to completely invent a new person but not reveal him to anyone. Just wait for the appropriate time and take off.

A trip through several graveyards in northern Connecticut finally turned up a headstone he could use: Randall Newman, born 1961, died 1967. Same birth year as Ivan's. He used his PC to make up a letterhead with the name John Newman at the top, using his condo as the address. A phone call to the county clerk in the town of Winchester had convinced her that he was a relative of the deceased Randall Newman, working on a complex family historical document, and he required a copy of Randall's birth certificate. No problem, she replied, just two dollars and an SASE with a cover note, and the request was taken care of. Hartman had instructed his mailman to deliver any mail addressed to either a John or Randall Newman to his apartment, since the men were relatives and would be staying with him on and off. And when he left, a commercial mail drop would be used to receive mail until Randall Newman had a permanent address.

With receipt of the birth certificate, the creation of his new ID became remarkably easy. First came a social security number, followed by four different bank accounts and two credit cards. A passport was next. The driver's license was tougher; he had to take both a written and a road test. His substantial profit from the sale of the construction business was invested under his new ID with several large brokerage firms. The small stuff—registered voter's card, library card, and local credit cards—would come later, depending on where his whim took him.

So here I am, thought Hartman as he sat at his dining room table, Rob Roy in hand. *Time to fight or flee*. Well, that was an easy choice. *Leave now to fight another day.*

He examined with pleasure all the items he had amassed to create his new identity. The bank books made him especially proud. Huge sums in each, having been deposited painstakingly in units under $10,000 each, so there would be no required bank report to the IRS. Total liquidity. Plenty of money to leave to charity when Randall Newman died of cancer. He carefully put the driver's license and credit cards into a new wallet from Bottega, embossed with the initials RTN. The bank books, social security card, passport, and birth certificate were placed in a large manila envelope and joined the bearer bonds in the shiny new Halliburton attaché case. Over $2,000 in large denominations were placed in his money clip, along with everyday small bills.

His new travel bags from T. Anthony were packed with an entirely new wardrobe. And a final strategy for altering his appearance was already forming in his mind: heavier, new hairstyle, different car, maybe a moustache. His scheme to implement his own disappearance, he reminded himself, needed polishing, but that would come soon. His new creative ideas always seemed to hatch just before they were needed. First would be a faked suicide, then Hartman would be replaced by Newman. Besides, with pressure mounting, he needed to get over the ID-switch hurdle carefully, because there was still a great deal of serious work to be accomplished for the good of society, and only eighteen to twenty-four months in which to be physically effective.

He finished his drink, popped a frozen meal into the microwave, and walked out to the mailbox, stuffed with mail he hadn't picked up in two weeks. His attention was immediately drawn to a notification to pick up a registered letter at the post office. Curious, he planned to sign for the letter first thing in the morning.

CHAPTER TWENTY-TWO

Farone decided to enter the rear door of the station house in order to avoid the media hordes who had assembled at the front door, awaiting his arrival.

Farone knew what the hubbub was all about. The media had been very efficiently handled by the commissioner's public relations officer, Isabel Hubley. She had fed them just enough information each day to allow them to continue to massage the serial killer story, or "Joshua" as many preferred to label it. But the slaying of Leon Kroll, a prominent New York attorney, had refueled the media feeding frenzy, national media included. TV trucks were assembled out on the street, antennae fully extended, like a swarm of praying mantises. Press photographers, reporters, and so-called TV journalists milled about, waiting for action, someone to hammer with questions. The abnormally hot weather did nothing to curb their impatience. And the bland, carefully worded answers of Officer Hubley were no longer easily tolerated. For the more sleazy of the media, for example, contrived stories, based on "private, unnamed sources" and "expert opinion" would appear.

However irritating the media may be, acknowledged Farone as he walked slowly to his desk, *they've got a great reason to pounce on us today, because it's our own goddam fault.*

He was still smarting over the chewing out he had gotten from Jonas James the night before. Several of the more prominent media had gotten word from "sources within the law enforcement community" that serious friction and conflicts of interest between the local police and the FBI had hampered the investigation from the very beginning. And the source of the problems had been laid in the lap of the police.

Lt. James had thwarted the calls as best he could, for a man who was not considered particularly diplomatic. But when the reporters had specifically identified his own man, "Lead Detective Farone," he began to lose his temper. He insisted that Farone and all his detectives and uniformed police had cooperated with the FBI and the state attorney's office to the fullest extent. He became even angrier, however, when the press claimed that they had evidence that the FBI had been excluded in the pursuit of several live leads and instead had been relegated to chasing possible leads that held little or no promise of panning out.

What's worse, the media announced that they would go with the story on TV that evening, and if the police department wanted its own side of the story told, they'd better produce Farone for a live interview the following day. Chief James alerted both Farone and Hubley to tune in to the local evening news in case the story broke, which it did—under the banner of NEWS ALERT! James had been relatively pleasant, though serious in his call to Isabel Hubley, partly motivated by the fact that she had done a good job in keeping the media at bay, and also because he needed her to help control the story and deflect the media from learning more about their leads, possibly jeopardizing the case.

When he had finally gotten Farone on the phone, however, he was livid. He demanded that Farone and all the cops working the case in the Stamford area keep their mouths shut and refer any media questions to himself or Hubley. He stated that he would make the same request to the Greenwich police. As for the FBI, one of Officer Hubley's inside friends in the media, a former boyfriend, had confided to her that a Raymond

Snyder was the "inside source." He had released the information, off the record, of course, which detailed the empty casting about for leads the FBI had been chasing, while good solid leads in the case had been hoarded by the Stamford police and not shared with his people. He dropped the name of Robert Farone, the lead detective, as the main bottleneck, a man "protecting his own turf."

James insisted that Farone be ready to appear with himself and Raymond Snyder to field media questions, their talking points being that cooperation was very good and improving daily, and that several good leads had developed and were being pursued by all elements of law enforcement working together.

James was equally angry with Farone and Snyder: Snyder because he had leaked the information to the press, although he had denied it when confronted; and Farone for having frozen Snyder and his people out of the four promising leads Farone's team had devised from the list of local cancer patients. He demanded that he cooperate with all other members of the team and end the grandstanding. James had controlled his anger with Snyder and had halfheartedly accepted his side of the story, though he knew that Snyder was a liar and an egomaniac. He vowed to get to Snyder through contacts he had at FBI headquarters in Washington, but only after the case was closed.

In addition to having to face the press with his newfound FBI buddies flanking him, Farone also learned that Agent Edward DeLong had been added to Head Agent Snyder's team, joining Jim Sisk in the investigation. The analysis of potential suspects by birth date had been dropped, with everyone's concurrence, because the net was too big and too full of holes. That left the suspect-as-cancer-victim scenario as the primary approach to generating strong leads.

Farone was also angry and disappointed with Chief James for making him the fall guy for the conflict of interest. The chief certainly had known that the FBI was being frozen out of parts of the case, and he had conveniently looked the other way, since it would be great politically for the department to get full credit for the eventual solving of the case and the capture of the perpetrator. But the leak to the press had changed everything, and the chief had to cover himself. Farone understood this, and his anger turned to increasing disillusionment with the amount of politics necessary to get ahead in law enforcement. At times like this he wondered if he really wanted to continue upward and drift into administration, handholding, and politics or return to law school, join his father's successful criminal practice, and spend the rest of his career defending the same kind of scum he now worked to bring to justice.

As part of the new process of cooperation, Snyder and James had agreed to a new division in the investigation of the four "cancer victims," with Agent DeLong pursuing Richard Battaglia, Agent Sisk assigned to Ivan Hartman, Detective Sloan handling Nestor Johnson, and Detective Nugent on the trail of Bart Daly. The arrangement, a compromise, of course pleased no one, but Farone at least conceded that the strongest lead in his opinion, Mr. Daly, was in his control.

After the assignments were parceled out and reviewed in some detail, the chief excused the agents and detectives from his office and directed Farone and Snyder to remain. His mood shifted, not too subtly, from professional to angry. "I want both of you to listen carefully to what I'm telling you now," he began as his steely gaze shifted back and forth between the two men seated before him. "We will not be having this conversation again, because if there is one more episode of glory stealing or of behind-the-scenes media leaks, you're both going off the case immediately. Is that understood? By both of you?"

Farone nodded affirmatively, tight-lipped, shoulders slumped uncharacteristically forward.

Chief Agent Raymond Snyder had a very different reaction, however. "My people and I don't happen to appear anywhere in your chain of command, Chief," he said angrily, "and we're not going to pretend to. The FBI was called into this case because of the kidnapping implications, if you'll be so generous as to recall, and also because we have more expertise and resources than you'll ever see. Don't threaten me or my people again. And don't lecture me about the media. If you and your alleged professionals had been honest and open with us, maybe even letting us handle the whole case, it would have been solved by now, and your so-called team would have gone back to writing traffic tickets and rousting bums."

With that little outburst over, Chief James bolted up from behind his desk and began attacking Snyder and the entire FBI as meddlers and glorymongers, people he would never have asked in on the case if he had had anything to say about it. This only provoked Snyder to respond in kind, and the meeting rapidly degenerated into a shouting match.

Farone, weary and disgusted, rose to his feet and announced, "I've had enough of this crap. I'll be at my desk when you get this back to an adult level and get organized to meet the media mob." His departure was barely noticed as he headed to the door.

The media was more irritable than usual, not so much from their endless waiting around in the hot sun, but from the practical reality of needing the lead time to prepare stories and video, edit, and make the next newspaper edition or news broadcast. When Chief James, Head Agent Snyder, and Detective Farone finally came out to the improvised podium arranged by PR officer Hubley, anger and annoyance instantly gave way to a scramble to roll footage, shoot pictures, and ask leading questions. Thanks to the coaching of Hubley, the three men were relaxed and congenial, and they spoke with one voice: a voice that proclaimed continual cooperation among all law enforcement personnel, new assignments to key leads in the case, and a spirit of openness with the press. Of course no specifics could be "divulged, in the interest of confidentiality," so the media came away with, as one of the reporters put it, "a pile of horse shit covered with Hubley's cologne." Several of the more experienced and resourceful reporters allayed their cynicism and instead moved to line up their inside police sources to get to the heart of the investigation through the back door.

Business as usual.

CHAPTER TWENTY-THREE

Sheila Ryan's garden apartment was part of a new condo complex that had been built in Riverside after the demolition of older rental buildings. There were only three buildings, surrounding a communal parking lot. The buildings were painted a sort of ersatz navy-gray, apparently in order to fit in with the community and project a seaside motif.

The two-bedroom apartment that Ryan owned was large, sunny, and comparatively quiet. It featured a small eight-by-fourteen balcony, designed to buttress the developer's description of "garden apartment." Ryan had done her part. The balcony was festooned with three hanging baskets of flowers, and another four pots with larger plants were seated on the balcony floor.

Ryan was relaxing out on the balcony, drinking bottled water and still sweating from the heavy workout in the nearby gym and the three-mile run which had followed it. She regretted that she had accepted a dinner date with a man she had been dating casually for five weeks. She really wished she could just remain home alone, shower, have a drink, graze the leftovers in the kitchen, and get lost in a mindless made-for-TV movie. But her sense of good manners never allowed her to break a date on the same day it was planned for, unless a bona fide medical or business emergency had taken priority.

Heaving a small sigh of resignation, she rose, polished off her Evian, and headed for the shower. As a small compromise, she decided not to work too hard at getting dressed for her date. Plain linen slacks, cotton shirt, summer-weight beige blazer, and everyday jewelry. She also remembered to plan on low-heeled shoes, since she was almost as tall as Alan Wolfe, her date. She was honest enough with herself to admit that she really preferred tall men, but then quickly became annoyed with herself for being superficial and giving in to some vague, juvenile emotional need to be folded into the strong protective arms of a big man.

Just as she was about to enter the shower, the phone rang. Mildly annoyed, she turned off the taps and decided to answer the call, hoping it might be Alan with a cancellation. Wrong guy, though. It was Bob Farone, and he sounded tired and depressed. They'd spent less than a minute on small talk when he characteristically got to the point, "Sheila, I know better than to make last-minute invitations, but I was hoping we could have dinner tonight. Nothing special, just pizza and a short night. No churning through past history. There's something I need to get your opinion on about Joshua. Please say yes."

Sheila was pained to hear the depressed, slightly desperate note in Farone's voice and realized that her feelings for him had never diminished. So it was even worse when she had to explain that she had plans. But she was clever enough to suggest that maybe they could have drinks at the bar of the Sheraton Hotel in Stamford, which was close to the restaurant where she would be having dinner. Farone agreed with the compromise and said he would be in the bar when she got there. She hung up, then made a quick call to Alan, informing him that she would meet him at the restaurant directly. He accepted the new arrangement gracefully, although he was slightly annoyed, since he had wanted to do all the driving, take her home, and be asked in for a nightcap. Maybe next time.

Ryan broke her own personal best record for showering and dressing and headed out to her car. She admitted that she was excited to see

Farone, even more than usual, possibly because she loved the idea of being wanted, especially by him. She drove her vintage BMW 325 convertible, quickly yet safely, east on the Boston Post Road, turning off on Atlantic Avenue, heading north to the hotel. The facility was, even by Stamford standards, grotesquely large, overbearing, and completely out of place in the middle-class neighborhood it grew out of. She wondered briefly if architects even bothered to consider the neighborhood or geography when they designed these large, impersonal concrete Kleenex boxes.

She also wondered, as she crossed through the large lobby and into the bar, if Bob would be drowning his sorrows in Scotch. To the contrary, Farone was seated at a small table, nursing a Corona Light and reading through a short police investigation report. He smiled as she approached, rose, and seated her, dispensing with the nearly mandatory air kiss. She ordered a vodka and tonic and quickly gave in to the feeling that she would much rather be with Bob than the man she was meeting later or, for that matter, any of the men she had dated since she'd broken off with Bob.

Farone forced a not-very-convincing note of jocularity into his voice to get things rolling. "Thanks, Doc, for fitting me in tonight. I'm trying to fight off terminal depression, and I could use your professional advice."

"Don't try to be ironic, Bob, it's not your nature. Just tell me what's going on."

"Only three little things, Sheila. I'm responsible for solving a string of serial killings and chasing an obviously smart man who strikes without warning, takes great chances, and leaves virtually no evidence other than his so-called signature. He's way ahead of us. For all I know he may be doing some poor bastard right now. We've got a partial ID on a red truck, a shaky witness—the Failsome woman—who can't even be positive on the FBI composite sketch she helped contribute to! And for that matter, the attack on her may have come from another guy, some kind of screwball who wants to attack pro-choice people, or possibly a copycat. And why not? The goddamned media prints every factoid they get their hands on. And that's one of my other problems: it's bad enough to have to be involved in a career shootout with the FBI guys, but to not get any backup from your boss—and worse, to have to pander to the media—makes my skin crawl. I'm beginning to wonder if I fit into the system anymore, or if I ever really did."

"Bob, you know as well as I do that you'll eventually solve this case. Wasn't it you who once told me that most serial killers eventually get caught because of a fluke accident, a mistake they finally make, or taking too big a chance, particularly when their twisted egos' needs become too pressing? And this mess with the FBI—isn't it at least cleared up for the time being? Just take the high road. Do your job. Share with others. If they play games, call them on it, but don't get into a pissing contest, OK?"

Farone finally cracked a smile. "A pissing contest? Wash out your mouth with soap, Doc. Such language. You've been around cops too long."

"OK, Sheila," he continued with hardly a pause. "I need your professional advice about something that's been gnawing at me for over two weeks. Our only avenues at present are tracking down four guys who suffer from some form of cancer and who have other evidentiary attributes, such as size and strength or a truck or seafaring links in their profile. All of which is pretty thin yet at least easy for us to check. But what's been bothering me especially is the question of each man's physical strength and stamina. After all, they're all probably dying from cancer and taking heavy loads of debilitating medication to boot. These crimes could only be committed by a man who is now, at least, still rugged enough to abduct people, kill them in outlandish ways, sling their bodies around like flour sacks, and not slow down the pace."

"That's a reasonable concern, Bob," Ryan replied calmly, "so I assume that's what you want me to do—give you an opinion as to each patient's ability to function. I'll do my best, but I would strongly advise you to get a second opinion from a top-flight oncologist, and also from each suspect's family doctor. That is, if you can do that in confidence."

Their waiter appeared abruptly and informed them that the complimentary hors d'oeuvres service (a large stainless-steel steam tray) was now opened, and he then inquired if they wished another round. Sheila glanced at her watch and announced that she must leave, so Farone settled the check and walked her to her car. On the way he paused, stopped her briefly, and handed her a slender police department report, official and confidential. He explained that the report contained all that was known about each of the four possible suspects, and that additional information would be added as the investigation developed under the direction of the new team assignments. But for now there was very specific data outlining the present physical health and treatments offered to each man. He asked her to read it as soon as possible and then give him her assessment of the capability of each man to perform the killings. He did not have to tell her to keep her report confidential.

"What's the story with this guy you're seeing, Sheila? I hear he's a whiz-bang, red-suspender stockbroker." Farone hated himself the moment he said it, but he could not stop himself from snooping into Ryan's personal life.

"Bob, knock it off. His name is Jerry Wolfe. He's actually a bond trader, and he does not wear red suspenders," she answered flatly, with no trace of anger in her voice.

"As long as I've already put you on the spot and humiliated myself, I would really appreciate one bit of information: is there anything serious with this guy?"

"Not really. We date, it doesn't really mean anything," she answered as they reached her car. "And don't apologize for being snoopy. After all, you're a cop."

"It means everything to me, Sheila. One last question: would it mean anything for us, together, if I stopped being a cop, maybe went into law?"

"Bob, let's talk about that another time. OK? You may be overreacting to a lousy week. It's kind of odd, though, that you would mention a career change. I've been thinking about one, too. I'll fill you in when I see you about the report."

She turned away and unlocked the door of her car, but before she got in Farone turned her gently around and kissed her on her forehead.

They remained motionless for a few seconds and then parted. She was tearyeyed but happy, in a way.

CHAPTER TWENTY-FOUR

Despite the specific agreed-upon assignments, Head Agent Snyder moved in aggressively to throw the massive resources of the FBI into the investigation. All four cancer patients were easily processed with available local demographic information plus a national ID, their social security number.

Agent Edward DeLong plunged into his assignment with great vigor, although he felt that the theory of cancer victim as killer was thin, a kind of grasping at straws, and not typical of a thorough, evidence-based investigation. But his job was not to critique the approach, but specifically to determine if one Richard Battaglia was a viable suspect. The information on Battaglia was skimpy, except for the summary of his physical condition: dying of prostate cancer, had declined further treatment, and was a heavy user of Ativan to treat a high level of anxiety.

I'd be panicked, too, thought DeLong as he reviewed the case file. Battaglia had been downsized from his employer, GT&E, several years before, and had eked out a living as a communications consultant to small local firms. His company group insurance had been automatically transferred to the government-mandated COBRA plan, an extension of health insurance designed to last eighteen months after he was terminated.

When the COBRA coverage had finally run out, Battaglia chose not to take over the full monthly payments needed to continue his coverage, because the rates were exorbitant. He planned to obtain cheaper, private insurance for his family but made the common mistake of procrastination. And then he was diagnosed with cancer, possibly spreading, and rendered virtually uninsurable. His wife, Jerri, had bravely insisted that they get a second mortgage on their house, and that their oldest son, a junior at Brown, drop out for a year and work to provide extra income. The problem, of course, was the incredibly high cost of treatment, including weekly radiation undertaken on the orders of their oncologist.

Battaglia, an engineer by trade, had been trained to work with facts, and the facts facing him were plain. He would probably be dead within the next two years, whether he continued treatment or not. The only guaranteed value of the radiation therapy was that it might add six to twelve months to his life. He considered that option to be a lousy choice, because the sheer out-of-pocket cost of treatment would deplete his family's resources, put his eldest son's college career on hold, and probably force the sale of their home. He controlled his mounting anxiety about the future of his family with Ativan and a sad effort to take on occasional consulting jobs in order to not become a burden.

Agent DeLong, using bank deposit records, had developed a list of several small businesses that had used Battaglia's services in the last few months. He was generally described as quiet and reserved, but nervous in a fidgety kind of way. The only emotion he apparently ever expressed was an outburst of anger when criticized or challenged, an anger that took several hours—or sometimes days—to cool off.

There was no good way to get any solid relationship between the days of the crimes and Battaglia's schedule, because he worked on-and-off hours interspersed with time spent at home. Therefore, one of the key pieces of any investigation—opportunity—would be difficult to detect, at least without a full interrogation, which was not called for at this time.

Battaglia's doctor also provided ambiguous information. She told DeLong that the patient's stamina and strength levels could vary widely from day to day. In the absence of medical treatment, he might spend many days feeling physically fit. Of course, she further observed, his condition would really start deteriorating as the metastasis in his lungs and liver began to seriously compromise the function of those organs.

DeLong decided that Battaglia should probably remain on the suspect list for the time being, because he fit the profile of a large, strong, white, male cancer victim who might still have the physical capacity to abduct and kill others.

The question of motive was tough to sort out, however, since the type of killings was insane. The avenging-angel theory was probably correct, DeLong thought, but Battaglia seemed more like the sort who would cling to his sanity, values, and morality and do the responsible thing, which in his case was take care of his family. A few angry outbursts could certainly be accommodated, given the total daily pressure of what he faced.

The local police had turned up very little with respect to the suspect's lifestyle. Only known hobbies were a weekly bowling league and occasional overnight camping trips with his family. One could hypothesize that Battaglia knew something about knots because of his experience as a camper, but that thought was so tenuous that DeLong had basically dismissed it.

The suspect had apparently never owned a boat, at least in the state of Connecticut, according to the registration bureau in Hartford. It was always possible, of course, that he could have kept a boat in the Stamford area, registered, however, in Delaware, a stratagem used by many boaters to avoid paying state sales tax on the purchase of watercraft. But the cops had done a thorough sweep of the six local marinas and clubs, and Battaglia's name had not turned up either as a club member or a renter of a seasonal slip.

In his report to Raymond Snyder, Agent DeLong recommended that Battaglia be retained on the suspects list but at very low priority. He sought approval for two more steps: to obtain existing or new photographs of the man and have them shown to Mrs. Failsome and the three jewelers they had interviewed, and to continue to probe for opportunity to commit each crime. This request was expected, but no one was too enthusiastic about it.

Snyder approved DeLong's next steps without a great deal of enthusiasm, primarily so that he could report that the lead was still under active investigation. He also reminded DeLong not to share any of his findings with the media and, above all, not to circulate his report to any of the local detectives.

CHAPTER TWENTY-FIVE

Bart Daly slammed his locker door shut and then kicked it savagely for good measure. He was furious, mad enough to kill somebody. Just minutes before, he had been told by his supervisor, Lloyd Parkhurst, that a cop, a pretty girl, had come around asking about him. And of course that faggot-asshole Parkhurst had cooperated instead of telling her to shove it.

Daly, though breathing hard and getting quite redfaced when Parkhurst finished telling him about the inquiry, held his temper in check. He understood that the warehouse company for which he worked—and Parkhurst in particular—were treating him decently, actually quite well, in allowing him to work on a staggered-hours basis to allow for time off to regain his strength after each bout of chemotherapy.

Daly was convinced he would beat liver cancer, despite the odds against it. In addition to his medical regimen, he had added his own therapies: a daily dose of apricot-seed-based tonic a buddy had obtained in Juarez; aromatherapy, which had been introduced to him by a cocktail hostess he was seeing; and a sharp reduction in alcohol, from eight to ten drinks daily to a sensible level of only three or four. Of course he was feeling weaker and more tired with each passing week, but he felt that his decrease in weight, from over 240 pounds to a current low of 215, signified improving health. His job as a forklift operator required occasional use of physical strength, especially when the loading pallets tilted or gave way, and a new pallet had to be reloaded. But for the most part he could manage most eight-hour shifts, as long as he could continue to take time off as needed to recover from the effects of the poisonous chemicals his doctor injected into his arm every ten days.

Daly's coworkers did not feel any particular sympathy for his condition. When well, and particularly when he was drinking heavily, he had been abusive to some of the men, on three occasions getting into actual fights. They agreed that after he had settled down from a brutal divorce battle—he was humiliated in court by endless accounts of spousal abuse—and accepted the financial beating he had taken, his aggressiveness and bad temper had cooled off some. Then he got sick and seemed to be somehow channeling his anger and eagerness to fight into combating the disease. Cutting back on the booze also helped him to soften. At least enough to be noticed.

When Lloyd Parkhurst had taken a call from Peggy Nugent and agreed to an interview, his first reaction had been to fear an investigation of why his company had failed to comply with a recent court order to install noise-abatement equipment outside the main warehouse, truck parking terminals, and loading docks. The order was at the insistence of the local neighborhood watch group, a coalition of low-income home owners and enterprising young politicians who had banded together to halt, or at least slow down, the relentless incursion of business into a formerly quiet residential area. Parkhurst secretly agreed with their agenda for environmental improvement, a concern his boss and others higher up loathed, because noise abatement would cut into profits and add nothing to the goal of improving customer service. However, Parkhurst grudgingly agreed with his management that the neighborhood would continue to sink, in terms of quality of life, despite increasing commercialization, because the more capable inhabitants had found a way to migrate to the suburbs, leaving those still in the urban sector to struggle with welfare, high unemployment, gang violence, and drugs.

As Peggy Nugent appeared in Parkhurst's modest glass-walled office to interview him, he was surprised to note how young and beautiful she was. With some haste and obvious embarrassment, he cleared a space amid the clutter of his desk for her to put her file down. She declined a cup of coffee, sat down, and got straight to the point of the interview—obtaining background and behavioral information on one Bart Daly. And although Parkhurst requested her reason for investigating Daly, she refused to divulge anything and made it clear that the interview would be onesided, with her asking all the questions.

Nugent opened her inquiry by asking for an abbreviated summary of Daly's work history, a request she had made over the phone two days earlier. Parkhurst turned it over with evident pride in his work, since he often was asked to prepare situation reports for his boss, an ex-army officer who still loved the military way of doing things. The report on Daly ran eight pages, with a convenient one-page management summary on top. Mostly mundane information was presented, which Nugent briefly scanned. However, her interest was captured by over nine odd accountings of probation handed out by the company in Daly's seventeen years of employment. She asked if that many reprimands was unusual.

"Yes, very unusual, Detective," Parkhurst responded, somewhat nervously, but at the same time feeling important and knowledgeable in the presence of a stunning young woman. "Over the years, Bart Daly has been a bit of an anomaly. Ordinarily, a worker with more than one cause for probation would be terminated. These men are easily replaced, since the type of warehousing work they do is semiskilled, pays decently, and provides competitive personal benefits. Daly, for better or worse, is quite exceptional. He is one of the best warehousemen we have ever had. First off, we experience a fairly high level of turnover at the lower levels of staffing here. Limited opportunity to move up, average wage increases at best, and general boredom take their toll. Daly has never asked for a promotion, never complained about his compensation, and never threatened to leave. Prior to his getting sick with liver cancer, he had never missed a day of work or, for that matter, punched in late. He is a hard worker and, despite the unsophisticated type of work he does, takes genuine pride in his work. And he is the best man we have ever had when there's been a need to train and break in new men."

"Tell me a little more about the probations, particularly those related to fighting," Nugent said. She continued to make notes for her report.

Parkhurst continued, a bit more cautiously. He didn't like Daly at all, but he didn't want to see him get in trouble either, particularly since his personal life had fallen apart, and especially now that he was seriously sick. "Daly does not take well to the kind of goosing around and coarse kidding, or ribbing, you always get on these low-level jobs. Probably some kind of hostility or boredom thing on the part of some of the men. Anyway, Daly puts up with little or none of that stuff and sticks to what he's doing. But when it gets to the point where he's really annoyed, which doesn't take long, he tells the other guy to 'shut up or else.' That almost always works, because he's big and tough. But on the few occasions it got out of hand, the disagreement was taken outside, as they say, and we had a real fight on our hands. In each instance, both men were put on probation, a week off without pay, with a warning that a repeat offense meant on-the-spot termination. Daly's been grounded at least three times since I've been here, but he takes his punishment without complaint. We violate our own procedures because we always take him back. He's just too valuable to lose."

"Well, knowing that you guys cave in, wouldn't Mr. Daly be more prone to assault?" Nugent asked pleasantly.

Parkhurst agreed that a part of Daly's belligerence and outbursts might be related to his growing feeling that "he could get away with murder," but he really thought that deep down there was another motive for his hostility, one hard to put into words.

Nugent pressed him to try, her cop's instinct for something important clicking in.

"Well, Detective," Parkhurst began somewhat tentatively, "Daly, in my opinion, is a man who, either through bad choices or bad luck, has not had very many things go right for him. His job here, such as it is, has, despite my report, worked out well for him and for us. And I think he knows that. So when there's a problem here with one of the other men out on the floor, and Daly gets into a fight, I don't think it's so much a personal thing, but maybe a situation where he is, in some crazy way, protecting the company from someone causing harm or disruption, at least as he sees it. So he punishes the man as an example to others not to disrupt the orderly flow of work by foolish horseplay and kidding around. Does that make any sense to you?"

"More than you might guess," Nugent responded. She thanked Parkhurst for his time and the effort he had put into his report and informed him that she might need to speak with him again.

As Parkhurst escorted her out, he was enthralled with the smell of her perfume, the lovely smile, the trim figure. *If only I had more self-confidence*, he thought, *I could ask her out, maybe for coffee.* But as she headed for her car, he knew he was just kidding himself. Once again.

• • •

When Peggy Nugent arrived back at police headquarters, she found the police report on Bart Daly completed, a copy on her desk. She opened up her sandwich and coffee container and began to read.

When she finished, she kept a tight rein on her growing enthusiasm. She realized she might have a strong chance to make a case of murder and charge Bart Daly sooner rather than later. The report listed six prior arrests over a fifteen-year period, including two for domestic violence, both later voided, because his wife had admitted they were both drunk and that the pushing and slapping were mutual.

The other four arrests, however, had resulted in two convictions after guilty pleas by Daly, one for simple assault, the other for assault and battery. Both convictions had resulted in jail time for Daly, less than thirty days, plus probation time and community service. The last conviction also included a mandatory course in anger management as part of his sentence. The prior arrests and convictions were certainly key to Nugent's developing case, but of equal importance to her was the alleged cause for the assaults.

One man, out for a walk with his dog, was severely beaten by Daly when observed to be kicking the animal for some infraction known only to the owner.

The more serious crime of assault and battery had occurred during an antiwar demonstration. Daly had reportedly been walking to the store when the demonstration, started by a group of what were described by police as "hippies," got out of control. Two of them had set fire to an American flag, to the cheers of the crowd, then tossed it to the pavement and began to stomp on it. Daly "went berserk," according to one witness. He threw one man to the ground, tore a peace sign from the hands of a female demonstrator, and began to beat the other male hippie with it. It clearly struck Nugent that a good prosecutor like Catherine Weiss could present a solid case linking Daly to the crab crimes on the avenging-angel theory.

And as further possible evidence, circumstantial perhaps, but nonetheless useful, a boat registration had been found for Daly. He owned, and prior to his illness frequently used, his Grady-White twenty-four-foot fishing boat, outboard powered by twin Yamaha engines, which was in a slip at a local public marina. A look at the craft by two uniformed officers turned up nothing suspicious—at least not enough to create probable cause and allow them to board the craft and search it. One of the officers, Marvin Pando, was a weekend sailor and knew something about knots. He noted in their report that the bow, aft, and spring lines that held Daly's boat to the slip were knotted properly and correctly secured to the cleats. Plus, the remaining slack in the line had been neatly coiled in the correct Bristol manner.

Nugent planned the next steps of her investigation carefully. First, to attempt to get a positive ID from the FBI composite sketch from Mrs. Failsome. If successful, to try to obtain the same result from the three jewelers turned up by the FBI. Next, to bring Daly into the station for an interview, seeking primarily to learn of his whereabouts on the days preceding each abduction. This approach was tricky, because the exact time and place of each abduction was not known, and a good defense lawyer could cast significant doubt on the presentation of opportunity as evidence. The big exception, of course, was the failed abduction of Mrs. Failsome, since the date and time of the assault were known exactly.

She also hoped that she might be clever or lucky enough to enrage Daly during his interview and that he might then bellow out a confession. A small hope, though, since such theatrics seemed to be in the exclusive province of TV cop shows.

She then decided to prepare a written report that summarized her findings to date and sought approval for her planned next steps. She would submit it to Catherine Weiss as well as Bob Farone, since there might be a need to approach a judge to obtain search warrants for Daly's house, his car, and his boat. And permission to put him in a lineup to see if Mrs. Failsome could ID him.

CHAPTER TWENTY-SIX

The FBI offices in Fairfield County were clean, comfortable, efficient, and devoid of any ambience. Strictly business. As head agent, Raymond Snyder was entitled to a small, well-furnished office with light-gray walls and one window, which he kept clear of any intrusive second colors or paperwork mess. Working files were neatly arranged in a rack on the table behind his desk, near his PC monitor and special secure phone to headquarters in Washington. The only adornments were three black-framed documents hanging on a side wall over a low wooden filing cabinet. Two were diplomas, one from Williams College and the other a law degree from Georgetown. A framed certificate of graduation from the FBI academy rounded out the display.

Snyder's desktop was basically bare, except for the typical in- and out-boxes, a speaker telephone, an expensive leather-bound calendar book, and the single working file of the case presently meriting his attention. As a small gesture to a personal life, a small framed picture of himself as an undergraduate, standing between his parents, perched on the far front edge of his desk. He glanced at the photo rarely, but when he did, he recalled the day it was taken—at homecoming weekend in October—which featured a return of loyal, occasionally drunk, alumni, and the visit of proud parents. The weather had been perfect, he recalled, a crisp, dry, brilliantly sunny fall day. The only disappointment had been the traditional football game, in which his team had been demolished by nearby Union College, thirty-one to six.

Mr. Snyder Sr. was arguably one of the wealthier parents. His father had been an immigrant from Warsaw, smart and aggressive. He had Americanized their name, learned the furniture business, and in twenty-five years, through hard work, luck, good bank loans, and the necessary level of ruthlessness, he had become the biggest manufacturer of aluminum lawn furniture on the East Coast. His son, Raymond Sr., was that rare second-generation businessman, someone who quickly built upon and improved the family business.

Agent Snyder suppressed the thought that he had disappointed his family by not going into the family business, especially after he had graduated from law school and could have applied his training to the administrative side of the firm, while his older brother, Jake, ran the manufacturing and sales arm. Unfortunately for the Snyder family, young Raymond had picked up some superficial patrician airs at Williams and had no interest in being known as a "furniture merchant." It was a particularly easy decision to reach, since his grandfather had willed large trust funds to him and his brother. What's more, he had been influenced by one of his law professors at Georgetown to consider legal aid or law enforcement work, both opportunities to contribute in some small way to society and provide some excitement, too. Having no practical need for a W-2 salary, the idea appealed, and Snyder had joined the bureau four months after receiving his law degree and passing the bar examination.

His personal life consisted of watching endless sports and cop shows on TV, a habit he vowed to break, or at least control. He liked to play racquet sports on weekends, depending on the weather. Tennis when pleasant, paddleball when it got colder. He had a hard time keeping up his eight-handicap rating in golf, because there was so little time to play. His social life was ordinary—visits to family and friends, occasional poker nights with his buddies, and trips to the firing range with FBI cronies on weekends. Women played a small role in his life, which did not bother him. His interest in them was driven primarily by a normal urge for occasional sex and companionship. He had better than average success with women, not because of his looks or personality, but because he dressed well, drove expensive cars, lived in a large private mini estate in back Greenwich, complete with pool and tennis court, and spent his money freely. He not only understood the superficiality of his attraction to women, he actually used it to justify his lack of interest in a deeper or more committed attachment to any woman— "Never want to work that hard," as sung by his favorite entertainer, Billy Joel.

Snyder opened the case file on the crab killings and turned to the short report on one of the suspects, Ivan Hartman. He had read the material, scant though it was, the night before, and looked forward to getting Agent Jim Sisk deeply immersed in the Hartman lead. And just as if actions always followed thoughts, Sisk appeared at his office door and asked if he could enter to discuss the case. Snyder waved him in, gestured to a seat, and buzzed his secretary, Betsy Underhill, to make more coffee.

Snyder had ambivalent thoughts about Sisk. He recognized that he was an above-average agent in many respects, most notably brains, loyalty, thoroughness, and excellent instincts for a case—something you can't teach. His record was excellent. However, Sisk had been repeatedly counseled—and sometimes reprimanded—by Snyder for two weaknesses. The first was Sisk's occasional failure to follow the facts exactly; instead he might choose to allow his instincts to make an early judgment and then massage the facts into a case that supported his hypothesis. This "guess and assess" approach, as Snyder labeled it, could lead to quick breakthroughs now and then, but it could also result in wasted time and money chasing a dead lead, or worse, accumulating evidence that was tainted or for some reason unusable in court, thereby weakening or killing an otherwise fruitful investigation. Snyder was particularly irritated by the instinctive approach, because it was so commonly used by normal street detectives, a group whom he looked on condescendingly.

Sisk's other weakness was his soaring ambition and need for the limelight. "Showboat" was a not-too-friendly nickname bestowed on him by the other agents. It bothered Sisk not at all, since in his view recognition led to promotion. And he had earned more than his fair share of recognition for his take-a-chance approach to solving crimes. Snyder realized that in some people there is a never-to-be-satisfied need for recognition and reward. Glory seeking. Sisk was this type of man, and as an agent his "kick in the door" approach, as his friends called it, worked more often than not. And it looked to Snyder as if the entire bureau was headed in that direction; a sort of unspoken reaction to the shackles imposed by needing to be politically correct, under the endless scrutiny of an irresponsible media horde that did not always respect the truth.

Sisk himself was tall, slender, and brash, though tempered with a good sense of humor. His brash behavior occasionally slipped over the line into rudeness, even arrogance. But results were results, and Snyder felt comfortable with Sisk on the trail of Ivan Hartman, whom he considered to be the best prospect in the short list of cancer-ridden suspects. *All long shots*, he thought glumly. *Why do these serial cases have to be so goddamned hard to solve?*

After a minimum of social chatter, Snyder got right to the point. "Jim, you've got an important role in this case. This guy Hartman is reasonably well qualified to be a suspect. Medical records show that he has been treated on and off for mental illness for over twenty-five years. Angry, vengeful kind of guy. Big, too. Tall, big-boned, and muscular. Certainly has the heft to overpower and snatch his victims. And apparently the type of cancer he has—melanoma—hasn't advanced far enough to debilitate him, so he is still capable of carrying out these types of crimes."

"But the medical report also stated that Hartman had refused further treatment. They wanted to remove his lymph glands in order to retard expansion of the disease into his major organs, stages three and four, where they generally check out," Sisk said.

"I know all about that, Jim. Also, they've apparently hired a new chief radiologist at Hartman's clinic who's getting many of their recent diagnoses peer-reviewed at Sloan-Kettering in Manhattan. Maybe his situation is not as severe as they thought, and he's got more time to create his little tableaus of vengeance. Or maybe his prognosis is worse than they think, and he may be heading rapidly into the final, incapacitating stages.

Be kind of funny if he died before we nailed him, like using death to beat a life sentence."

Sisk felt the urge to reveal to his boss an idea that had formed in his mind shortly after reading Hartman's medical file. "Ray, what if the latter scenario is true—that this guy might go down sooner than we think and escape justice? That's a real possibility. So is the chance that he might sense law enforcement is on his tail and flee. He's smart, obviously a planner, resourceful, and has plenty of money to run on.

"Here's my idea. Let me pick him up right now, on any basis, even that bullshit about 'person of interest,' and try to get a positive lineup ID from the Failsome woman. With that in hand, even the dumbest judge in this area would sign a search warrant, maybe even approve an arrest and temporary custody with no bail. What do you think?"

"No," Snyder said emphatically. "Look, Jim, this guy is not about to keel over now, and my sense is he's not ready to run. He has no reason to believe he's going to die ahead of schedule, and he may have plans to take a few more people with him. Also, I don't buy into the thought that he's beginning to hear footsteps, that he's running scared. He's had lots of success, if you could call it that, and only one screwup so far. And speaking of that, this Failsome woman is shaping up as a lousy eyewitness. She dithers on every ID. 'Too dark, too scared, looks like a lot of men,' blah, blah, blah. If she did make a positive and unequivocal ID of Hartman, I would go with your approach in a nanosecond. But if she failed to identify him or came up with some lukewarm bullshit like 'could be the man, but I'm not sure,' we're screwed. Because not only would any subsequent case against this guy be weakened, but if he is the killer, the mere process of being brought in for an interview and put through a lineup would trigger an immediate destruction of evidence on his part, and possible flight. I'd rather build a case and nail him right here than see him take off and have to wave a useless arrest warrant around."

"OK, boss," Sisk responded, his enthusiasm undiminished. "What we have is a big, white middle-aged male, average looks, drives a red pickup truck, fits the cancer-victim-as-avenger concept, but does not have a boating or knot-tying profile. So what I plan to do is go back to the yacht club and interview that stuffy vice commodore again. I have a feeling he was not fully cooperating. Also, when the local cops were running boat registrations, they came up with a big sailboat registered to a Lansing M. Hartman. It's a common family name, but our guys are doing a quick check to see if our suspect and the other Hartman are related in any way. OK to proceed, Ray?"

Snyder readily agreed and asked Sisk to also set up a procedure for wiretaps and, possibly, surveillance of Hartman's home in the event probable cause could be established and a court order obtained.

Sisk excused himself promptly, eager to get back into the field. He was immensely pleased with himself and hoped he hadn't shown it, because his ruse with Snyder had gone off without a hitch. He knew that the plan to pick up Hartman and stick him in a lineup wouldn't fly with Snyder. Therefore, he had assumed correctly, his next step—to return to the yacht club—would be easily OK'd. He had deliberately withheld a key piece of his investigation: after three rounds of drinks with the Mianus Yacht Club dockhands, Sisk learned that when old man Hartman passed away, everything he owned had been left to his son, who was also named executor and trustee of the estate. And part of the estate was a forty-four-foot sloop, an expensive Morgan named *Coy Mistress* and berthed at the club. So a boating link was clearly forged for Ivan Hartman. Circumstantial evidence, to be sure. A lot of men knew how to tie nautical knots. But if the crab theory was correct, then the sailing connection would become critical to the success of the investigation and prosecution.

Sisk's plan was to quickly interview the vice commodore to extract as much specific and useful information about the suspect as possible and also to inspect the boat itself, seeking any reason for probable cause to search it. He felt that if he got a reasonable amount of information at the yacht club, then he would locate and approach Hartman solo, interview him, and possibly arrest him, the latter occurring with a tip-off to the media—a tip-off he would later deny making. Sure, the local cops would be pissed off, but if the collar resulted in an arraignment, they would be told to shut up by local politicians, who would be very relieved to have the case progress, maybe close. Snyder would not be very happy with his grandstand arrest either and would chew him out for lack of "team play," taking risks with a high-profile case, and not following the chain of command. And just as before, he would apologize to Snyder for "moving too fast, cutting corners," all the mea culpa crap, knowing fully that when Snyder cooled off, he would commend Sisk in his report to Washington for "perseverance, imagination, and exceptional initiative."

It's a good time to take risks, Sisk thought. The bureau was no longer the media's sweetheart—maybe nothing was anymore—because of blunders, internal investigations, and the critical remarks made by cynical and bitter retired former agents. Sisk agreed that the bureau could use stronger leadership, but somehow it had to find a way to maximize the media value of its many exceptional investigations. Sisk had full confidence in his emerging mastery and victory in the Hartman case and realized that the subsequent conviction would make the FBI look good. *Do a lot for me, too*, he thought. *First job is to take care of number one.*

CHAPTER TWENTY-SEVEN

Dr. Ryan planned to meet Detective Farone at her lab on Tuesday afternoon, in order to present her thoughts to him on the comparative abilities of his four suspects to carry off the crab murders. Her conclusions were ready, but she was not.

Twenty minutes before Farone was to visit her office, an ambulance had arrived from the Stamford General Hospital bearing the bodies of three children, one boy and two girls, who had been killed that afternoon in a terrible accident. Ryan's job was to determine the cause of death in each case, not an easy job given the nature of the accident. The children, a brother and his twin sister, age nine, along with a friend of the same age, had been picked up in a Toyota Corolla after school by the friend's mother and were en route to a dance class at the CivicCenter. The mother, Florence Summerman, had pulled into a gas station, unscrewed the gas cap on her car, and started to refuel. She set the automatic hold-down clip on the gas nozzle into its slot so that she could get back to her car and use the cell phone while her tank filled automatically. Multitasking. She returned to the pump to extract the nozzle. Her car exploded in flames when her hand grasped the gas nozzle. The fire inspector would later report that static electricity, picked up on the mother's slacks from the car seat, had discharged when she grabbed the metal nozzle and triggered an instantaneous explosion when the spark hit the pooled gas fumes at the mouth of the tank.

Incredibly, a large Lincoln Navigator was in the process of pulling in behind her to use the rearward pump when the explosion occurred. The driver of the Lincoln, a short middle-aged woman who was not familiar with her huge SUV, reflexively stabbed at the brake pedal a fraction of a second after the explosion occurred. Unfortunately and tragically, her foot had crashed down upon the left edge of the accelerator instead of the brake, sending the five-thousand-pound behemoth flying into the rear of Mrs. Summerman's flaming Toyota. The occupants of the Lincoln dashed to safety as their own vehicle threatened to become engulfed.

Mrs. Summerman, alive but badly injured, had been flung aside by the blast, breaking her right elbow and pelvis. She was also on fire, but quick action from a motorist parked in front of the station's food/snack store saved her from serious burning; the good Samaritan had grabbed a blanket from the rear seat of her car and rolled the victim in it, smothering the flames.

A surprisingly rapid response to the accident brought two fire trucks to the scene, along with one rescue truck and two private ambulances. Three police cruisers, wailers constantly blaring, arrived last. The cops sealed off the scene and immediately began obtaining witness statements, while the firemen finished extinguishing the blaze and started to rescue the three kids who had been in the back seat of the Toyota. The idea of rescue was quickly discarded with a glance at the children's still-smoking bodies. None had been wearing seatbelts, and the only airbags in the car were in the front seat. Though they had deployed, they did no one any good. In addition to being horribly burned, the children's bodies were twisted into gross positions, either by the force of the blast, the impact of the Lincoln, or both. In any event, they were disfigured and dead.

The paramedics, after performing first aid on Mrs. Summerman, transported her and the three kids to the nearest hospital. The children were received as DOA, while she was heavily sedated and treated for her injuries. In cases like this, the hospital was obliged to remove the bodies of the deceased and transport them to the medical examiner, who would seek to learn the exact cause of death. In this case, the possibilities were asphyxiation, burns, or impact from the accelerating Navigator. The ME's report would weigh heavily in the subsequent investigation of both the police and fire departments. Claim agents and accident investigators, representing the companies that insured both vehicles and also the gas station chain, would be filing their own reports, but overarching all this activity would be Sheila Ryan's conclusions as to the cause of death of each child, because her decisions would set in motion the claim-and-blame game always associated with big accidents. Greedy, aggressive contract lawyers representing the families of the victims would be moving fast to initiate charges of negligence in civil courts against the firms and manufacturers most likely to be found culpable...and to have the deepest pockets. Lack of the mandatory static-electricity warning posted at the gas station? Improper ventilation of the Toyota gas tank? Unintended acceleration by the Lincoln? Improper vehicle operation by its driver? *Problems for the justice system to solve*, Ryan thought as she began her task of examining each small burned body.

She asked her assistant to greet Farone as he arrived punctually at 4:30 p.m. The assistant explained to him that Dr. Ryan had a bit of an emergency on her hands and he would have to wait. He was free to go into the lab and join her while she worked, but she thought he would probably not want to do that.

And she was right. Farone had certainly seen his share of dead people over the years and had gotten over his squeamishness, but little kids were another thing, so he asked the assistant to check with Dr. Ryan about meeting him for a drink later, if she wished, at Zeno's Bar and Restaurant on Atlantic Street, a place where few, if any, cops ever hung out. The assistant returned and said Dr. Ryan was "good to go" and would meet Farone in the bar in about three hours.

• • •

Farone plopped himself on one of the green leatherette barstools at Zeno's, ordered a beer, carefully avoiding anything from microbreweries—too yuppie, he felt—and settled into his favorite lager, the immodestly named king of beers, Budweiser. He was grateful that the regular bartender, Mike, was off, since he didn't feel up to the usual barroom banter. He normally would expect Sheila to be right on time, since she respected punctuality as much as he did. But he knew all about the explosion and collision at the gas station and realized that she had her hands full and might be late. So he was pleasantly surprised when she appeared minutes later and ordered a cosmopolitan with a glass of ice water back.

"Hard booze, eh, Doc?" Farone smiled at her. "Yeah, well, I know what your last job was this afternoon. It was on the scanner. The guys were talking about it, and the media's all over it. One hell of an accident."

"I'm not finished either, Bob. It's a tricky case. The windows on the car were all rolled up, so the fire, when it pushed through the floor and rear of the vehicle, would have eaten up the small amount of oxygen very rapidly. So we can't rule out asphyxiation. Not yet. The boy seems clearly to have died from the impact. His neck was broken and there was severe trauma to his head. Looks like he was thrown directly into the back of the driver's headrest. The girls? Well, the jury's still out. I guess that's me. But if the impact didn't kill them, the burn trauma probably did. You know, Bob, there's usually a little bit of mystery in what we do at the lab, adds a weird sense of glamour to the job. Makes me feel like a big-time detective like you," she added with a slight smile. "But not this time. Not this case. They were only nine years old, for God's sake, hardly begun to live, hardly..."

Farone offered her his hanky to dry the tears, put his arm around her shoulder, kissed her temple gently. It killed him to see her cry, to be in pain. He loved her so much it hurt him.

Farone worried that Ryan might leave abruptly, so he took the easy way out and ordered two cosmopolitans, although he wasn't really sure what was in them and really didn't care. He made a lame attempt to change the subject to something light but realized unhappily that he couldn't come up with any topics. His flailing about for neutral material was interrupted by a welcome mood swing in Ryan, who said, "Bob, you invited me here to talk about your suspects, not my day, so fire away."

"This is really nice and relaxing, Sheila. First we talk about the dead, now the dying. Won't get the fun couple of the year award with that material. So are you ready to educate me about the physical capabilities of our dying suspects?"

"Sure. What do we call it—the Topic of Cancer? Seriously, Bob, you should probably check with a good oncologist after I give you my opinion on these four guys. This is not exactly my field, OK?"

"Maybe it isn't, Sheila, but I'd still rather have a good top-line summary from you than get snowed by a superspecialist I don't know. C'mon, speak to me."

"I see only two possibilities out of the four men you're investigating who still have the potential strength and stamina to abduct and kill people and then deposit their bodies somewhere else: Daly and Hartman. I just can't see how the other two would have the capacity to carry out these crimes unless they had accomplices, and you've told me that these types of bizarre crimes are almost always committed solo, which doesn't surprise me, Bob. Hard enough to believe one person could be deranged enough to do these horrible things, let alone two."

Farone felt suddenly uncomfortable discussing the case on a barstool and suggested that they move to a corner booth. The waitress brought over their unfinished drinks, a surprise to Farone, who usually attributed that level of personal service to higher-end restaurants. She also left two menus and a wine list with the couple, assuming they had moved to the table to have dinner. So Farone suggested that they order something and was pleasantly surprised when Ryan agreed.

Dinner consisted of two large feta cheese salads, lamb shish kebab, and a bottle of Greek wine. Farone made the shift out of small talk back to the case without much finesse. "So you don't think we should bother with Battaglia or Johnson?"

"I suspect Battaglia's major organs have already been compromised, and since he declines further treatment, he can only get more debilitated. Nestor has lung cancer but continues to smoke, and don't forget that his torn rotator cuff would cause him severe pain if he tried to lift and carry or even drag a large inert body. Not impossible, but highly doubtful in my estimation.

"This man, Ivan Hartman, is a much better candidate. As you recall, his medical record shows repeated treatment for mental illness, probably with little effect, particularly the psychoanalysis sessions. And I learned through back channels that he stopped taking his antipsychotic medications at about the time he was diagnosed for melanoma. I'd hazard a guess that he may feel his life is slipping away anyway, so why bother with mind-altering drugs? Maybe he's gone completely off the deep end and is willing to take the risk of killing people because he has nothing else to lose."

"What about his physical capabilities at this point, Sheila?"

"Probably OK for now. His disease progresses through four stages. It presents and starts to move in stage one, but there's no immediate effect on the patient's daily activities. Hartman has just crossed over from stage two to stage three, where the cancer will progress to the lymph glands. The usual procedure at this point is the removal of some of the glands, in order to arrest the spread of the destructive cells, but he's declined this procedure. Right now, therefore, I would guess that he's feeling OK, since unfortunately the first discomfort comes with the treatments—radiation, surgery, or chemotherapy. If I'm right, he's certainly got the ability—a big guy, only forty-eight—to successfully attack and subdue someone. Add to it the fact that he's psychotic, and you've got a potentially serious suspect."

"So where does our last guy, Bart Daly, fit in? You mentioned that he's also a good possibility."

"He is," Sheila responded with more enthusiasm. "In fact I might place him as your number one suspect. He's your youngest subject, only forty-two, and he's probably in great shape from working in a warehouse. His liver cancer will certainly cause his death, unless a successful transplant can be arranged. Daly's apparently a fighter. He's been taking his chemotherapy treatments about every ten days and has indicated a willingness to have an infusion pump implanted near his liver in order to direct the medication precisely to the cancer with minimal damage to healthy cells. I would imagine that the game plan he's agreed to follow with his oncologist is to continue treatment to control, if not mitigate, the disease, and pray for an organ donor. There's also the possibility of a resection of his liver, but he may be a little too late for the surgery to do any good."

Farone was puzzled. "Sheila, if this poor bastard's getting hammered with chemo every ten days or so, and its effects are as rough as everyone says, how could he find the strength to stalk and kill?"

"You mean the diarrhea, nausea, and vomiting, don't you? Well, there's probably some of that, but remember, the newer drugs are generally less intrusive than the drugs prescribed only a few years ago. Plus, there's been some improvement in antinausea medication, so the unwelcome effects of chemotherapy are something the patient can better tolerate. In my opinion, Mr. Daly could rebound to his normal level of physical ability, or near that level, in the interim between treatments. On a strictly medical basis, I would say that Daly is physically capable of committing these crimes, at least for the time being."

"I'm still a bit surprised that you rank him ahead of Hartman," Farone said. "He's a little younger but not by that much."

Ryan chose her words carefully, knowing that her answer might irritate Farone, but to duck his question would have been impossible. "Bob, listen, I don't want you to get upset or anything, but I ran into Peggy Nugent at the mall yesterday, and we had a light lunch together. The case just came up casually in conversation, and she mentioned that she had been assigned to investigate Mr. Daly. So I told her about what I was trying to do to help you out, and we got to talking about Daly. She told me in so many words that the patient had prior arrests and one or two convictions for assault and battery. Also, they found out he had a fishing boat and apparently knew something about tying knots. Add it all together, and I think you've got enough reason to bring him in for interrogation."

"We call it an interview, these days, Sheila. All part of being politically correct." Farone tried to keep the annoyance out of his voice, but he was upset that Detective Nugent had been blabbing about the case in the mall. He'd have to speak to her about that. "Well, in the spirit of keeping score, crack investigators of the FBI have learned that a large sailboat is registered to Hartman's deceased father. The boat was berthed at a local club, but I walked around there with Kenny Fusco, their harbormaster, who said the boat had been moved by Hartman the younger. Destination unknown. Jimmy said that Hartman was, however, a crack sailor and had grown up with boating. Snyder is sending his hot-shot agent, Jim Sisk, out to the club tomorrow. He'll find out what I already know."

"Then what's next, Bob?"

"I'm going back to old-fashioned police work. I plan to canvass all the local boatyards myself, probably split up the job with Nugent and some uniforms. The name of the Hartman boat is *Coy Mistress*. Thought we should check it out, maybe find probable cause to search. Or get a warrant. You know, Doc, I'd really love to have you be my partner in crime detection, but it sounds like you've got a lot on your hands, determining exactly what killed those kids."

"As a matter of fact, I planned to take the weekend off. Quite honestly, my job has been getting to me lately. Maybe I'm not really cut out for pathology. The deaths of these three little kids today really hurt, and that's not supposed to happen in my profession. Totally uninvolved, you know? Anyway, I'd like a break. I definitely need one. I'll tromp around boatyards with you tomorrow, Bob. I've already assigned my cases to two good assistants who don't mind working weekends, so we won't be losing any ground on the accident. What time will you pick me up in the morning?"

"Eight on the nose, Sunday morning," Farone answered, unable to keep the note of enthusiasm out of his voice. "Wear your boat shoes and slicker. It's supposed to sprinkle. Right now have an anisette with me and talk about anything but work, OK?"

Ryan instead rose to her feet and gathered up her purse. "Robert, darling," she said with not quite enough irony in her voice, "I'm exhausted. I want a hot shower and beddy-bye. One more drink here will lead to another, and then we're into relationship territory. Not tonight, Bob."

"Not ever?"

"Not tonight," she answered softly and headed for the door.

CHAPTER TWENTY-EIGHT

Early morning. Beautiful summer day, particularly over the sound, thought Vice Commodore Tod Morgan. It was one of the rare days when he regretted seeking and being elected vice commodore of the club. Lots of headaches, minimal thanks. Could have been out sailing today, or, just a few years ago, enjoying a long client lunch at the Four Seasons Grill in Manhattan. His law practice had been good to him, both financially and as a conduit to making new friends. Now, retired for two years, he and his wife had made few new friendships. They found themselves with time on their hands and laughed ironically that on the precise day of Morgan's retirement party, the stock market, on which they relied for income, had begun its biggest slide in recent memory. He felt that he should be grateful for his post at the club, along with several other pro bono volunteer assignments, because they filled the hours. But there were drawbacks, like the one he faced today. That pushy, grinning FBI guy, Sisk, had requested another interview, and he had sounded less pleasant on the phone than he had the first time.

Sisk pulled into the club parking lot and cast an admiring glance at both the large array of expensive sedans, SUVs, and roadsters soaking up the sun and several of the female members, dressed conservatively but still alluringly, either on their way to their boats or heading into the club. *Just what I've got to look forward to,* he thought, *work my ass off for thirty-five years while the little woman enjoys her recreation and gossip with the other women. No wonder they outlive us by seven years. But do they really live?*

Agent Sisk reminded himself of his game plan as he approached the older man: kiss ass, then kick ass. Usually worked. The first interview was really positioned as just that, a pleasant request for cooperation and information, packaged in good manners, a nice smile, and honest man-to-man candor. But if enough information was not forthcoming, the next interview would be staged with plenty of intimidation, coercion, and threats as necessary to yield real cooperation. *This is the phase we're in today,* Sisk thought, *and it sure beats being Mister Nice Guy.*

The two men shook hands stiffly and sat down in two uncomfortable chairs out on the lawn. *No offers of coffee this time,* observed Sisk, *guess my body language must be working today.*

"I'm glad you were able to see me today, Morgan. It's now clear to me that we've got some unfinished business between us, business that could have been taken care of the last time and saved me another trip out here."

"What exactly is it that you want of me, Agent?"

"Cooperation. Full cooperation," Sisk said coldly. "We've learned of a boating connection between Ivan Hartman and this club. Something you could have filled me in on while I was out here."

"As I believe I told you, Hartman was not a member of this club and did not own or sail, as far as I know, any boat named *Lobster* or *Crab*, or whatever name you were checking up on. And as I believe I told you, any number of men and women wear our logo shirts and sweaters, including nonmembers," Morgan replied with a faint air of condescension in his voice.

"It's what you didn't tell me, and probably could have, that is a real problem. We learned that a sloop named *Coy Mistress* was berthed at this club and was owned by a member, a guy named Lansing Hartman. Name ring any bells?"

"Of course, Lansing was a member and a personal friend. And naturally he kept his boat here. An excellent sailor, now deceased, as I'm sure you've learned."

Sisk leaned forward abruptly and pointed his pen toward the slips, "What we've learned," he snapped sarcastically, "is that Hartman left his boat and everything else to Ivan, his only child. And that Junior spent a great deal of time out here over the years sailing with his old man. What I want you to do—right now—is to walk me down to the boat and answer all my questions about Hartman. You should understand," he added coldly, "that any refusal to answer questions or refusing to cooperate can be construed as obstruction of justice, and we could bring you in."

Morgan rose and looked at Sisk straight in the eye. "I'll be more than happy to answer your questions, but I would like you to know that I am a retired lawyer, quite familiar with criminal law, and totally unintimidated by your little game of obstruction of justice. So please, show more respect for both of us and knock off the bullshit."

"Fine. Where's the boat?"

"I have no idea. Young Hartman appeared here, at my request, several days after your visit. He and I had very little to say to each other, since I happen to dislike him intensely and he, it seems, dislikes everybody. In any event, I explained that he had the right to join the club as a legacy, so-called, since his father had been a member in good standing. I was delighted, but not surprised, when he declined, and I'm sure that the other people on our membership committee are pleased as well. I told him that we wanted the sloop moved off the club premises as soon as possible and arranged for the use of a travel lift and two dock workers."

Sisk cut in, a cold smile on his face. "Yes, I know one of them. That's how we got the information you refused to volunteer."

Morgan made a mental note to speak severely to the man who had blabbed. It was a serious mistake to discuss club matters with outsiders, even cops, unless pressured.

"Well, then, Agent, the man you spoke with must have told you of the destination of the boat."

"His name was Fusco, and he didn't have a clue. This Hartman apparently keeps his mouth shut. So I'll ask one more time: do you know the whereabouts of the sloop or not?"

"As I believe I have already made clear, I have no knowledge of the whereabouts of the Hartman boat. Since Hartman is not, I presume, a member of any other sailing club, he probably has taken the boat to any one of dozens of public marinas and rented a slip or a mooring. If I hear of anything, I will call you, but it is highly unlikely."

"Why didn't you tell me about the old man's boat in the first place? It's nothing to you."

"Quite frankly," replied Morgan, "I probably would have if you had been more straightforward in expressing your reasons for the inquiry. Short of that, my natural instinct is to protect the integrity not only of the club but also of Lansing, a fine man. His son, Ivan, is crazy, but in an odd way. When he came out here, it was always in the company of his father and sometimes a sailing companion of his father's."

"A young babe?" Sisk interrupted, making it obvious that he had obtained a complete rundown from the dockhands. "Tell me more about Ivan."

Ignoring the remark about Hartman Senior, Morgan answered, "Ivan is big and strong and hostile. He made people uncomfortable just by hanging around. How he ever made a success of his contracting business I'll never know. He was always involved in fights, both as a kid and as a young man. But he never picked on anyone. He wasn't a bully."

"Then what motivated him to smack other guys around?"

"Some strange kind of sense of right and wrong—as though he was a self-appointed judge, jury, and executioner—when he came across behavior that offended his values. There was one instance, if I recall correctly, when he was home from college, out here at the club. One of the members' boys, a high-school kid, was trying to train his Labrador to retrieve. But when the dog got bored with the routine, he just picked up the training dummy and lay down. The kid got angry, immature of course, and went over to the dog and started beating it with the leash. Not only did Ivan run over and pull the kid away, he beat the hell out of the kid with his own leash. Caused a big stink around here, especially embarrassing for Lansing Hartman, who agreed to keep Ivan away from the club until he grew up. But immaturity wasn't the problem. Ivan has a screw loose. He's very angry and very vindictive, and he acts out when he's provoked."

Sisk made notes carefully. Then he put down his pen and asked, "This dog-whipping incident. Sounds like young Hartman was making the punishment fit the crime. Do you agree?"

"I never thought about it that way, but yes, I would agree."

"OK, there's one last Hartman topic I want to cover with you. The last time I came out here, you didn't respond to my question about Hartman driving a red truck, and as I pointed out at the time, there is no truck registered to him. We've got some other vehicle information on him, but I need to know from you what the guy drives."

Morgan chose his words carefully. "Ivan generally drives a red Jaguar roadster, at least when I've seen him, and that's only been here. I've also seen him behind the wheel of a dark-green SUV, maybe a Mercedes Benz, I'm not sure."

"So still no connection to a red pickup truck?"

"Well, in a way, perhaps. His father drove one now and then, probably a carryover from his contracting days. But he had the good sense to avoid using it to visit the club. We're apparently too stuffy to appreciate pickup trucks filling our parking lot," Morgan answered with a slight smile. "However, you might wish to check with vehicle registrations, as young Hartman probably took over the truck as part of the estate."

"Have you ever actually seen him driving his father's truck? I mean, after the old man died."

"Perhaps once or twice. He showed up a few weeks ago to take some sail bags off the boat, stuff too big for his SUV."

Agent Sisk, satisfied that he had gotten any and all useful information out of the old salt, reverted to his pleasant, bland personality, made his good-byes, and urged Morgan to call him immediately if Hartman showed up again.

As he headed back out to the Boston Post Road, Sisk was feeling slightly euphoric. He was convinced the case was about to break—his way. It was time for an audacious step: withhold what he knew from Snyder and, especially, the local cops; pay a solo visit to wherever Hartman lived; and check out the truck if it was still there. If there was enough evidence, arrest him on the spot. And maybe get lucky and locate the boat. Check it out, too. But that was the second priority.

CHAPTER TWENTY-NINE

Jonas James was relieved when Agent Snyder and Detective Farone scheduled a review meeting with him. They billed it as a progress report, a detailed rundown on the four cancer-afflicted suspects they had agreed to investigate. He hoped like hell that they would give him something useful to feed to those media morons who plagued the department daily with questions. But, of course, he couldn't give the media anything really specific or the publication of it might blow the case. It was odd, he thought, that in any high-profile crime you had two groups of investigators: the cops and the media. And because of the coverage the First Amendment afforded the media, they, in many ways, had far more latitude to investigate than the cops.

James's secretary, Lois, buzzed him to let him know that his people and the FBI people had arrived. She was directing them to interview room one. Fresh coffee, but no rules of engagement, she added sardonically, knowing full well the antagonism between the bureau and the department.

But in reality, much to James's relief, the meeting was short, cordial, and conclusive.

After an acceptable and minimal amount of shuffling and small talk, Farone got right to the point. "Chief, this group has done a fine job individually in preliminary investigations of our four suspects. If you agree with our recommendations, you can tell the media that we've narrowed the list of suspects down to two men, and that they're being actively investigated."

"Who are they?" asked James, pushing himself slightly forward in his seat.

"Bart Daly and Ivan Hartman, Jonas," answered Lead Agent Snyder. "We've eliminated Richard Battaglia and Nestor Johnson at this time, for reasons that DeLong and Sloan will outline. Hartman and Daly are another story. We'll fill you in and then try to leave this room in agreement on the next steps. It's a good opportunity to demonstrate teamwork, keep everybody reading from the same page."

Agent DeLong was asked to begin, since his suspect, Nestor Johnson, was least promising. DeLong revealed that Johnson had no priors but did have a record of disputes with the IRS, including some foolish threats by him to "get even." But there was no suggestion of any past criminal or antisocial behavior. His known associates had nothing much to offer, saying that he was a regular guy, worried about what would happen to his family when he finally died of cancer. Copies of his photo, obtained from his employer, bore only a slight resemblance to the bureau composite, and further, Mrs. Failsome did not feel that he looked like her assailant. DeLong said that he would keep an eye on Johnson but that in his opinion there was little reason to knock on his door.

The take on Richard Battaglia was a little more complex, according to Detective Brian Sloan. First off, a recent photo of Battaglia did bear some resemblance to the composite, although Mrs. Failsome had not made a connection other than to state there was "a vague resemblance" to the attacker. In informal interviews with six of the suspect's former coworkers and other friends and associates, all agreed that the man was always susceptible to mood swings, but in the last year, what with his termination and the onset of cancer, he was very angry and didn't care who knew it. On the other hand, though, no prior arrests, no threats to anyone specifically, and no history of physical violence. He had served in the navy, but his duties ran to various assignments in the engineering departments of large cruisers and one aircraft carrier. No sense of knot-tying skills. He owned no boat and no truck, but he did go camping with his family, which provided a very tenuous link to the knot-tying scenario. But all in all, not enough evidence to warrant picking him up. Like Agent DeLong, Sloan agreed to keep an eye on his suspect, but he was certainly available for additional duty.

At this point, Raymond Snyder announced that Agent DeLong was going to be reassigned to assist Agent Sisk in the Hartman investigation, and then he asked Sisk to report on what he had accomplished to date.

"Not enough to approach him yet, but it's clear to me this guy Hartman is a prime suspect," Sisk began confidently. "First off, he's a screwball. Extensive medical record for paranoia and reactive violence. Has had extensive psychotherapy, all kinds of medications for bipolar behavior, panic attacks, you name it. To give him credit, though, he started a commercial contracting business and really built it up. Had a lot of experience working for his father when he was young. He sold out last year. We're talking about twenty-two full-time employees, two utility buildings, one large storage facility, and four or five vehicles. Annual sales over twelve mill. Hard to believe a nut case like him could run a business like that, but he did. Sold the house and all that was in it, too, the whole ball of wax. He's not a boat owner, but I did run down the MYC logo lead and learned that his father was a club member, and he kept a fancy sailboat at the club. And our guy, Hartman the younger, basically grew up sailing—local cruising and racing, even some blue-water racing. Certainly knows knot-tying backward."

"What about vehicles?" asked Chief James. "And what about motive and opportunity?"

"I think there's plenty of motive if you look at his background carefully. And I did. He has quite a history of fights and scuffles, primarily as a schoolkid and then a young man. But the pattern, so far as I can piece it together from people who've known him over the years, is that he needs to feel like he's squaring things or putting things right. A teacher he had in prep school recalled that one of the few friends Hartman had, a black kid from Washington, got shoved around one afternoon by a townie who called him a nigger and other similar garbage. Next day, Hartman walks up to the townie, doesn't say a word, and knocks him flat. But that's not the interesting part. After he's got the idiot down, Hartman sits on his chest and smears the guy's face with something like black grease. A little lesson. This screwy notion of punishing people in some way related to their apparent crimes reflects the crab killer's MO. That is why each of these killings has no tie to another other than the charm. They're all linked in Hartman's mind. That is, these people need to be punished, and further, made an example of.

"As for opportunity, Chief, that will have to be determined after we bring him in and check his whereabouts on each day, which will be tough to do, since the bodies were found two or three days after the vics had gone missing. Other than that, the guy doesn't work. He rents a furnished home, so he's not busy there. He had apparently broken off with a woman he was going with, ended it about the time he was first diagnosed with the melanoma. He generally has a hell of a lot of spare time on his hands. Plenty of time to take up kidnapping and murder as a hobby.

"There is a possibility that he may've spent some time sailing since his father's death. Maybe he's on the high seas right now. I learned from some old salt at the club that Hartman had kept the old man's boat and certainly knew how to sail it."

"Maybe, maybe not, Jim," Farone interrupted. "We checked out the boat registration trail, too, and learned that the boat, a classic, forty-four-foot Morgan named *Coy Mistress*, has been dry-docked, actually sitting in her cradle, at the Mianus Yacht Club for the last year or so. Hartman is known to have moved the boat recently, but no one knows where. I think it's a priority to find the boat and check it out for possible evidence; a lot easier to do at this point in the investigation than getting a warrant to search the guy's home."

"I agree," responded Sisk in even tones. "Didn't know the boat wasn't in use for all this time, so I guess that fact actually provides even more time for this guy to do his thing. And since the crimes committed were all local, and the victims were generally accessible, there's theoretically plenty of opportunity."

"What's the story on the truck, Bob? Any registrations or rentals?" asked Chief James.

"We didn't turn up anything, Chief. As we had learned via the checks, the suspect owns a Jag convertible and also a Mercedes SUV, but no truck. Although it's never occurred to me—what about the vehicles that Jim mentioned, the ones that were a part of the construction company?"

"That's a good question," Sisk replied disingenuously. "We ran that one down and learned that all the trucks, the Case loader, and the Bobcat went with the sale of the business and are in use now by new owners."

Sisk was immensely pleased, although he maintained a poker face, to know that he was still the only one in the room to know that Hartman had kept his father's personal truck and had not bothered to title it over to himself. And that the truck was the best possible source for evidence and making a case. Not that fucking boat. But he concluded, "Now that I've got Eddie joining me, our priorities seem pretty clear. First, let's coordinate a search for the missing boat. I'm sure you can assign a few teams of uniforms to canvass the local boatyards, and I'm sure Ray will give me all the people I need. While that's happening, Eddie and I will split the list of people known to have associated with Hartman in the last year in order to generate new leads or ideas. If you have any further ideas for us, Chief, we'd be glad to pursue them."

"I will, if I can come up with any," replied James with a slight smile. "Meanwhile, put a full-court press on what you're presently doing, Jim. Looks to me like you've got a good investigation going. Congratulations. Now let's hear from our gorgeous crime fighter on the Daly investigation. What have you learned, Peggy?"

Detective Nugent was well schooled in hiding her annoyance at being singled out for her looks. If James had been a female chief, she wouldn't have to put up with those dumb-ass remarks. But to be fair, she had never had any reason to be offended by her immediate boss, Bob Farone, who treated her like one of the boys. Well, maybe. She had mentioned that trait of Bob's to her friend, Cathy Weiss, a bit of a cynic but pretty accurate, too. Her quick response was that first of all, all men are slavering dogs at heart, and Farone was no different. Second, who knew what crossed his mind when he worked with her? And worst of all, he had had a very intense relationship with the assistant medical examiner, Ryan.

Back to the business at hand. "Bart Daly has three or four of the ingredients needed to make him a prime suspect, Chief. He is a violent guy who has six priors for assault and two convictions. And who knows how many other scrapes he's been in where there's been no formal complaint or arrest? He's big, strong, and has a terrible temper. He's also a drunk, but never on duty—I mean on the job—and a mean drunk, I've been told. Somewhat like Hartman, Daly's roughing up of other men, which in his case has taken place almost exclusively at work, has a crude idealistic quality. It's as if he feels that some guy has to be punished for messing up, for letting the firm down. At least that's his supervisor's interpretation, and he struck me as a savvy man.

"Daly also owns a boat, a small fishing boat. Fishing is apparently his primary leisure activity, although one of the guys at the marina where he keeps his boat told us that Daly hadn't used it for a while. But at least we have a good knot-tying connection. Incidentally, he's cooperating like crazy with his doctors. He apparently feels he can beat the cancer or maybe, like Hartman, he feels a strong need to stay alive to do his thing, as they say."

"Maybe, Peggy, but Hartman refused all treatment," Sisk interrupted.

Nugent chose to ignore the remark, although it annoyed the hell out of her. "As I think some of you know, Bart Daly drives a red pickup truck, Connecticut tags, silver tool box in the bed. It's a Chevy Silverado, crew-cab model. I know the tow-truck driver gave us the statement that when he saw the perpetrator drive off the night Mrs. Failsome was attacked, he ID'd the truck as a Dodge Ram. But we've taken a look at both the Dodge and the Chevy models, and from a distance they look very much alike."

"Excuse me, Peggy," Sisk interrupted again. "Our guy is a professional tow-truck operator. That's all he does. That's his business. If anyone can make a positive vehicle identification, he can."

Farone said, somewhat coldly, "I believe that's already been considered, Jim, and we give the tow-truck man the benefit of the doubt. But it was at night, a dark night, and the red truck was peeling off as fast as possible. So let's pursue the Daly truck as potential evidence for now. Where do we go from here, Peggy?"

"More of the same, boss. Interview a few more people who know Daly, see if he's been acting unduly hostile lately. Look over his truck while it's out in the parking lot at work, see if there's anything potentially incriminating in it. And when we get to where we think we may have a case, pick him up and ask for his cooperation. One key question we would ask is his whereabouts the night Mrs. Failsome was attacked. I didn't hear this tactic mentioned in connection with the Hartman investigation, but it's obviously a primary consideration since, as far as we know, that's the only specific night that we can tie to an attack. If anything comes of that, then we go straight to a lineup. OK?"

Agent Sisk was irritated at the rebuke but didn't show it. *Stay cool*, he told himself, *this meeting's just about over*. Adding DeLong to his team was both a blessing and a curse. The added manpower would clearly speed up his investigation and arrest of Hartman, but along with it would be the risk that DeLong would tip off Snyder that they were bending the rules. But even if there were some boundary problems, he reassured himself, that kind of petty crap goes away fast when you have a big win. He could hardly wait to score.

Just as Chief James was concluding the predictable motivational speech about the value of cooperation and thanking them for doing a great job, Farone politely interrupted. "If anyone needs more encouragement to go with our decision to focus on Daly and Hartman, I'm the man to talk to. Remember when I said we would get an estimate of each suspect's physical ability to do these crimes? Well, I had an opportunity to speak with Dr. Ryan on the topic; you might recall that she was the first to review the medical histories of each man. She also followed up with phone calls to their various oncologists and MDs to help make an assessment. The bottom line, she told me, is that Johnson and Battaglia are in no shape to carry out the crimes personally; they would need an accomplice. But there's no indication of any accomplice in the small amount of evidence we have. So that leaves Daly and Hartman. They're our best shot, according to Ryan."

Speak with Dr. Ryan, thought Peggy Nugent, as she closed her attaché case and arose from the table. *Poor Bob. He tries so hard to play it cool, when anyone who knows him at all knows he's still crazy about Sheila. Give it up, boss. You're too nice a guy to waste emotions on a dead romance. Didn't you hear that unrequited love's a bore?*

CHAPTER THIRTY

Another Sunday. Beautiful day. Not too hot, not too humid. A great day to be on the job, thought Farone wryly. He decided to skip his normal compulsions: six-mile run, the *New York Times*, Bloody Marys, brunch, introspection, nap, TV. Instead a quick shower, OJ, granola, and coffee. Standard dress: khakis, polo shirt, and boat shoes, no socks. Farone headed out to his car with the items necessary for the day's boat search: Nikon FM2 SLR camera with Nikkor zoom lens, notebook, list of southern Connecticut boatyards, gun, badge, and thermos of ice water.

Farone had made two decisions about the day's investigation. The first was that he would check only those marinas east of the Stamford metro area, where no crab crimes had been committed. The assumption was that Hartman would have moved his boat close enough to be handy, but away from the sphere of his crime spree. The second decision, to invite Sheila Ryan to go with him, had been tougher to make. The fact that he had already invited her was unchangeable, but the real problem he was forced to acknowledge was that being with her caused him to vacillate emotionally between pleasure and pain. She was the woman he wanted and couldn't have, and proximity merely dredged up all his feelings. On the other hand, some atypical strain of optimism inspired him to see her and hope for some signal or event that would convince him that things could change.

Ryan and Farone had changed plans. Instead of Farone picking her up, they agreed to drive separately and to meet at Cummings Park. *No awkward dropping-off scenes at the end of the day*, thought Farone, *probably for the better*. Ryan had driven up exactly on time, one of her many good qualities, Farone conceded. And, of course, she looked gorgeous. Just the right makeup for a sunny day, EK sunglasses, blousy cotton T-shirt, white shorts, and rubber-soled white moccasins.

Ryan had no objection to playing second fiddle and handling the map and marina list while Farone drove. He had admitted that their chances of stumbling on to Hartman's boat were slim, but it wasn't a bad way to spend the day. Ryan wasn't as pessimistic.

It turned out that neither was correct. Farone had pulled into Harbor Marine in South Norwalk on only their third stop, located the harbormaster, and was directed to the docks where the larger sailboats were berthed. They found *Coy Mistress* neatly tied up on the sixth slip in, fresh water and shore electricity connected to the dock. There was no one on board. The harbormaster had gone about his business, so Farone stepped aboard, a violation of the right to search, he guessed, but no chance of being reported. Ryan handed him the camera and notebook and followed him aboard. The hatchway door was locked, not surprisingly, but the lock would have been easy for Farone to pick. He decided not to push his luck and to confine the investigation to the cockpit and deck.

The boat had been kept in meticulous condition, thanks no doubt to Hartman having the money to hire a professional cleaning crew to keep the boat detailed and maintained as needed while in dry dock. Since there was little to observe, photography and taking notes took little time, with one exception. Farone, a decent skipper himself, noted that the boat was outfitted with a power windlass on the prow, a large Danforth anchor with shackles, and a white-coated chain anchor rode neatly stowed in chocks on the foredeck. Exactly what this boat would call for. Yet there were also two coils of heavy anchor chain and two large plow anchors, all obviously new, stowed in the cockpit. What for? Farone decided to ask the local cops to swing by the marina daily to check on the status of the boat. He also instructed the harbormaster to phone him immediately if the boat was moved. He decided to hold off on asking for a search warrant for the boat for at least a week, on the hunch that there might be other, more crucial developments on both the Hartman and the Daly leads.

"I didn't realize your job was this easy," Ryan smiled as they left the parking lot and headed back to Route 1. "You get paid all that money for driving around in a nice convertible on a beautiful day and taking pictures. What a good deal!"

"Reality check, Ryan. This is supposed to be my day off. The nice weather's not my doing. I've got monthly payments on the car. The boat took mostly luck to find, and it didn't provide any useful evidence, as far as I could see. And with respect to making big money, I'll quote my father: 'The only rich cops I know of are either in jail or soon will be.'"

"Bob, really. You know as well as I do that you could have asked one of your detectives to phone every potential boatyard and get a check on whether *Coy Mistress* was berthed there or not. I think your real motive was to put in for overtime pay today. Admit it."

"My real motive was to be with you, Doctor. But not to worry. Strictly platonic, just old buddies, comrades in arms, playing within the boundaries, just—"

"Oh, knock it off, Bob," Ryan interrupted. "I'm famished. Let's have a late lunch, OK?"

"I agree completely. You have excellent judgment. Here's my exciting recommendation: we'll pick up some greasy sandwiches and a six-pack of Genesee Ale, head for the beach at Tod's Point, and have a picnic. OK?"

"Done deal, Detective."

The beach was crowded with the usual Sunday-afternoon groups of young families and teenagers hanging out and flirting. So Farone decided instead to head for the barbecue and picnic area, where they could have some privacy, shade, and a beautiful view of the water.

Small talk blended in with lunch and ale up to a point. But Ryan became uncharacteristically serious during a lull in the conversation.

"I've decided I just can't take it anymore, Bob. And it isn't just the three little kids. This whole ME business keeps you continuously exposed to the worst in society. Some pathologists can keep their reactions in bounds, stay balanced, realize it's just a job—an important job. But I'm not one of them. I don't want to spend the rest of my life seeing the dark side of human nature, the cruelty, the lack of responsibility. I've got to leave as soon as they can get a replacement."

Farone was, for reasons he could not readily identify, not at all surprised by her attitude and decision. He probed gently. "Have you told anyone about your feelings? What do you plan to do, Sheila?"

"Just you, Bob. I guess I wanted a sounding board. What's your reaction? You know how much I respect your opinion."

"Given your feelings, I think it's right for you to leave. But if I were you, I'd wait until I had an alternative plan in mind before bailing out. Do you have any thoughts about the future?"

"Yes, I do. That's what's going to make this a lot easier. I want to go back to med school and specialize in pediatrics. I've been thinking about it for over six months. You know that I'm a person who really hates change, but frankly, this current case has made up my mind for me. I'm going to see my boss tomorrow, tell her I'm leaving, and let her decide how much longer she will need me before she's hired my replacement."

Farone began to feel guilty about his selfish reaction to her anguish, but he couldn't deny it. *If she changes careers and has nothing more to do with cops,* he thought, *there's a reasonable shot for us to make it together.*

As they walked slowly and quietly back to the car, he realized he was already back into bargaining. Several years ago, Farone had sensed that the death of a relationship, or the loss of anything of great emotional value, might follow the path that psychologists had plotted for an actual impending physical death: first the denial, then the anger, followed by bargaining—what does it take to get back to normal? And when the bargaining didn't pan out, the depression set in, followed sometime later by final acceptance. He hadn't thought about his theory in years, but suddenly he realized that, with respect to Sheila, he was coming quickly out of depression and moving back up the scale to bargaining. A cheesy word for the elation it was giving him, he thought, but true nonetheless.

And then he stopped thinking, stopped walking, put his arm tightly around Ryan, and kissed her softly on the lips. And the kiss was returned in kind, no reservations. Farone knew pure joy for the first time in months.

CHAPTER THIRTY-ONE

Half a loaf is better than none, thought Peggy Nugent as she left the courthouse with Cathy Weiss. They had obtained a signed search warrant from the judge that allowed them to search the truck and boat belonging to Bart Daly, but permission had been withheld to search his house, at least temporarily, until more promising evidence had been turned up.

"Checking out Daly's boat is a waste of time, Peggy," offered ADA Weiss. "The uniformed guys checked it out, and as I recall from their report, it's a small open fishing boat. Nothing to search, really. Why don't you focus on his truck, take some photos, and maybe show them to Marjorie Failsome for an ID? Agreed?"

"Yeah, I know the drill, Cathy. One step at a time. Look, assuming Daly's well enough to go to work today, I'll head over to the warehouse and see if there's anything we might use as evidence against him. I've already e-mailed photos of Daly to the jewelers who sold to the perp. Got a no from one of them and a thin maybe from the other man. I'm going to see Mrs. Failsome at the clinic after lunch and get her reaction to the photos. Nowhere to go but up. Got any interest in visiting the warehouse with me? I'm heading over there now."

"No, thanks anyway, Peggy. I've got a real mess to straighten out back at the office: DUI hit and run," Weiss replied, then added seriously, "Peggy, listen to me. There is some likelihood that Daly is a killer, and there's no question that he can be violent. Why don't you play it safe and take some uniforms with you, just in case?"

Nugent answered firmly and pleasantly, "I know, and I appreciate that you're looking out for me, Cathy, but I can take care of myself. And to be perfectly honest with you, I think that being with uniformed cops and their squad car might provoke him more quickly than if I'm alone. Now answer this question: would you have given the same advice if I were a guy?"

"Yes. Good luck."

· · ·

Nugent's investigation had drifted from lukewarm to cool. Her visit to the warehouse parking lot had, at first, looked very promising. Daly was at work. His truck was in the parking lot, a red Chevy Silverado pickup with a tool chest in the bed. Also in the bed was an eight-foot length of nylon line, quite similar, if not an exact match, to the rope used in the serial crimes. And the line was smeared in spots with a dark red substance. Nugent confiscated the line in order to submit it to CSI for analysis. The passenger-side door of the truck was unlocked, but an examination of the interior revealed nothing of significance: a few maps, chewing gum, ballpoint pens, notebook of phone numbers, three empty prescription pill bottles, and the predictable registration and insurance papers.

Her next stop was a visit to the abortion clinic where Mrs. Failsome worked. The visit did not please Nugent at all. Her personal views were definitely pro-life, so the clinic itself felt like a step into hell. And the interview was a serious disappointment as well. Marjorie Failsome was of the strong opinion that the picture of Daly bore little resemblance to her attacker. Further, she had no positive reaction to photos of Daly's truck. Then she went on to criticize Nugent and the entire police department for not producing the killer. After all, she pointed out, there was no reason to think he wouldn't try again.

The forensics people were next in line to dash cold water on Nugent's investigation. The nylon line obtained from Daly's truck showed signs of having been used in connection with boating. The line exhibited large traces of embedded salt water that was chemically identical to the water in the sound. And the dark-red stains had turned out to be smears of bottom paint, the type used to coat the hulls of boats to prevent buildup of barnacles, worms, and other destructive saltwater pests.

Nugent reviewed her progress, or lack of it, with Farone and Weiss. It was agreed that Daly would be asked to come in for a brief interview, but unless something he said sparked further probable cause, no warrant would be sought to search his house. The matter of arrest was, at present, completely out of the question.

Daly, who had had trouble with the police over the years, was not overly surprised when Nugent approached him as his shift was ending. Without discussing specifically the department's interest in him, she told Daly that his red pickup truck, together with the line in it, had made him one of a number of "persons of interest" the police were eager to talk to with respect to several recent violent crimes. Daly had agreed to show up at the precinct house for an interview. He acknowledged with a wry smile that he was aware of the recent series of killings, and he figured his record qualified him for a serious investigation by the police. Nugent had made no reply and said she was looking forward to sitting down with him.

Daly showed up on time, acting neither apprehensive nor hostile. He declined a cup of coffee in the interview room on the basis that it might be bad for his health and said he had no problem with the interview being taped.

Farone had advised Nugent to keep the preliminaries to a minimum and get right to the most important question: where was he at the specific hour and date of the thwarted attack on Marjorie Failsome? Farone had also insisted that Detective Sloan be present at the interview, since he might pick up on something Daly either said or omitted, and also in case Daly got abusive or violent.

The interview was over in less than twenty minutes. When Daly heard that the night he was being questioned about was a Thursday, he broke into a sly smile. Thursdays, for the last six years, had meant poker night with five friends, and even though he was sick, he had never missed a session. The games were the high spot of his week. He easily provided Sloan and Nugent with the names and phone numbers of the other players and further explained that they always met at the home of one man—a bachelor—and played cards from about eight to eleven o'clock. Farone, observing the interview, realized that the Daly lead was virtually evaporating, since it was clear that five responsible alibis for Daly's activities on the evening of the attack at the clinic would eliminate any possibility for an immediate arrest and would consign further investigation of him to very low priority.

Well, what's next? Easy. First, let Nugent know that she did a fine job on the Daly investigation, which she had. Next, let Snyder and Jones know that the Daly lead is, if not dead, at least severely wounded. Since he had already informed them of his discovery of the Hartman boat, with no apparent evidence, a warrant to search Hartman's rented house would have to be approved by a judge immediately, and a coordinated plan would have to be set in motion to pick up and interrogate Hartman ASAP. And what if it turned out that the Hartman lead went dry, too? Farone dismissed the thought from his mind. *Too discouraging to think about.*

CHAPTER THIRTY-TWO

Ivan Hartman was, atypically for him, worried. The media pressure and resulting news stories, some actually accurate, had at first given him pleasure, even feedback, because he realized that despite what the police and media labeled him, his message was getting through to the general public. He had felt that, on his death, his remarkable achievements in calling attention to the misdeeds of human scum would be viewed as bizarre by some but ultimately heroic by many. And perhaps others, inspired by his feats, would take up the cudgel. But now the media focus had turned more toward the FBI and local police, featuring stories and interviews that highlighted their investigation and not the evil that he was attacking and making an example of.

Having been treated for years for a variety of mental illnesses, Hartman realized that some of his increasing worry might be garden-variety paranoia. Fear that he was being followed had become chronic. When he drove, he now used his Mercedes SUV exclusively, because it was relatively inconspicuous. The Jag and the Dodge truck were locked away in his garage, now too obvious to drive.

Worse, his failure to abduct and punish the Failsome woman had really created a mess. Now he had to worry about her ability to identify him, if and when the time came, and he also had to sweat out the fear that she or someone else had noted his truck's license plate number. He forced these thoughts out of his mind, allowing cool logic to extinguish the rising heat of panic. After all, if the police had run the license number, they would have come up with Hartman Sr., and it would take some time to trace the truck to him.

But then the phone call from Harbor Marine this morning. The office manager had asked Hartman to stop by and pay a minimum of four months' slip rental in advance, in addition to the two months already paid for. When Hartman questioned why, the manager agreed that it was unusual for the marina to request a long advance payment—especially in cash—but a police officer from Stamford had checked out the boat over the weekend and asked to be informed if the boat was moved. The manager acknowledged that the cop had not revealed his interest in the boat, but the marina had to protect itself in the event there were some sort of problem, such as a lien on the boat, and it had to protect itself in the unusual case of a customer suddenly taking off and leaving unpaid bills and so on. It had happened before. Hartman responded coolly that he had no idea what the cops were snooping around for, but "what the heck, I'm a businessman, too," and he agreed to put up the security deposit that afternoon.

After leaving off the cash deposit, Hartman reviewed his next move calmly and carefully. It was obvious that some element of law enforcement was in the process of actively seeking evidence against him. And with the pressure on the police from the media, a warrant for his arrest would not be difficult to obtain, even with a thin case. *Time to play defense*, he thought. He drove out to Meyers Avenue, off the Merritt Parkway, where he knew of a third-rate motel, straight out of the fifties, the Three Elms. The actual big elm trees after which the motel had been named had died, unfortunately, in 1960, succumbing to Dutch Elm disease, but the name was never changed. The facility itself was a typical old-fashioned, one-story affair, designed so that each guest could park his car in a space directly across from the door to his unit. It had been the first commercial business in a middle-income suburb destined to be developed into a strip mall.

Hartman registered under a false name and address and paid for four nights' lodging in advance with cash. He asked for and got a corner room in the back, not visible from the street.

Hartman knew the motel well. In slack times, about ten years before, he had submitted a bid for a small job at the motel, rebuilding the roof, which was suffering from dry rot, thanks to a nonexistent ventilation system, courtesy of the original building contractor. The hoped-for strip mall that developers had sought to build in the area had never come to pass, because local citizens, coming out of their comatose state after the surprise construction of the Three Elms, realized that their quality of life and, more important, the value of their homes would head south fast if the strip mall development proceeded as planned. Luckily, one of the residents had had problems with the local planning board, since resolved, over the construction of his septic tank and leach field. What he had learned through his own bitter experience was that the area had vast deposits of clay in the underlying ground, making drainage very difficult and the construction of so-called soft-commercial buildings an environmental no-no. So after only two review meetings, the planning board withheld approval for construction. The strip mall and the developers moved on.

The motel had survived throughout the years because it was a popular spot for those bent on a little extramarital cheating, renting a room for a night even if only for a few hours' use. A succession of owners had made out reasonably well by pocketing the cash often paid by guests and then underreporting their gross income to the IRS. The "No-tell Motel," as it was popularly called. Perfect for Hartman's immediate needs, he thought, as he headed back to his rental home for a final visit.

• • •

Jim Sisk was a good agent: smart, aggressive, well trained. Had a good track record. But too many other agents possessed the same qualities, which made it hard to break out of the pack, get recognized as exceptional, and move up the ladder. Sisk's ambitions were limitless but bound by common sense. He realized that most breakthroughs in bureau careers came about due to assignments to high-profile cases or by getting extraordinary breaks in solving, almost single-handedly, a major crime. A crime, for example, like the crab killings. If ever there was a chance to make a big case with minimal repercussions for bending the rules, this was it. He developed a simple plan for his solo investigation.

 First, he would have to distance himself from his new partner, Agent DeLong. Simple. He would instruct him to obtain a search warrant for the Hartman boat, in conjunction with the local cops, and then to drive out and perform the search. Meanwhile, Sisk decided to investigate the Hartman rental home alone, without benefit of a search warrant, and without informing either Snyder or Farone of his plan. His hope was that Hartman would not be at home, that he could poke around the premises, maybe even enter the house or garage, and find enough evidence to warrant probable cause, leading to his arrest of Hartman. Of course, if Hartman was at home, he would interrogate him and maybe dredge up an admission of guilt, giving Sisk the ability to take Hartman into custody immediately and to perform the "first" search of the house and grounds. He planned to lie if and when asked whether the suspect had been informed of his Miranda rights, assuming that, at that time, it would be his word against Hartman's, and through his interview and discovery of damning evidence he would be believed. The anticipation of the media coverage was almost too exciting to bear and more than outweighed the lukewarm criticism he would get from Snyder, Farone, and company. After all, his stance of personal initiative versus bureaucratic doctrine was the American way, was it not?

 It was early afternoon when Sisk drove down Sweetbriar Road, an upper-scale neighborhood in North Stamford. The address had been easily discovered by both police and FBI with simple inquiries to the local phone company and electric utility. It was a good time of day to investigate, especially under somewhat clandestine conditions. Kids were at school, working parents at the office, cleaning ladies inside, and only one so-called landscaping service, really a "mow and blow" team, was at work well down the street. A small lane afforded some coverage for Sisk's car. He parked and walked briskly up to the side door of a three-bay garage. No sounds or any indications of someone being home, Sisk sensed. Maybe he would get lucky.

And he did. The small door on the side of the garage was unlocked. He slipped inside and spotted a vintage Jaguar convertible, top down, nothing instantly apparent inside. But parked next to the Jag was the mother lode: a red Dodge Ram crew-cab pickup truck. He quickly noted the license plate number, planning to run it as soon as possible through the state database.

A quick look into the truck bed convinced him that he had found the killer, or at least his truck. The dimpled metal tool chest was at the top of the bed behind the cab, as reported. But the big finds were a shovel, still marked with dirt, a large coil of three-strand white nylon rope, and what appeared to be dried and congealed bloodstains. An apparently bloodstained tarp was also carelessly piled in the truck, used to cover up bodies and gear, Sisk surmised. *God, what balls this guy has*. He strode quickly to the door connecting the house to the garage, hoping to find it open and no one at home.

A dark Mercedes SUV meanwhile had pulled up behind Sisk's car. Hartman coolly observed the vehicle, one of Sisk's mistakes. The car, a Ford Crown Victoria, was part of the detectives' fleet in the local police motor pool. Sisk had borrowed it for a few days while his own car was in the shop for bodywork. Unfortunately, the borrowed car screamed *cops* to Hartman: cheap oversized tires, spotlight with handle on the driver's side, red flasher light resting on the passenger seat. Hartman entered the house through the front door and paused to listen for sounds of the intruder. He was rewarded by the sound of the lock being picked on the door connecting his garage to his kitchen. He silently positioned himself in the small pantry and waited patiently for the kitchen door to be opened. Once again, he felt the comforting calm of the hunter awaiting his prey.

After a lot of false tries, the lock finally released under the less-than-expert probing of Agent Sisk. The door swung open to reveal an empty kitchen. However, Sisk had an eerie sense that he was not alone. He reached behind him under his suit jacket and pulled a Smith & Wesson .40 caliber semiautomatic pistol from its holster. He cocked it, laid his index finger alongside the trigger guard, as trained at the academy, and then dropped the weapon to the floor as the shock of a thirty-thousand-volt Taser stun gun knocked him off his feet.

Hartman quickly picked up the gun and patted down the agent's body. He was surprised not to find a backup gun in a leg holster. Maybe he had seen too many cop shows on TV. He did find a pair of handcuffs, along with a lockpick set, and put the cuffs on Sisk, still comatose on the kitchen floor. Hartman had assumed from the appearance of Sisk's car that he was a local detective and was surprised to see from the ID that the guy was an FBI agent. No sign of either an arrest warrant or a search warrant, though. Hartman reasoned that if the cops were planning on an arrest, or a search, or both, they would have appeared in force, not just one guy with a lockpick set. Obviously a glory seeker, a sneak. Needs special punishment.

Hartman went out to the garage, grabbed a roll of duct tape, and returned to his victim. He put a short piece of tape over Sisk's mouth and another long piece around his ankles.

He then went upstairs to pick up his prepacked garment bag, a black T. Anthony two-suiter bag, an old duffel bag, and any remaining medications and toiletries from the bathroom that had not been already packed. After he brought his gear down to the kitchen, he went into the den and picked up his leather attaché case, his Halliburton metal case, and a small, lockable metal file box. Like the luggage and the prey, they were all deposited on the kitchen floor.

Hartman removed two bottles of Evian from the refrigerator and took them out to the car. *Doctor's orders—hydrate*, he thought, the irony not lost on him. He backed the Mercedes up to the open door at the side of the garage, popped open the rear tailgate door, folded away the rear seat to make a larger bed, and unceremoniously tossed the FBI man in the back, along with the luggage and other gear. He closed the rear door and slowly drove away, headed north for the Merritt Parkway and the Three Oaks Motel. He stowed Sisk's gun in the large CD storage compartment between the seats and made a mental note to hit him with another jolt of the Taser after the first shock wore off.

CHAPTER THIRTY-THREE

Hartman had always been fascinated with the concept of luck. What one person might celebrate and attribute to good luck, another would feel was simply his due. And the same, in reverse, held true for bad luck. The best thing about luck, he felt, was that it almost always counted, though it was not earned: the lottery winner, the marine who returned from battle unscathed. And so far, Hartman realized, his luck had certainly held out. Particularly now, as he backed into his motel parking spot with virtually no one around and unloaded his gear and a slightly wriggling cop.

But he was sobered by his alternative view of luck: the streak always ends. It was obvious that this glory-seeking FBI guy would be missed, and the same line of evidence or reasoning that had drawn the man to Hartman's house would also be followed up by other cops. And even though this motel was obscure, and his car was not in view from the street, his movements would be limited, the SUV itself a subject of search. If not now, soon. He accepted the fact that his priorities had changed, his plans accelerated by the unexpected accuracy of the cop's detection. What could they have possibly found that would make him an obvious suspect? Well, it didn't really matter now. They had him made, and he was on the run. Just needed a little more time to question this guy, Sisk, and to come up with a creative way to punish him, something that made an example of Sisk's folly of hyperaggressiveness, impulsiveness, and duplicity.

Hartman tossed Sisk's slowly recovering body onto one of the two queen-size beds in the room. He set his boating gear bag on the other bed and then removed the victim's handcuffs in order to take off his suit jacket, which he hung neatly on the plain pipe that served as a closet. The handcuffs were then replaced in order to take no chances of a struggle, a sensible but probably unnecessary precaution, thought Hartman, because he was considerably bigger and clearly stronger than his prisoner.

Sisk at this point had almost completely recovered from a second shock of the stun gun and was slowly orienting himself. *In a second-rate hotel room. With a big, oddly pleasant-looking psycho. Hands cuffed, bound by something at the ankles, mouth sealed.* Sisk forced himself to remain calm and review what he needed to do to stay alive: *if the gag was removed, try to establish some emotional connection with Hartman, listen sympathetically, use his name, be agreeable, don't argue, don't fight. At least until you're in a position to kill the twisted son of a bitch.*

Hartman, who had been arranging a few ballpoint pens and some paper on the round table that served as a desk, noticed that Sisk was alert. He walked over to the bed and unceremoniously yanked the duct tape off Sisk's mouth. He then hit Sisk hard with a backhanded slap to the face, knocking him sideways. In a tone of voice completely devoid of any passion or feeling, Hartman gave Sisk a short warning. "This place is remote and pretty much empty. Don't bother yelling for help, because there isn't going to be anyone coming, and you'll only get a lot of pain for your trouble. Don't speak until spoken to. We'll talk later, after I finish writing some notes. Enjoy the TV show. I'll be with you shortly."

Sisk scrunched up against the simulated-walnut headboard of the bed and looked around. The room was fairly dark except for the light dangling from the ceiling over the round table, at which Hartman—*remember to call him Ivan, to build rapport*—was writing. The curtains were drawn tightly over the one window and duct taped at the edges for additional security. The only other light came from the TV set, now showing a rerun of *Law & Order*. Sisk remained silent, as ordered, but now that his head was clear, he began to plan how he could escape a probable death and maybe even wind up on top of the struggle. There could be no reliance on cops or other agents coming to his rescue, because even though they would have determined that he was missing and would probably head for Hartman's house, where Sisk's borrowed car was parked, there would be no way they could trace him to this motel, wherever it was. He was on his own.

It took Hartman over forty-five minutes to complete three notes, two of which he placed in his attaché case, and the third he left on the table alongside the roll of duct tape he had been using. He was slightly nervous that time was flying by, precious time. It was obvious that the cops would be calling on the rental house, seeing this agent's car, and concluding that he was missing. But it was not possible that he could be readily traced to the motel room. The real concern was that they might head immediately for Harbor Marine, seize *Coy Mistress*, and completely foul up his plans to eliminate Hartman and replace him with Randall Newman. No time to waste.

Hartman pulled a chair over to the bedside where Sisk lay still. He turned the chair around backward, then sat down on it, facing Sisk. "We're going to have a very short talk, Mr. Lawman, and the quality of your answers to a few simple questions will determine whether I leave you here dead or alive. Do you understand?" asked Hartman.

"Yes, Ivan, I do. What do you want from me?" Sisk answered in an even and respectful tone of voice.

"I want you to knock off the mind games. Don't call me Ivan. Don't use your own name. Don't be charming or submissive. Don't risk a severe punishment. We'll start now. How did my name get on your list of suspects, assuming that you have a list?"

"It was basically your signature, the crab charms you left on those deserving to die," Sisk answered, his words chosen very judiciously. "Someone finally determined that the sign literally stood for cancer, the disease, so a survey was taken of all the local doctors, particularly oncologists, and cancer clinics, to develop a list of all men presently afflicted with some form of cancer. You were on the list."

"But I refused treatment. Melanoma's a one-way street," Hartman argued.

"Frankly, that's the opinion we developed. Maybe someone who felt his days were numbered might be motivated to get on with the task of avenging certain crimes and misdeeds that have gone unpunished," Sisk answered pleasantly.

Hartman struggled to repress a rising anger. "Vengeance has very little to do with my work. It's all about seeking justice and making an example of all sorts of scum, hopefully generating enough notoriety that other scum will take notice and cease their filthy activities. This is my way of giving something back to society before I go. Understand?"

Hartman probed Sisk for more information about his being targeted as a suspect—big guy, knottying, MYC shirt, negative comments made by vice commodore. But no solid make on the red truck, and other leads did not pan out. Hartman actually began to lose interest in the development of the case as related by Sisk. What was done was done. The challenge now was to leave the FBI guy, probably unharmed. No strong reason to punish him for just doing his job. Just another glory seeker. And he had been straight and forthcoming in his answers about the case, even admitting that his superiors knew nothing of his one-man investigation.

"May I ask you for a favor?" Sisk asked nervously. Getting no response, he persisted. "Look, please, I have to use the bathroom. Could you please cut me loose for a few minutes and let me go in there?"

Hartman didn't respond, but he knew that the bathroom was serviced with a ventilator. There was no window, no chance to break out. Wordlessly, he removed the handcuffs, but not the duct tape around the ankles, and motioned for Sisk to use the toilet.

By hobbling and steadying himself with his hands against the wall, Sisk managed to get into the bathroom and nudge the door shut. He unbuckled his belt, unzipped his fly and let his pants drop. He reached into his briefs, really a professional crotch holster commonly used for deep-concealed carry, and pulled out a small so-called pocket pistol, hardly bigger than a deck of cards. The gun was a Seecamp .32 caliber semiautomatic, a weapon so in demand by law enforcement as a highly concealed "last-ditch" weapon that it had taken over fourteen months to get the gun after ordering it. The weapon had its shortcomings. Not very accurate, prone to jamming, overpriced, and, worst of all, it fired a very anemic round. But Sisk and thousands of other customers weren't concerned with the Seecamp's drawbacks. Accuracy didn't matter that much at close range, and the price was unimportant if you felt you were ensuring your safety, maybe your life. The cartridge itself, long popular in Europe, had been improved in recent years, particularly by the Fiocchi Cartridge Company in Italy. Their round was a full-metal-jacket, seventy-three-grain bullet. Though not matching the effectiveness of larger calibers, it still produced a reasonably potent hit, and in good hands it was lethal.

Sisk checked that the magazine was seated properly inside the grip and that a round had been chambered. Locked and loaded, ready to fire. He set the little gun down on the top of the toilet tank while he pulled up and zipped his pants. With the pistol in his right hand, Sisk hobbled over to the bathroom door, a mixture of fear, excitement, and revenge making his heart race. Taking down the serial killer solo, while beaten and tied up, with no backup. He would be a new bureau legend, open road ahead. His plan was simple: push the door open, acquire the target, and kill the bastard.

Hartman was kneeling on one leg, repacking a sailing bag, when the door to the bathroom swung open suddenly. Sisk began to fire. The first round was high, plowing into the top drawer of the dresser. The second round ripped through the left side of Hartman's shirt, barely grazing his ribs as he charged. The third round struck Hartman's left bicep and exited neatly out of the rear of his arm. The next round jammed, no time to clear it, as Sisk was bowled over, gun knocked away, and severely kicked and beaten.

· · ·

After securing a badly mauled, handcuffed, and gagged FBI man to the bed, Hartman tossed the little gun under the bed, collected the three spent cartridge casings and tossed them into his sailing bag, and began to treat his wound, which he knew wasn't serious. He cleaned out both the entrance and exit wounds, fortunately both small because of the small diameter of the bullet and the fact that it wasn't a hollow point. He found the boat's medical kit—a fairly large one, since the yacht had enjoyed many long-range cruises—in the sail bag. He stitched up both wounds, suffering the pain of the needle without anesthesia, and then he wrapped his arm tightly with large sterile pads and first aid tape. He took three Excedrin for the pain and then sat down for a few minutes to reorganize his thoughts.

First, he reviewed his plan of leaving. No changes necessary at this point, but no more time to waste either. Second, what was a suitable punishment for a man whom you treated generously, and who then lied to you to set up an ambush? A simple plan soon developed.

Hartman emptied the contents of his sail bag, removed some items of clothes from his suitcase, and tore up the note left on the table, which he had planned to tape to the outside of the front door when he left. The note had merely stated that Sisk was inside the room, watching TV and awaiting his FBI colleagues. A good idea at the time, because it left him the option of punishing Sisk, or merely holding him captive, indicating at the same time that there might be a hostage situation, thus slowing down the entire process of breaking into the room, buying time. Of course, he would have already fled in either case.

Hartman took the phone off the hook. He assembled some items on the empty bed. He returned to the table to compose a new note to leave on the front door and a quick outline of a new replacement note he would leave aboard *Coy Mistress*.

CHAPTER THIRTY-FOUR

FBI Agent DeLong was a strictly-by-the-book investigator and junior to Agent Sisk. So he accepted without question Sisk's instructions for him to check on Hartman's boat, based on the information provided in Detective Farone's report. DeLong, however, like most good cops, was a born skeptic, and he realized that he was being shunted off on a fool's errand; clearly there would be nothing more to investigate on the boat until they obtained a search warrant, forced open the hatch, and searched below decks. DeLong figured out that Sisk's remark about needing time to "check some other details on the case" was pure BS, but he didn't want to push the matter. He decided instead to approach Lead Agent Snyder and ask innocently about the status of the subpoena the cops were supposed to obtain from the judge in order to search Hartman's boat and rental home.

"About one more hour," Snyder had replied. "Judge Wellborn takes forever on these things. He wants to know every last detail. Our bad luck he was on the bench today. Incidentally, where is Jim? I told him last night that after Farone picked up the warrants we would head out as a team to Hartman's place."

"I don't know Jim's exact whereabouts," DeLong replied, pleased that he'd be getting even with Sisk without doing or saying anything questionable. "He told me that he had some details on the case to clear up, Ray. He also told me to go check on the boat, so should I do that now or wait until we get the warrants?"

Snyder jerked up from his chair. "I can't believe this shit. Sisk was reprimanded three or four years ago in Columbus for trying to break a case on his own without following procedure. Almost lost us the collar. Did he say anything to you about going out to the Hartman house on his own?"

"No, sir, not a word."

"Well, you can bet your sweet ass that's exactly what he's doing," Snyder barked as he slammed his fist on the desk. "Try his cell phone or pager right now. I've got to head him off."

DeLong was not surprised when he got no response from Sisk. The guy was definitely out there on his own, and one Raymond L. Snyder was very pissed off. Farone was soon told of the problem and wisely refrained from berating Snyder for failing to control an impulsive agent. Farone also agreed to ask ADA Weiss to use her personal friendship with the judge to get his signatures on the warrants ASAP. Weiss was as good as gold, delivering the signed warrants in fifteen minutes with a pleasant, "You owe me one, Bobby," directed at Farone. Snyder had already lined up a forensics team and instructed them to follow him to the home. He handed the boat search warrant to DeLong and told him to delay a trip to the marina until further instructed. Meanwhile, Farone and Peggy Nugent piled into one car, a squad car with uniformed officers in second position, Snyder in the third car and, ending the convoy, the forensics technicians.

It took only twenty minutes to reach the house, and the first thing Farone spotted was a detective car from his own unit. Nugent told him that Sisk had checked out the car because his own vehicle was in the shop. The car was locked and empty, Sisk's cell phone and pager left on the passenger seat.

The group fanned out for security purposes as Farone, gun drawn, moved quickly up to the front door of the house, rang the doorbell, then peeked through the windows. No response. Then one of the cops called out that the side door to the garage was open, and they all pushed through. Farone instantly had mixed reactions: no SUV probably meant that Hartman had fled, but then where was Agent Sisk? On the other hand, the red pickup truck was an obvious find, potentially a major piece of evidence. The forensics team immediately cordoned off the truck and started accumulating their inventory of evidence and submitting it to field tests. They also decided to take photos of the truck and make sure that the towing company was alerted in case the vehicle had to be impounded.

The investigation continued rapidly as the group streamed through the open kitchen door, the detectives moving quickly rapidly through the first floor, the cops through the second floor. No Hartman, no Sisk. Big problem, especially for Snyder and the bureau.

Farone remembered talking shop, many years ago, with his father, who was engaged in the defense of a man charged with the first-degree murder of his wife. The prosecutor's case was so strong, the senior Farone had said, that he planned to plead the case out, maybe go for a murder-two homicide sentence rather than go before a jury. He had referred to the search of the couple's home, the scene of the crime, as providing the police with an "orgy of evidence." The phrase had always stuck in the younger Farone's mind, because he had never had an overwhelming amount of evidence on any case.

Until now. In the back of the truck was a shovel with dirt on it, three-eighths-inch nylon rope, apparent bloodstains, and a toolbox with an axe and a bloodstained machete. A bloodstained blue nylon tarp, still secured at two tie-down points, rounded out the immediate evidence. A spot computer check in Hartford had already confirmed the fact that the truck was registered to Hartman's father.

The house itself had initially yielded no evidence. Guest bedrooms were apparently never used. Nothing obvious in the living room, dining room, and kitchen. They struck pay dirt, however, when they searched the den. Newspaper media accounts, stacked in chronological order with the most recent on the top of the pile, described each murder. The clippings had apparently been deposited in a legal-size manila file labeled PROGRESS

REPORT and brought out for a final reading. On top of the den desk was another file, labeled JUSTICE REDUX PENDING. It contained newspaper accounts of the activities of three men: the first under current investigation for rigging votes in a recent election; the second man had been convicted but let off on a short probation period, for the crime of animal abuse and neglect at a petting zoo he half owned; and the third man was out on bail, an alleged child pornographer who taped and distributed his material through underground pornography sources.

Nugent reported that most if not all of the clothing, shoes, and personal items in Hartman's bedroom were intact, in slight disarray. It looked as though he had perhaps taken a few items, but not necessarily the best, since a black belt with a solid-gold Tiffany buckle, his initials engraved, had been left hanging in the closet. She had also discovered a Rolex Oyster Perpetual watch and a pair of gold cufflinks, both engraved with his initials, on the top of his dresser. Meanwhile, Farone and Snyder went through the desk carefully and turned up the rental slip for *Coy Mistress*. But the big find came last: three gold charm bracelets, each adorned with a crab charm.

Enthusiasm quickly evaporated as reality set in: the perpetrator had fled, probably taking Sisk with him, dead or alive. But where? In the first cruise through the house, Nugent had noticed an open phone book on the couch next to a telephone in the living room. She told Farone she examined it for a lead. A break—the book's yellow pages were open to the section on hotels, and a motel, the Three Elms, had been neatly underlined. Nugent quickly filled in Farone and Snyder on her find, then called the motel. The desk clerk said he had no one registered by the name of Hartman, but that a big, middle-aged white guy had taken a room—requested that it be in the back of the building—earlier that day. And yes, he drove a Mercedes SUV, dark green. Snyder, meanwhile, had called a special number at the phone company, and they readily confirmed that a call had been made from Hartman's number to the motel three hours prior.

Farone quickly implemented their next moves. He called ADA Weiss to get her started on an arrest warrant for Hartman. He then called in for an APB on the SUV, sealed off the Hartman home, and impounded the

Dodge Ram pickup as evidence. Two FBI SWAT teams were requested for immediate duty by Snyder. They were to report ASAP to the Hartman home for a quick briefing on the situation. Then they would join the police convoy headed out to the motel.

Farone had simultaneously given the same instructions to three squad cars of uniformed cops and then told Nugent to remain at the Hartman house with the two cops and the forensics people to investigate, supervise photography and evidence collection, and secure the premises. Farone and Snyder reached a virtually tacit agreement to delay notifying Lt. James of the breaks in the case, since the possibility of a leak to the media might cause them to lose the perpetrator and, worse, to get Sisk killed, if he wasn't already dead.

The entire company of law enforcement was organized within the next thirty minutes, and with Farone leading they headed for the motel.

CHAPTER THIRTY-FIVE

Ivan Hartman carefully examined his latest work of redemption with great pride, tempered with the chronic worrier's concern that something might be wrong. But no, the tableau was perfect.

Agent Sisk had been beaten just enough to break his spirit, making the rest of the job easier. Even straddling Sisk's chest and stitching his lips together with surgical thread had gone better than Hartman would have thought. When he had finished the suturing and cleaned the remaining drops of blood off Sisk's lips and chin, the rest of the project was child's play. Off came the handcuffs. Then Sisk's shirt and tie were removed and tossed into a pile, destined for the Dempsey Dumpster in the parking lot. Next a red V-neck sweater with a prominent MYC logo replaced Sisk's shirt. He was then dragged, still groggy and listless from being beaten, into the bathroom. From his tool kit Hartman dug out wire cutters and a long roll of thin stainless-steel rigging wire, crimped to hold the wire together. He folded down the toilet seat lid and placed Sisk on it.

"Cooperate, don't fight back," he warned Sisk. "I'm not going to kill you, and I don't want to hit you anymore. I'm going to tie you to this toilet with wire, and when I finish, I'll leave."

He removed all remaining duct tape and then bound Sisk's legs together with wire, looped the wire around the back of the toilet, and crimped it tightly together. The same procedure was used to secure Sisk's upper arms to his torso, and then the entire trunk of his body was bound to the toilet tank. This wire was unbreakable and better yet, not instantly visible. Hartman next removed the magazine and a chambered round from Sisk's Smith & Wesson and tossed them into the pile of Sisk's other belongings. A liberal smear of Krazy Glue was applied to both sides of the pistol's grip, and then the gun was placed in the agent's right hand. To keep the weapon pointed generally straight ahead, he wrapped a final hank of wire tightly around Sisk's wrist, guided up through the right-hand sleeve of the red sweater, down diagonally across his back, secured around his left wrist, and then wrapped tightly around his left thigh. His left arm was now totally immovable, and his right forearm, hand glued to the gun, was pointing forward, unable to be brought down.

Sisk slowly began to realize that he was being set up, sacrificed. He couldn't scream or speak and could barely move anything but his head. The real panic set in when Hartman put something around his left wrist. He knew it was the charm, and he knew what it meant. The finishing touch to the scenario was the snug placement on Sisk's head of a tan, long-billed yachting cap. Hartman backed out of the bathroom, closing the door behind him, pleased with his work.

The room's phone was disconnected, and the main circuit breaker was pushed off. All the agent's personal stuff would be tossed into the Dumpster. *What would the cops find?* Hartman asked himself. *A room with no phone and no agent, but maybe a suspect holed up in a dark bathroom behind a closed door,* Hartman thought approvingly. He replaced all the materials he had used in the back of the SUV, along with several motel letterheads, and as a parting touch he taped a new note to the outside door of the room with a small strip of duct tape.

He wondered if the logic of his latest example would be understood by the police and the media: that the agent's duplicity—bending all the rules to get the arrest he wanted—was matched by the deadly duplicity Hartman had now imposed on his appearance. *Well*, he thought, *hope for the best and plan for the worst.* He slowly drove out of the parking lot.

CHAPTER THIRTY-SIX

The law enforcement entourage, headed by Detective Farone and Agent Snyder, approached the Three Elms Motel as unobtrusively as possible with seven police vehicles. No wailers blaring, no lights flashing, no emergency tactics.

The first step upon arrival was easy. After being shown a picture of Hartman, the desk clerk agreed that he was the "big guy, kinda quiet" who had checked in earlier, but he had apparently used some other name. He confirmed the Mercedes SUV, but not a plate number, since Hartman had not pulled up near the office when he registered, and anyway the motel no longer bothered with vehicle ID on its registration forms. He confirmed that room 29, around the back, had been paid for in cash. There had been no commotion of any kind after check-in. The clerk also indicated the seven other rooms in the rear of the building where other guests had checked in, and handed Farone a key to Hartman's room with a request not to break it down.

Uniformed cops were dispatched to evacuate all rooms currently occupied. They were to place their vehicles at both ends of the parking lot to block any chance of an attempt to escape by car. The evacuation went smoothly, with one exception—a semiclad, prominent doctor who was married yet sharing his room with a young physician's assistant named Keith.

Lead Agent Snyder attempted the obvious, a call on his cell phone to room 29. Constant busy signal. A check with the phone company confirmed that the phone was off the hook.

It was getting dark rapidly; lamps were glowing in most of the occupied rooms, but not in room 29. The lights were out, curtains tightly drawn. A tight perimeter of cops with guns drawn was set up. Snyder and Farone, along with the agent heading up the six-man FBI SWAT team, could not agree on the best way to penetrate Hartman's room. An obvious tactic was to call to him on the bullhorn and demand that he come out. Another idea was to order the SWAT team to toss a special phone through the room's window and give the negotiator an opportunity to talk the suspect into surrendering via phone. A final option discussed was also obvious: breaking into the room with no fanfare and hoping for the best.

Imponderables did not make the task of deciding any easier. Since there was no SUV in the parking lot, Hartman might have already fled, and time was being wasted. Agent Sisk was missing. And it was not even clear if the suspect had heard or seen the police force descend upon the scene.

Snyder, characteristically, submitted that breaking into the room with no warning was the best approach. No one there, no problem. Hartman there, worst-case scenario—we kill him. Sisk there, takes his chances. Admittedly, the suspect may have kept Sisk's gun, since he obviously had disarmed him, but a quick check of local and state records showed no hunting permits or pistol permits were on file for him. Hartman and his crimes did not indicate any use or knowledge of firearms.

Farone disagreed, noting that their lack of information about Agent Sisk's whereabouts was a major concern. Both Hartman and Sisk may have fled by car. Or maybe Sisk was being held hostage in the room. Possibly Hartman had fled, leaving Sisk in the room, dead or alive. Finally, there was no evidence to indicate that Sisk was ever in the room. Maybe he had been killed or dumped off somewhere. And there was the obvious need to interrogate a live Hartman as soon as possible in order to discover the whereabouts of Jim Sisk, in the event he was still alive. Snyder, surprisingly, seemed to be agreeing with Farone's arguments.

While Snyder and Farone debated the options open to them, one of the SWAT officers reported what looked to be a small note taped to the door of the room. The desk clerk said the note had not been placed there by him, so Farone and Snyder decided to retrieve it prior to any break-in. Two SWAT team shooters, nine-millimeter sidearms drawn, slipped silently along the row of motel rooms until they reached room 29, and the lead officer slowly peeled the note from the door.

Snyder, Farone and the SWAT leader read the note over three or four times, trying to agree on what it meant:

> Cheers!
> Agent Sisk was kind enough to explain how you got on to me. Death by sunburn. Sad, right? So you must realize that I have nothing more to lose. What have you got to lose? Life? Liberty? Pursuit of happiness?
> Kick in the door. You'll then learn where I left your agent. And you'll also learn how brave you really are when you face a truly fearless man, one with nothing left to lose. Welcome!

The SWAT team leader, Agent Ellner, took the note to be a direct challenge for a confrontation and urged that they force their way in immediately, using as much surprise and intimidation as possible. Farone pointed out that perhaps that was what Hartman was hoping for, that he would be killed by the police, an ever-increasing national phenomenon that had been dubbed "suicide by cop." Ellner's cold response was, "So what? It's what the bastard deserves." Agent Snyder reluctantly agreed with Ellner, but he urged that every effort be made to subdue the suspect, since they needed to learn where Sisk was if not in the room.

Without belaboring the point, the three men agreed that the probable outcome for Jim Sisk was that he had been murdered in some strange grisly way and left as one of the suspect's last crimes. Evidence pointing to the location of such a crime would probably be found in the room, even if Hartman was killed in a fight and couldn't be interrogated.

A break-in was agreed to, and although Ellner and his team had never performed one in a real-life situation, they were well trained and knew the drill backward. The only glitch, Ellner thought, as they assembled silently in front of room 29, was that Snyder had insisted on being part of the break-in team. The plan was simple: two team members would position themselves on each side of the door. Two other team members would be tasked with using a heavy steel ram to break down the door, on Ellner's count. Snyder and Ellner would be positioned directly behind the break-in duo. When the door gave way, the team member opposite the hinged side of the door would toss a flash/bang grenade into the room. The team members would then enter the room, guns drawn, in a much-rehearsed order. The grenade was a commonly used device, highly successful in forced entries. Although harmless, the explosion and the simultaneous flash stunned and disoriented those in the room, sometimes causing people to freeze, other times frightening them so much they instantly hit the deck. Under these circumstances, the possibility of capturing people greatly increased; and when armed resistance was still a hazard, the odds were in favor of the attacking force.

With everyone in position, a secondary perimeter of detectives and uniformed cops set up, guns drawn, Snyder gave the command— "Go!"— and the ram smashed into the cheap motel door, knocking it inward instantly. A split second later, the pin was pulled on a grenade; it was tossed in and exploded. The team poured into the dark smoky room, ready to fire, but no Hartman. Snyder noticed the closed bathroom door and demanded that the suspect come out immediately, hands on head. No one on the team, including Snyder, really thought that there was anyone in there, but adrenaline and fear had everyone on maximum alert. Agent Ellner, suspicious of a trick and unwilling to lose the momentum, whispered, "I'll pop open the door. If he's in there, defend yourselves. No heroes."

The door swung open, and in the low light all that registered was a man seated on the toilet, wearing a red MYC sweater, a yachtsman's cap, and pointing a gun. In less than one second, Agent Snyder and two SWAT team members opened fire, a total later recorded as sixteen rounds, twelve hitting Agent Sisk, killing him instantly. Sisk's last moves had been to frantically swing his head from right to left and back again as if to say no, and within the limited range of motion of his right arm, to try to point the firearm sideways. Snyder's scream— "Stop shooting!"—came about two seconds too late to help Sisk. The yachting cap had been literally blown off his head, and although one other round had struck him in the forehead, creating a massive exit wound in the back of his head, he was now clearly recognized as a fellow agent, now a victim of death by cop.

Farone, hearing no more shots fired and picking up the sounds of men's voices in the room, stepped from behind the vehicle he was using as a barricade, holstered his SIG SAUER .45 caliber pistol, and rushed toward the hotel room, asking, "What's going on? Do we need to call EMS?"

Raymond Snyder was first to leave the room. He saw Farone, heard his questions, and then vomited into a row of scruffy yew bushes that separated the cars from the rooms.

CHAPTER THIRTY-SEVEN

The Three Elms Motel suddenly became the epicenter for major excitement in Fairfield County, for at least one hour. The EMS ambulance was first to respond, lights flashing. But the medical technicians realized immediately that there was little to do except wait for the crime-scene people to finish their investigation and photography and then remove the agent's remains and transport the body to the morgue. A Mr. Harvey Altman, who announced that he was the owner of the motel, as well as a practicing tort lawyer, demanded to speak to the officer in charge, who now turned out to be Detective Farone, since Head Agent Snyder was busy explaining via phone to his immediate superior the inadvertent and tragic killing of Agent Sisk.

Altman had driven to the motel as soon as his desk clerk had informed him of the arrival of a police convoy. He was of two minds about the killing occurring on his property: in the long term, the publicity might be good for business and make the place easier to unload on some careless investor, perhaps an Indian group, since they were becoming prominent in this business lately. But maybe the place would be stigmatized and what business they did get would fall off. Regardless, for now his need was to badger Detective Farone to accept responsibility for the cleanup and repair of his facility. He also wanted appropriate paperwork—probably a copy of the police report—that would serve as evidence of his claim, in case he had to go to court to demand payment.

Farone was in no mood to argue over a bloody, shot-up motel room, but his training in dealing with the public helped him to suppress his desire to tell this creep Altman to shove it. He handled the matter with the approved blend of official courtesy underpinned with bureaucratic inflexibility. He finally managed to palm Altman off to an extremely upset Raymond Snyder, reasoning that the FBI had made the entry and was responsible for the incident. Altman, suspicious that he was getting the runaround, stalked off to confront Snyder, who was in no mood to be diplomatic or remotely concerned with claims for a trashed motel room. The shouting match that developed could be heard out to the street.

Farone's report to Jonas James had not been a pleasure either, and both realized the situation would only get worse as the realities of politics took over the reaction to the shooting. To round out an increasingly lousy day and night, the desk clerk, just to be self-important and maybe obtain a little glory, had called two of the three local TV stations. The remote-broadcast trucks had arrived at the motel almost instantly. They set up their mobile transmitters and fifty-foot antennae and sent their Steadicam roving camera operators off to get background footage of the scene. Farone acknowledged that he had at least gotten one break: Lt. Hubley of the department's public information office was on the job and had informed a relieved duo of Farone and Snyder that she, and she alone, would deal with the media.

Upon realizing that Hartman was missing, Farone had called in to headquarters to check if there had been any response to the APB issued for the suspect's SUV. None yet. He then instructed Detective Nugent to alert all airports, train stations, and bus depots to be on the lookout for Hartman and to arrest him on the spot. Background information, as well as one poor photo of the suspect and copies of the arrest warrant, would be faxed or distributed to each transportation site, as well as the media.

Snyder was relieved to be out of the loop for the time being. He and Ellner had been ordered to report ASAP to bureau district offices in

Hartford in order to begin an official inquiry into the killing of Agent Sisk. As lead agent, Snyder knew that the bureau would do its best to shield him from the media, which would be all over the case, but that internally he would be severely reprimanded and probably transferred to a remote bureau outpost, a real career killer. Curiously, the only feeling he had for Jim Sisk was anger, not remorse; if Sisk had gone by the book, none of this mess would have occurred. And that was the pitch he intended to make to the higher-ups who were looking for a fall guy.

Lt. James, meanwhile, choked down his anger and fear of political retaliation as he watched the first of the so-called breaking news reports on TV— "An FBI agent was killed by friendly fire in a strange new twist to the crab slayings..." He and Farone agreed that the only real response to settle down the media now would be the capture of the killer. James, for his part, was canceling leaves, time off, and less pressing assignments to place as many detectives on the case as possible.

Farone cursed himself for actually being relieved at not being made the police department scapegoat; maybe that would come later if the case dragged on. He suffered some guilt and self-doubt for not having been more forceful, more successful in convincing the bureau guys not to break in. *But*, he thought, *that's literally about to become yesterday's news.* Time to get back to police work.

In a follow-up phone call to Lt. James, Farone, composed and professional, told his superior that he and Detective Sloan were going to drive out to the marina to check on Hartman's boat. He would report back to the precinct, about 10:00 p.m., to file his report of the night's events and to be available for any follow-up meetings that were necessary.

As they drove away from the motel, Sloan confessed that he was relieved to be leaving that unhappy and screwed-up motel scene. He went on to say that they were presently on a wild goose chase.

"What makes you think so?" Farone asked, as they eased on to Route 1 heading east.

"Remember, Bob, we told the head office guy at the marina to call if Hartman's boat was moved or took off. I checked headquarters and there have been no calls, so I assume the boat's still there. I have a real problem believing that Hartman's aboard, just waiting for us to show up."

"I do, too," Farone answered, "but you never know. There might be something different about the boat. Maybe it's for sale. Who knows? At least we'll be away from the boss and the press for another hour. Maybe things will calm down. But I kind of doubt it. The string of murders and now this crazy shooting by friendly fire will keep the media feeding for days. We really need a break. And soon."

・・・

The boatyard was dark. No evening activity, a light on in the harbormaster's office, which doubled as a rental office. Seated behind a desk was a tall, thin man about forty years old, reading a back issue of *Playboy*. He looked slightly annoyed as Farone and Sloan entered the office, displaying their shields and noting the man's name tag.

"What are you men doing out here?" the man asked. "We haven't had any problems tonight."

"We're checking on a forty-four-foot sailboat, *Coy Mistress*," Sloan stated. "Any recent activity? Boat still here?"

"Funny you should ask," the man answered with a slight yawn. "Big guy went aboard about three hours ago, just after I came on duty. Didn't say nothin' and didn't want any help untying the boat. Tossed off the dock lines and split. Don't know where the hell he went. No racin' at night. And I got no idea when in hell he'll return."

Farone did a good job of suppressing his rising anger and asked, "How do you know he'll return?"

"Well, that's not too hard to figure out," the man answered, a slight sneer on his face. "First off, he left his dock lines coiled up on his slip. Also, see that fancy Mercedes over there?" he pointed out into the dark parking lot. "I doubt that vehicle's going to get home by itself."

"Was this the man?" Sloan asked, showing a photo of Hartman. "And was he alone?"

"He was definitely alone, had a sail bag and some other gear with him to stow on board. Can't really say if that picture is the guy or not. Didn't get much of a look at him. They don't bother me, I don't bother them. That's my philosophy."

Farone felt himself losing it and began not to care. "That's your philosophy, is it, Socrates?" he snarled as he pulled the man to his feet. "My philosophy is to cuff and stuff any asshole who won't cooperate with the police. The guy we're talking about is wanted for murder one, and the instructions we gave you people said you were to call us the minute the boat was being moved." He pushed the man back into his seat. "I don't want to hear any bullshit or fucking philosophy," Farone yelled. "Why didn't you call us?"

"I was busy. Guess I forgot."

"Get his statement, Brian," Farone said, suddenly very dejected. "I'll check out the SUV. We'll probably have to get it impounded. You know, there's over ninety miles of Long Island Sound out there. Plenty of little harbors and gunkholes to anchor out in. Moonless night, too. Why the hell can't we catch a break?"

Sloan completed the statement quickly and checked with Farone; nothing obvious about the car, which appeared to be empty. They decided to have it impounded anyway. Never can tell. They notified the coast guard to start looking for the sailboat and met with a very grudging response. They also called in to Peggy Nugent and asked her to call all the police departments on both the Connecticut and Long Island sides of the sound to be on the lookout for the boat.

"Bob, do you want me to tell Chief James about Hartman's getaway?" Nugent asked. "He's still in his office."

"No thanks, Peggy. Just transfer me over to him. I'll tell him myself. More great news from the front lines."

CHAPTER THIRTY-EIGHT

Another press conference was called for ten o'clock the following morning on the steps of the precinct. Farone knew that he looked like hell: little sleep, too much worry, and recriminations about how they could have done a better job. But he dutifully took his place among assorted politicians and various other law enforcement people, behind Lts. James and Hubley, who stood at the microphones fielding questions from the media.

As the police department representatives smoothly handled the press, sticking to their talking points and giving every impression of openness and objectivity, Farone was glad that it was their job to manipulate the press and not his. He knew that he would screw things up if he had to handle the media often. The tug-of-war between the media's feeding-frenzy need to find something wrong with everything and the cops' and politicians' need to appear professional, correct, and above all, productive, was not going to end anytime soon. *Certainly not during the time I serve*, he thought. Farone tried to dismiss the increasing sense of disillusionment he felt about his job. Too many factors to contend with, the media being only one of them.

The media, of course, had two major storylines to exploit, both bad for the image of the police and the FBI. The first was the dramatic news of the killing of the FBI agent by his own people. The second news subject—the inability of the police to apprehend the killer and take him into custody—was almost secondary but certainly still on the agenda.

Lt. James adroitly handled the killing of Agent Sisk by passing the buck; he announced that the FBI would schedule their own press conference after their preliminary investigation into the tragedy was concluded. And no, he did not know when that would happen, and no, it wasn't the place of the police department to offer commentary or opinions on the activities of other law enforcement agencies. And as to the killer running free, James proudly asserted that the investigation phase had been successful, was over, and the new focus was on bringing the known suspect, Ivan Hartman, into custody. He revealed nothing more in terms of specifics, particularly the apparent flight by boat, "in the interest of not revealing any confidential details of the pursuit." But he did acknowledge that the detectives in his department were following a solid trail and results could be expected in the near future.

As Lt. Hubley took over the conference, speaking warmly of the excellent job the FBI had done, Peggy Nugent walked quietly across the improvised dais, pulled her boss aside, and indicated he should come with her. Important phone message. Farone followed Nugent off the platform and into the precinct, heading quickly for his desk. Once out of range of the microphones, Nugent told him urgently that a Captain Rogers of the New London coast guard station was on the phone. Two men from Old Saybrook, out trolling early for bluefish, had come across the *Coy Mistress*, adrift near Orient Point and apparently abandoned. Sails were reefed, diesel engine shut down, hatches battened down.

Rogers had put two of his crew aboard and instructed them to sail the boat to the docks in New London, under power only, and secure it under armed guard, since it was part of an ongoing police investigation. Farone requested that the boat be brought down to Stamford for greater ease in the inspection and investigation the police would perform, but Rogers cut him off abruptly. "If you want to see the boat, I suggest you drive up to New London and see me first. We do have jurisdiction over the boat, and we simply cannot hand it over to you without the necessary paperwork. You'll also have to provide a timetable for removing the boat—the sooner the better—before we can release it."

"Why can't we do all the paperwork in Stamford?" Farone responded, a trace of annoyance in his voice.

"Because my men have better things to do than spend hours ferrying a sailboat for delivery in Stamford. In case you people haven't heard, the coast guard is now tasked with the war on terror and the war on drugs, as well as coming to the aid of every idiot civilian who heads out to sea on weekends without checking the weather or even topping off his gas tanks. All this and not a goddamned nickel from Congress for additional staffing and patrol boats. I'll see you when you get here."

Brian Sloan and Peggy Nugent stocked the unmarked car with a street map of New London, several bottles of water, and half a dozen evidence bags. They also helped their precinct photographer load some of his gear in the trunk.

With Farone at the wheel they set off for New London at noon, a forty-five-minute trip. It had been estimated that the *Coy Mistress* would reach the dock at about eleven forty-five, so they could board immediately and get down to work.

Farone's mood had brightened. It was good to get out of Stamford for a few hours, away from the precinct and the press. And it was good to have a specific project to accomplish, even though they would be looking at an empty boat, probably little indication of when and where Hartman had fled. *Hunches were for horseplayers*, Farone thought dismissively, but he could not let go of his cop's hunch that they were close to the end of the trail, even though the boat had been found empty.

They arrived at the coast guard dock and asked to see Captain Rogers. They were informed that he was attending an important conference at the academy; however, a Lieutenant Mackall was on hand to supervise the paperwork and to escort them on board. Farone left Nugent to fill out the necessary forms and asked Sloan to interview, via phone, the two fishermen who had found the sailboat. They had been instructed to await a phone call from the Stamford police. In addition to being excited about being part of a real police investigation, they wondered if there might be a reward for their discovery. "Maybe we'll get salvage rights," one said to the other.

Mackall escorted the detectives to the boat and instructed the NCO guarding it to allow them to board, remove whatever contents they needed, and obtain photographs as necessary.

The fishermen had sworn to Brian Sloan that they had not moved or taken anything from the boat when they boarded her, and Sloan was inclined to believe them. *One good thing about cop shows,* he thought. *They teach civilians some useful things about police work, like not screwing around with potential evidence.* The two coast guard men who had ferried the boat to the dock, however, explained that they had gone below decks to make absolutely sure that no one was aboard. They also corroborated the two fishermen's story that there were no heavy anchors and anchor chain in the cockpit, as Farone had recalled.

One item the coast guard crew had missed, however, was an envelope sealed and addressed simply to "Police Force," lying on the forward bunk. Farone tore it open and extracted a handwritten letter, penned on Three Elms stationery, along with a long, thin key. He unfolded the letter and read it aloud to Nugent and Sloan, while his photographer took a few photos, quietly disappointed that there was nothing of dramatic interest to shoot.

The letter itself was addressed to Police Chief James, chosen, Farone guessed, because Jonas had been their TV spokesman and had probably been seen by Hartman.

>Cheers!
>
>And congratulations. You managed to get to me sooner than I expected. Too bad one of your more clever men chose to be sneaky, not a team player. I had to punish him, but you got to participate, too, according to last night's news. You should thank me.

And while we're on the subject of gratitude, I feel that over time I will be thanked, if not admired, for having the courage and creativity to make examples of some of the worst scum in our society. I hereby freely admit to being the instrument of death of those you found with my golden crab signature, so don't waste taxpayers' time and money looking for another man. Better to spend any time left on this case to clearly explain my motives and goals to the media. You will find attached to this letter a long and detailed so-called confession of my acts recently. Enjoy!

You may also wish to inform the reporters that I planned to punish at least three more evil people before I became weak and sick from the cancer eating me alive. But your quick work put an end to further activities.

I accepted no treatment, no medication. Needed to be sharp to do my work. But now it's time for me to retire, as they say, at the top of my game. My life has no meaning to me anyway, other than exacting justice. Why would I want to suffer, grow weaker, die a lingering, painful, and certain death in some hospital? Not a chance. I've always planned to kill myself, even before the melanoma. The time is nigh. After I finish this letter, I plan to weigh myself down with a length of anchor chain shackled at each end to a heavy anchor and slip quietly over the side. Easy death, no burial, no problems.

I leave behind some final requests. The three charms are to be given to the three scums you no doubt found in newspaper clippings in my home. Let them know that they were next. The key enclosed is a safe deposit key for a box I rented in the Stamford National Bank. In it you will find my will, properly witnessed and attested to, along with a notarized statement that I have no offspring, no siblings, no heirs. The will appoints the president of the Stamford ASPCA as sole executor and trustee of my estate, which I have left to his organization. Titles to vehicles and this boat are in the safe. Any personal effects left in the rental house should also be turned over to the executor. All other assets of my estate have been converted to cash and bonds and distributed as I wished several months ago. My work is done. May others carry on.

Sincerely,

Ivan Hartman

Farone handed the letter to Sloan, who placed it in an evidence bag along with the key and the charms.

"Let's call it in to the boss," Farone said to the others as they stepped off the boat. "I imagine he'll be very pleased with the news."

"It'll mean another grueling press conference, Bob," Nugent said quietly.

"You're right, Peggy. But as far as we're concerned, it will probably be the last one on this case. Besides, they've still got the bureau's carcass to pick. I really don't like Ray Snyder, but I feel bad for him. What an incredible setup. That shooting could have happened to any of us; instinct, training, and adrenaline. Too bad the guy on the toilet wasn't really Hartman."

"Do you think drowning's a better death?" asked Sloan.

"In the case of that sick bastard, any death is a good one," Farone replied. "Let's get the hell out of here."

CHAPTER THIRTY-NINE

The revelation of Hartman's confession and suicide brought on a renewed media frenzy, with coverage even extending to the national networks and the all-news networks. The media was delighted with something new to report, and interviews with Chief James, along with local and state officials, dominated the headlines for several days. Of course all the credit given to the police for solving the case was balanced by the media's need to create its own news, which in this case meant a backlash of criticism for not locating and arresting the suspect rather than letting him run.

But in general the public was pleased with the outcome, and its interest soon turned back to more mundane news. Some small questions still remained, the most prevalent being the status of the case in official terms. Chief James announced in a low-key news briefing that law enforcement had no reason to believe that Hartman had any accomplices, but given the severity of his crimes, the police department would continue to sift through every element of the case to ensure that the final police report was accurate and thorough, so that he could announce officially, "Case closed." In his briefing to the press, he estimated that closure would take about two more weeks. In his private meeting with the mayor, the commissioner, and other dignitaries, however, he declared the case to be over with and suggested they might wish to spread the word later that a great deal of time and money had been saved by not having to go through the circus of a jury trial, in addition to possible civil suits.

The only other remaining news was the story of the FBI's internal investigation of the accidental shooting of Agent Sisk. Hard news was tough to come by, not unexpectedly, since the bureau was as adroit in protecting its reputation as it was in solving crimes. No one at the scene of the motel shooting provided any hard information or even opinions, to the press, since "an official investigation was being conducted."

Farone, for his part, had received commendation from the department, not his first, for his work on the case. But for the first time in his career, he took no pleasure in the recognition and was happy to have one week off to go fishing, do some dumb personal errands, and think seriously about what was going on with his life.

The medical examiner's department was hosting a good-bye party for Dr. Ryan that evening, and she had asked Farone to escort her to dinner after the cocktail reception, the awkward speeches, and the small gift presentations were over. *My little vacation is getting off to a great start*, he thought.

CHAPTER FORTY

Three days later, two twelve-year-old boys, hanging out near the Port Jefferson docks to see the big ferry boat from Connecticut dock, got lucky. They had been keeping a careful watch on a small Zodiac inflatable rubber dinghy which had been slowly washing ashore with the incoming tide. The little craft was missing one paddle, and the only cargo was a large orange life jacket. The boys waded out the last few yards and pulled the dinghy ashore. It was a little too heavy to carry, even for the two of them, so one boy decided to bike home and ask his father to drive down with the truck to help them pick up the Zodiac and bring it home. The other boy remained with the little boat, hoping fervently that no grown-up would come by to claim it.

In less than thirty minutes, the first boy returned with his father in their truck, and together they lifted the boat into the back of the vehicle, along with the second boy's bike. As they drove off, the father declared that the kids could keep the boat, on the condition that they check the marina bulletin board and the classifieds in the local newspaper for at least two weeks to see if the Zodiac had been reported missing.

...

After tossing the anchors and chain line overboard, Hartman went below and placed his suicide letter and confession, along with a bank key and three crab charms, in an envelope and tossed it on the galley dining table. He carried his Benetton attaché case, his metal Halliburton case, and a black T. Anthony two-suiter up to the deck and closed the hatch behind him. The sails were properly furled, and the engine had been cut for over twenty minutes, the key left in the ignition. *Coy Mistress* drifted just off the entrance to the Port Jefferson harbor, slowly heading east with the current. Hartman calculated that she would probably drift to the end of Long Island Sound before she was spotted in broad daylight the next day.

He had already inflated the small Zodiac dinghy with an electric pump and launched the boat in the water, lashed fore and aft to the sailboat with two lines that had been looped over the deck rail. A small five-step swim ladder was hooked securely over the gunwale. Hartman calculated that he was at least three hundred yards from shore, a long row for certain, but one that he knew he could handle. He had declined to use the small outboard motor that came with the Zodiac in order to be as inconspicuous as possible. The Zodiac, though quite stable, did not tolerate excessive tipping and overloading, so Hartman lowered his gear carefully into the craft with the help of several small pieces of rope, then buckled on a life preserver and slowly descended the swim ladder. After balancing the dinghy as well as possible, weight distribution being of primary importance, he lifted the swim platform upward to free it of the gunwale, then pulled it down and tossed it into the water. He next unknotted the two lines holding the boats together and pulled them around the deck rails and down into the Zodiac, freeing her from the sailboat looming over it. Hartman began his long row to shore, no last glance at his father's boat.

When the dinghy reached shore, Hartman hopped out, hauled it halfway out of the water and quickly unloaded it. He then gave the little boat a strong shove back into the sea and watched the current sweep it east along the shoreline, minus one oar, which had gotten loose of the oarlock. He had decided to leave the life vest in the craft since he was now faced with clambering up a small embankment with his belongings and then crossing the marina public parking lot to his new car, a BMW. First, he stripped off the latex gloves he had been wearing, in order to avoid leaving his fingerprints on the Zodiac and its oars, and tossed them in a convenient trash barrel at the top of the embankment. He loaded his gear into the trunk of the car, then swung into the driver's seat, started the engine, and took off.

At 11:00 p.m. there was little traffic heading west on the Long Island Expressway, a far cry from the bumper-to-bumper commuting traffic that would begin at seven. Hartman drove conservatively, radio tuned to the all-news-all-the-time station in New York City, eager to hear of any news of his latest exploits.

After crossing over the East River via the Throgs Neck bridge, he headed south on Interstate 95 toward New York City. His left arm had begun to throb with pain again from the small-caliber gunshot wound, so he popped two more Motrin. He hoped that his cleansing and closing of the wound, crude as it was, would hold up so that he would not have to run the risk of seeing a country doctor. But...if a problem came up, he would know how to solve it.

At twelve fifteen he checked into an Econolodge motel in northern New Jersey and registered as Randall Newman. Address, a mail drop in Bridgeport, Connecticut; room, prepaid with cash. After moving all his gear into the room, he asked the night manager to call a local pizza parlor or any place that delivered to get some food and soft drinks to his room; he gave him twenty dollars for his trouble. While choking down a cold Big Mac and soggy french fries, Hartman stayed tuned to the local news channel in his room. He also rechecked all of his new IDs: driver's license, passport, auto registration, auto insurance, birth certificate, social security card, and title to the BMW. Once he obtained a legitimate permanent address and consolidated his many bank balances, he planned to get new addresses on all the documents and apply for a few credit cards.

A lot accomplished today, he thought, suddenly realizing he was exhausted. He dropped into bed after hanging a Do Not Disturb sign on his doorknob. Still no news, but that could wait till morning. Hartman was dead, and Newman was heading west.

CHAPTER FORTY-ONE

In two weeks the crab killer case was officially labeled "closed," and the media hardly took notice. Chief James and his family finally took an oft-postponed vacation trip to Nova Scotia, Brian Sloan got married, and Peggy Nugent dropped her latest boyfriend, an out-of-work advertising copywriter with wannabe plans to become a screenwriter.

Bob Farone was happier than he had been in years. He saw Sheila Ryan every night, every weekend. He was terribly happy that she was going back to med school and planning to return to the medical field as a pediatrician. But he was also a little envious that she had so easily decided on a specific career change, while he was still discontent with his job on the force. Joining his father's law practice was always an option, but he had a hard time accepting the fact that he would be earning his living defending the same kind of people he had been arresting for the last nine years.

Ryan accepted his love with only one reservation: no commitment to a marriage until they both agreed that their professional lives fit together as well as their feelings for one another—feelings which neither questioned anymore. Farone agreed, although he thought that the burden of deciding on a career change was putting most of the relationship pressure on him. Maybe a blessing in disguise; his Hamlet act was getting tired.

Farone's mother had checked into LenoxHillHospital for an extensive annual physical, which included an overdue colonoscopy. She had decided to remain in the hospital overnight, although her doctor said it was unnecessary. Farone and Ryan had decided to drive into New York to visit his mother, check that everything was all right, and then have dinner with Farone Sr.

As they left the hospital, Ryan remarked, "I don't think that you and your father have anything to worry about with your mom, Bob. I spoke to her personal doctor, and he said she's fit as most thirty-year-olds. Probably bury us both."

"Well, she sure as hell looks healthy," Farone replied. "But pass along that remark to Dad when he joins us for dinner. He worries about her as much as I do."

"It's genetic, Bob. You Farones worry about everything."

After a short drive south to the Village, Farone pulled into a parking garage. They walked a half block to the Broadway Bar at University and Seventh Street, a favorite restaurant of theirs in Manhattan. Joe, one of the owners, greeted them warmly, showed them to a nice banquette, and promised to personally greet Bob's father when he arrived. The arrival of two Bombay martinis, straight up, and the announcement that Jack O'Reilly would perform at the keyboard that night increased Farone's sense of well-being. And the fact that the good doctor was squeezing his hand under the table was frosting on the cake.

Jerry Farone arrived promptly at eight thirty, hugged Sheila warmly, then also hugged his son, substituting manly backslapping for the air kisses exchanged with, he hoped, his future daughter-in-law. A dry Rob Roy on the rocks quickly appeared for the senior Farone, and after a brief, upbeat discussion on the state of Mrs. Farone's health, Jerry began to do what he did best: ask questions. Jerry was one of those unique people to whom friends, acquaintances, even strangers would reveal the most intimate aspects of their lives. An excellent asset in a trial lawyer, although sometimes one didn't really want to know too much about a client. The senior Farone somehow gave off the aura of being nonjudgmental, somewhat sympathetic, and able to keep confidences. And in his case, these attributes were true. Bob Farone sometimes thought that his father might have made a great confessor in some medieval period.

Small talk quickly gave way to two career discussions the older Farone was interested in hearing about: one for Sheila, the other for Bob. Ryan quickly explained how she had decided to make a 180-degree swing in her career, from a doctor charged with helping to explain death to one responsible for sustaining health in newborns.

For his part, Bob had little to report to his father that was new. He repeated his growing concerns about the level of politics in law enforcement and the rivalries between different arms of the law, as well as the endless pandering to the media. He admitted that he wanted out but couldn't decide on what to do, except resign, take some time off, and figure it all out later. His father interrupted with the old caution about monkeys: when swinging from tree to tree, they don't let go of the first limb with one hand until they have a solid grasp of the second limb with their other hand.

The conversation quickly swung to the crab case, the details of which were endlessly fascinating to Jerry Farone. "Tell me, son, when do the cops expect to see a floater, the remains of this guy surfacing somewhere?"

"Probably never, Dad. Remember, he weighed himself down with about two hundred pounds of anchor gear, more than enough to take him to the bottom. We passed on doing any dredging, too. Too damned deep and no real way of knowing where he went overboard."

"No, Bob. I understand why the idea of dredging makes no sense, but I think that there's a fair possibility that he might float. I remember from a case we tried years ago that a forensics expert testified that it takes about five or six times a man's body weight to keep his body on the bottom after being tossed overboard. Has a lot to do with the gases in the corpse gradually expanding and slowly floating the body to the surface. You know in those old movies about the mob, victims being poured into cement coffins and tossed overboard? Now those guys knew what they were doing! Anyway, what do you make of it as a medical person, Sheila?"

"Jerry, I really don't know. You're right about the floaters coming to the surface because of gas expansion in the torso, but none of the cases I've ever seen involved the weighing down of the body. I really don't know what amount of added weight would be needed. Each case is different anyway. For example, if the body hit shark-infested water, I think you'd be lucky to find small pieces, if anything. On the other hand, in an environment like Long Island Sound, probably the biggest threat to the corpses would be crabs, so there would probably be a much greater possibility of a floater."

Crabs. Ironic, thought the senior Farone.

"Hold up, guys," Bob Farone signaled for a time-out. "Diane is headed our way with some great T-bone steaks and all the goodies. So let's knock off the talk of body parts, at least human ones, OK?"

The excellent food and wine did not deter Farone's father from persisting between courses in what his son jokingly referred to as cross-examination. "Tell me, Bob, why are you so sure this screwball really killed himself? There's no body. You may never find one. Anyone can write a suicide letter. Happens every day. This guy is fiendishly clever, as the Brits used to say, and he was still free and on the run after he took off from that motel. Why throw in the towel and kill himself?"

"I take your point, Dad," Farone answered, "especially since there's no body. But you've got to remember that Hartman was being pursued by us, and we were getting closer, despite how clever he was. He also knew the melanoma was going to take him down eventually. He had no options. I personally thought that he might think about confronting us. The FBI agent responsible for the shooting of his subordinate thought so, too, one of the few things we agreed on. But now that I've had time to think calmly about the entire case, it's fairly obvious to me that, to Hartman, his actions and crimes were justified. Creating a confrontation with cops and hoping to be killed by them would not fit his MO, or what he thought was good for his legacy. Suicide was his last act of personal control."

"One more question, Bob, and then I promise that we can enjoy dessert and coffee, a little anisette, and Judy's first set of stride piano. How do you know that Hartman really killed all those people? Any nut can write a confession, particularly since the details of each assault were printed in the paper. You have no witnesses. There's some circumstantial and scientific evidence, of course, but there's no specific link to each individual crime except the bracelet, and any copycat killer can plant one. Incidentally, Bob, I'm as sure as your people are that Hartman did these crimes, all of them, but I'm still interested in your reasoning."

"As you no doubt would know, Dad, the case files are locked up and may be permanently sealed by the court. However, the prosecutors have been through every detail of the case ad nauseam, particularly the confession letter. In a nutshell, there are details of each crime that only the killer would know, so it's clear to us that not only is Hartman responsible for these murders, but that he was clever enough to describe certain details of each crime in his confession letter, so we would accept without question that he was the killer. In his twisted mind, he wanted to make sure that he got full credit for each crime. We've also got one other bit of reasoning for making Hartman the sole serial killer; Chief James called it the Williams syndrome. Does the name Wayne Williams mean anything to you, Dad?"

"Well, yes, it rings a bell, Bob," the elder Farone answered with a smile, having a good idea where this was going. "Wasn't Williams the gay black guy who was convicted for killing all those young men and boys in Atlanta years ago?"

"Right. After Williams was arrested and tried, a lot of people claimed that he was innocent, that the police hadn't done a thorough job, and that the real killer was still out there. A few years went by, Williams was still in jail, and either a DA or one of the top cops commented to the media that the fact that the killings had ended completely after Williams was incarcerated seemed to prove beyond doubt that Williams was the killer, not a fall guy. Anyway, that's the analogy we draw with our case. All is quiet, all is calm."

"Bob, you were going to tell me what happened to the FBI investigation," Sheila Ryan said. "Whatever happened to those agents involved in the shooting?"

"Nothing good, believe me. Ray Snyder was transferred to a small office in Billings, career dead end. His ambitions will have to be satisfied some other way. Luckily for him he's got his own money, so he can choose a new career once the heat dies down or simply chill out and have fun for a while. His other agent on the case was promoted and transferred somewhere, probably in order to keep his mouth shut. And as for the murdered Agent Sisk, he was given high honors, and his wife got something out of it, too. The odd one is this guy Ellner, who led the SWAT team. He quit the bureau and plans to open a restaurant featuring Russian food and vodkas in LA. He's going to name the place Comrades."

Julie brought over the check after the first set of jazz was completed with a spirited rendition of "Ain't Misbehavin'," and Farone Sr. paid it, remarking that the next one was on his son, assuming he still had a job.

His son picked up his car at the garage, and he and Sheila dropped off his dad at home on upper Park Avenue. Farone entered the FDR Drive to Connecticut at East Ninety-Sixth Street, but while being held at the red light, he reached over and commenced a long slow kiss with Ryan, which was eagerly received. The light turned green, and the cabby behind them immediately laid on his horn, his face reflexively contorting to a mass of disgust.

"I love New York, sweetheart," Farone said. He slowly swung up onto the FDR.

CHAPTER FORTY-TWO

After seven leisurely days on the road, Hartman arrived in Kimball, Nebraska, at about six o'clock and decided to spend the night. Before looking around for a chain motel—his favorites were Holiday Inn and Econolodge—he pulled into a busy Burger King and ordered a large coffee, a Whopper, and fries at the drive-in window.

After years of carefully avoiding tasty, fattening fast food, Hartman still felt a twinge of guilt in the three or more stops he made each day to the various roadside and truck-stop emporiums. But he had to admit, he was beginning to gain the extra twenty-five pounds he planned to put on, even though it was flab. *Randall Newman's a bit of a slob*, he decided, *probably a big jock gone to seed*.

His physical creation of Newman had been easy. The wearing of nonprescription Porsche designer glasses had taken a few days to get used to, but the change in appearance was well worth it, particularly when he wore the second pair, tinted and polarized for driving. Keeping Newman's head shaved was an annoying chore, as was the careful trimming around the newly growing goatee and mustache, but the end result would be effective, particularly when complemented by his completely new wardrobe of expensive Italian designer clothing and shoes, packed neatly in two new T. Anthony pieces of luggage with the initials R.N. embossed in the supple leather.

Newman finished his snack in the Burger King parking lot and decided it was time to finally cut all remaining ties with Ivan Hartman. He unlocked the trunk of the car and removed the new Benetton attaché case. Once again he glanced over his luggage and the shiny metal Halliburton case that held over two million dollars in cash and bearer bonds. He closed the trunk, got back into the BMW, lit a cigar—a new affectation—and removed several articles from the case. Four newspaper clippings, cut from different newspapers as he had headed west, still gave him great pleasure to read. Hartman's honest confession and manly suicide had obviously brought that great cliché—closure—to many: the police and the FBI, the families and friends of the people who had been punished, and Hartman himself, he thought with a smile. He put aside his annoyance that the media had completely missed the point of his contributions, portraying him as "disturbed," "a loner," "a self-appointed vigilante," and other obvious labels. No mention of the positive impact that his dramatic scenarios of retribution would have on others: influencing evildoing scum to change their ways and encouraging other decent courageous men to take up the cudgel.

Newman put aside the clippings for the last time and turned his attention to a letter he had received shortly after the failed attempt to abduct the abortionist. He had read and reread the letter so many times that he could almost quote it, but since the message in the letter had completely changed his plan for the remainder of his life, he thought he would indulge himself by rereading it one final time. The letter was from Dr. Ransom of the Fairfield Dermatology Clinic.

> Dear Mr. Hartman:
> As you may recall, our dermatology practice contracts with several radiology practices in order to obtain diagnoses of biopsy tissue. In your case, and three others, the need for a second radiology opinion was recently identified at our clinic, due to professional disagreement over the initial findings and diagnosis. We asked the Eaton & Ross

Radiology Group in New York to provide a second opinion on your case, in a timely fashion, of course, since your initial diagnosis indicated malignant melanoma, and serious medical intervention was contemplated. Therefore, we received a second diagnosis of your excision recently, and senior members of our staff reviewed it with great care and interest. A detailed report of the radiologists' findings has been sent separately to your primary physician. An abbreviated report is included in this letter.

Unfortunately, you apparently have not been pleased with our approach to your case and have neither returned our phone calls nor responded to mailed requests to schedule a follow-up appointment to review our findings, which are good news for you. As a result, we have chosen to contact you directly via registered mail and to provide you with a new diagnosis of your case.

We urge you to discuss the new findings with your primary physician when you feel more comfortable with the subject. Time, however, is no longer of the essence. You do not have cancer.

. . .

ROSS & EATON RADIOLOGY GROUP
PATIENT: Hartman, Ivan

The slides we received from the Fairfield Dermatology Group have been reviewed here and show a compound nevus with architectural disorder. We have concluded officially that the mole is a benign melanocytic nevus. This is good news for the patient and confirms our initial impression, in which we were not able to identify any areas of malignancy, and given that the margins were free of nevus, we believe that this has been thoroughly excised.

. . .

As you have no doubt gleaned from this report, Mr. Hartman, the process of radiology is sometimes as much an art as a science.

Notably so in your case. We are pleased that we were able to provide a positive and definitive conclusion to your diagnosis. So please, get on with your life.

Very truly yours,
Grant W. Ransom, MD

Better follow doctor's orders, thought Hartman, quietly amused. He crumpled up the letter, tore up the newspaper clippings, and dumped them, along with the remainder of his meal, in the food chain's Dempsey Dumpster.

Newman pulled out of the parking lot and headed slowly down the strip, looking for a motel. A billboard advertising a household cleaning product caught his eye— "New And Improved!" He smiled and thought, *Got that right.*

CHAPTER FORTY-THREE

Phone conversation. Boise, Idaho.

"Hello. You've reached Majorsky Jewelry Distributors. How may I direct your call?"

"Let me have my sales rep, Sandy Fox."

"He's out of the office today, sir. Can anyone else help you?"

"Yeah, his manager, Leonard Whitehead. Is he in?"

"Yes, sir. I'll connect you."

"Hello. Whitehead speaking."

"Hello, Leonard. This is Harris Goldman, Goldman and Sons Jewelers, in Boise. Remember me?"

"How could I forget? Terrific store. Nice people. And the important part, you pay on time."

"If the schmooze is over with, Leonard, I'd like to go over my current order, OIP 746200."

"Hang on, Harris. OK, it's up on the screen. Looks like your order is mostly for Swatch watches, nine different rings, six faux tennis bracelets—"

"Hold it, Leonard. I know the order. It's OK. I'm calling to add an additional item, to see if you have them."

"If we don't, we can always call the manufacturer and get the merchandise FedExed, Harris. What are you looking for?"

"I need twelve fourteen-karat charm bracelets with only one charm on each—a Zodiac sign, the scale of justice. It's supposed to cover the end of September into October."

"We have a supplier in Chicago. Bear with me for a few minutes while I bring their catalog up on the screen. OK. Yeah, they still manufacture the items. Fourteen karat. Bracelets we can get overnight, looks like they want five to seven days on the individual charms. Can you wait that long?"

"No problem. How much for the lot?"

"Thirty-six dollars apiece, including tax. Shall I place the order?"

"Leonard, you know the saying 'I was born at night, but not last night'? Thirty bucks per is the highest I'll go."

"To be perfectly honest with you, that's not much more over our cost, but you've got a deal. I must have gotten too much sun in Mexico last week. The items ought to be in your regular shipment one week from Friday, OK?"

"That works out fine. Call me if there are any holdups, though."

"Harris, if you don't mind, I'm a little curious about your order. Charm bracelets are out. We never get any orders. I'm afraid that your son—your grandson, God willing—will be carrying these bracelets in inventory for the next twenty-five years. And why not at least order a variety of charms, give yourself a better shot at moving the goods?"

"Give me credit for a few smarts, please. I know the bracelets are dogs, but a customer came in an hour ago, and that's exactly what he ordered, no variation. Maybe he's starting a club or something. Didn't say much. Wasn't in the store more than five, six minutes."

"If you don't mind, ask him what the deal is with the charm bracelets when he picks them up. Might be the start of a new national fad or something. I'd appreciate the heads-up. By the way, if you didn't know what the wholesale price would be, how could you quote him a price?"

"Leonard, gimme a break! I'm in the business thirty-six years, and you think I can't come up with a price? I charged him one ten a pop, plus tax. This is a guy in full Armani, by the way, didn't say a word, and paid upfront in cash."

"Rich guy or not, better hope he doesn't spot the same merchandise in Walmart for forty-eight bucks someday. He might get really pissed off."

"So what's he gonna do, Leonard? Kill me?"

THE END

Made in the USA
Lexington, KY
05 November 2014